About the Author

At twelve, walked into the racing stables, asked for a job, began cleaning the toilets, ended up travelling the world as a horse whisperer, in between making his living as a professional National Hunt jockey. Became an international koi carp judge, staying in the Yamaguchi Mountains of Japan with the descendants of the Matsunosuke samurai; became even more connected with the spirituality of man and the animal kingdom, a world where deception plays no part. Enjoys the theatre, having played Shakespeare through to pantomime. Now spends much of the time as a singer-songwriter, tormenting the world with his songs.

The Watcherer

Alan Scobie Coogan

The Watcherer

Olympia Publishers
London

www.olympiapublishers.com
OLYMPIA PAPERBACK EDITION

A CIP catalogue record for this title is available from the British
Library.

ISBN: 978-1-80074-425-7

This is a work of fiction.
Names, characters, places and incidents originate from the writer's
imagination. Any resemblance to actual persons, living or dead, is
purely coincidental.

First Published in 2023

Olympia Publishers
Tallis House
2 Tallis Street
London
EC4Y 0AB

Printed in Great Britain

Dedication

I dedicate this book to my wife, Janet, who put up with me for forty-five years till we parted at the door of breast cancer.

The taxi's nearside wheels slipped over the soft verge. No sooner had the cab stopped, Michael Grogan was pushing the fare and more into the grateful driver's hand, anxious to get to Oliver, his brother by a different mother, who had slumped over the bonnet of his beloved XJS Jaguar, his devoted wife, Ninal, rubbing the space between his shoulder blades. The color had abandoned his face; tiny bubbles of saliva had formed at the edge of his mouth.

'You look like you've seen a ghost,' the famous dagger stare, usually confined to the racetrack, glared back. Ninal, hiding her concern behind a veil of light-hearted sarcasm, explained that although she had pleaded for him to follow advice and not go into the house alone, this fearless jump jockey whose motto is, "If I can't ride it can't be rode", decided once again to disregard any advice and do his own thing.

'Needless to say you will observe he got this one disastrously wrong and I present to you one Oliver Grogan, quivering wreck.'

'Thanks for the sympathy,' said Oliver who was regaining some composure. 'Next time you are riding a racehorse and it decides to deposit your gorgeous bottom unceremoniously onto terra firma, forgive me should a wry smile tickle the edges of my month in remembrance of this day.' She punched him playfully between the shoulders then hugged his back.

'Where are the keys to the house?' Michael asked.

'Still in the front door,' Oliver replied. 'Such was my haste to vacate that the small matter of retrieving the keys must have slipped my mind and you are not going in that house without me, just give me a minute to gather myself.'

While Ninal fussed around her shaken hero, Michael

slipped up to the front door and turned the key, stepped inside and slid the bolts home. He turned to face the hallway, a dark narrow space where the stairs to the left led up to the second floor. The old secluded farmhouse nestled the edge of the Fens some three miles outside the market town of Soham.

Michael walked the few steps to where the kitchen branched to the right. The view of the magnificent cathedral at Ely could be seen through the grimy windows, the long fingers of ancient black soil pointed straight at the spires, a testament to the ploughman's craft. The Fens, desolate and beautiful, beguiling and dangerous, the larder of a nation.

The cathedral, "ship of the Fens", stood like a fortress in the black lands, a mighty beacon to the lost.

Michael had sat in the front pew with the bishop less than forty-eight hours previous, having been summoned by His Holiness.

'Michael', the bishop had said, 'we are in need of your special talents.'

The late vicar at St Andrew's in Soham had requested help. The problem had dramatically unnerved him, and may well have led to his untimely death.

A terrible tragedy occurred eighteen months ago when a car driven by the wife of a young couple, Bernadette Green, lost control, shot up over the bank and plunged into the Great Ouse on the back road from Ely to Queen Adelaide. Witnesses report that the young woman had freed herself but repeatedly dived back down into the muddy waters in a vain attempt to release her children, five-year-old Ben and six-year-old Amy. They found her body the next day further down the river, while the two children's bodies were recovered from the scene.

Needless to say the whole community was devastated. Husband, Martin, who had been harvesting sugar beet, was inconsolable, believing he was responsible. On Fridays he usually drove the family to his mother's for tea but that fateful afternoon, had asked his wife to go without him so the children didn't miss their grandparent time, while he could make best use of the fine autumn weather.

The Greens had been keen worshippers and very active members of the congregation. The wife, Bernadette, helped with the Sunday school. She was extremely popular; it was a dreadful time for all concerned.

The upshot was that the husband never set foot in the church again, believing that God had turned his back on him. He became a recluse, his character changed from the amicable fun-loving blade that was the life and soul, to a sad, sombre being. Even that character morphed into an angry, sinister man who oozed menace.

Friends were abused, his parents were subjected to torrents of gutter language, his sister, Elizabeth, determined to help, was met at the door by her naked brother with his phallus pointing skyward, his jaundiced eyes spewed evil only matched by the wicked grin. Angry and undeterred, fueled with rage, she shouted to her brother, she said that growing up she was always a match for him mentally and physically. But this was different: he simply picked her up with one hand, held her above his head and walked to the living room where he threw her across the room. She landed on the sofa which tipped over revealing the pentagram, the Devil's star painted on the floor. It was at that moment that she realized her brother had sought solace in the dark arts, "seek and ye shall find", and he had found, for no longer was her brother walking with Christ.

Torpedoed by grief, spiritually crawling on his belly, he had met the serpent, he had been possessed.

Rising to attempt a defence against the advancing brother, when her sibling stopped and retreated half a step, staring transfixed between her breasts. A pendant of Christ crucified had slipped from behind her blouse and she recalled that in that strange moment it seemed to glow, although only a nanosecond, her brother seemed to recoil, gripped by conflict. She was aware of a dark shape forming around him, growing in intensity, the room temperature seemed to plummet, her frosted breath arrowed towards her brother. In the flick of a horse's tail she was past him and heading breakneck for the open front door and the sanctuary of the car which thankfully burst into life at the turn of the key.

   With little regard for speed limits, she found herself racing the streets of Soham abandoning the car outside the great medieval church of St Andrew's. Inside she found the Reverend Gough, a long-time family friend and pastor. Such was the intensity of distress shown by his visitor that the vicar immediately abandoned his discussions with the purple-haired ladies and left them to position their flower arrangements unhindered.

   Leading Elizabeth to the quiet of the vestry, he listened with growing unease to the unfolding story. During his years of devotion he had seen many strange things, in the main deeply spiritual and uplifting but occasionally he was sure he had seen the work of the Devil; although not a modern fashionable explanation for events he was sure evil was at the tiller.

   "Possession". That was different, he'd heard stories, he

remembered during training, how as young curates they'd tried to scare one another, but the passage of time had seen him doubt their validity.

Now rose fears from the pit of his stomach. Visions of spinning heads, of stomachs punched and pounded from the inside, buckets of foul, spewing with flamethrower accuracy. Entities crawling under the skin seeking exit. Reverend Gough steadied himself by clutching the back of the ancient carved wooden chair.

The condition of his parishioner left little doubt as to the accuracy of her testament, with dread he realized that here was his test, the next few hours would confirm whether a career minister or the deeply committed Christian he thought he was. If the former the encounter would cost him his life. If the latter, like any soldier, he could suffer lifelong trauma from the battle. Now he faced his hour: he must face the enemy as a soldier of God.

There were procedures. After ensuring Elizabeth was in the safe bosom of her family, the bishop had been contacted and permission granted to initiate the process which meant that the Reverend Gough should visit alone to judge the situation.

He prayed before the altar. He prayed with an earnest long forgotten. He prayed from his soul. It was a spiritually invigorated God soldier that walked the thin tarmac path from the vestry door to the small car park that abutted church and playing field. There was no hint of the trepidation that racked his being as he climbed into the small Astra, smiling and waving at the families enjoying the swings and slides of the small park.

The drive across the beguiling flatlands with its water-filled ditches brimming with this year's roach fry, darting kingfisher harvesting the bounty while countrymen armed with their tractors worked the land. The scene completely at odds with the sense of foreboding that gripped the clergyman.

The old farm cottage perched in the corner of an eleven acre field, the small concrete bridge fording the dyke, a source of inspiration for any pen or brush man.

This day the beauty of the flat lands had passed him by. Thoughts of Gethsemane and Mount Sinai where the Christ had been tested bounced around his head, his heart pounded in his chest. He was ill-prepared to meet with the Devil or any of his cohorts.

It was a clammy hand that closed the car door with more force than was necessary, laboured feet moved him towards the front door which, strangely, was slightly ajar.

The procedure required him to be there alone to validate or not. Rumours of ghosts and goblins were the fatted cow for the starving media, serving only to hinder in the rare occasions powers of evil were to be confronted.

The reverend pushed open the door, calling out to Martin as he stepped inside. In his soul he knew, this was one of those rare occasions.

Martin's nude body hung from the balustrade, the flex from an extension lead rendering him lifeless. His face, though contorted, had a strange hint of peace, a serenity borne of release; he had seen the look countless times, when those burdened with pain were released from life.

He felt compelled to kneel and pray. He prayed for Martin and he prayed for himself, thanking God his fear had been groundless, built solely on the testament of a half hysterical lady who had mixed extreme mind-busting depression with possession.

During his incantation of the twenty-third psalm "Although I walk in the valley of death I fear no evil" the reverend became aware of the chill, an arctic blow unhindered by clothing leached at his body causing it to shiver, his teeth began to chatter distorting the words of the psalm.

Movement caused him to look up. The mundane and daily plod of the reverend Gough's journey towards heaven evaporated with his first real encounter of the enemy; his heart, fit to burst, pumped fear to every capillary.

The head on the body was moving, slowly turning by staccato increments, gone was the serene countenance, the lips were stretching, pulled past the teeth to the gum line. Two thin slivers of tongue pushed past the teeth creeping down below the jawline searching and tasting the air, each tongue an independent entity, two asps stalking their prey. The rotating head came to rest facing the curate. The eyes pinged open. The contents of the corpse's stomach spewed splashing from floor to holy man.

Reverend Gough staggered from the house aware of a tightening in his chest. He needed a hospital; he needed to speak to the bishop. Driving in a haze, aware of the pain engulfing his upper body, he pulled over and dialled the bishop.

His report to His Holiness had been thorough and accurate; prior to disconnecting the mobile he mentioned the pain. He lowered the back of the seat, an attempt at relief; it was up to the bishop now.

He thought of his beloved wife and the wonderful life they

had had before God had called her home. She was only lent to me, he thought. In the half-light of half-closed eyes he saw her in amongst the golden corn smiling and waving at him to follow. He smiled, the pain ebbed, his eyes closed, never to open.

The bishop dispatched the emergency services who recovered two bodies. The Soham edition of the *Ely Standard* reported the two tragedies, the suicide of the young farmer and the death from suspected heart attack of the much loved local vicar.

The bishop conducted the funerals of both the Right Reverend Liam Gough, his colleague and friend.

As farmer Green's funeral was to precede the reverend's internment he had offered his services which were gratefully accepted by the grieving family.

A harrowing day saw the bishop heading back to Ely a worried man, dark clouds were hurrying past the cathedral's spires, eager to pummel the earth with their watery arrows.

What he had heard that afternoon only served to deepen the foreboding that seemed to be forcing itself deeper into his being, for several months he had been aware of the growing presence of the dark one.

'If you believe in God then you must believe in the Devil,' his father had often told him as he was about his missionary duties in the small villages surrounding the town of Imbala in western Zimbabwe.

Any lingering doubts about the validity of the Soham incarnation had vanished when the local undertaker, Mr. Phillips, mentioned that his family-run business had been in turmoil since the arrival of the two bodies from the mortuary.

After cajoling from the bishop, Mr. Phillips had told him that the morning after their arrival he was checking the chapel of rest, his daily ritual, the same ritual his father and his father before him had performed. He had been completely stunned to find the body of the suicide face down in the coffin.

Someone was playing some kind of sick joke. Everyone suspected everyone else, the working atmosphere changed from congenial to hostile. It plummeted into the permafrost when on the second morning Mrs. Phillips found graffiti, crafted in excrement, written in the language of the gutter plastered on the wall of her small office, accusing her husband of a sexual liaison with her sister.

Nightly, coffins shifted their positions a few inches. Artifacts and letters placed in the coffin beside their loved ones were strewn across the chapel of rest.

Mr. Phillips told the bishop that last night he had hidden himself in the chapel attempting to discover the culprit.

It was the early hours when he first heard a grunt which returned his focus sharp from his dozing.

Judging by the stink he assumed that some drunk vagrant had accessed the chapel. A door or window must have been left open for the temperature had plummeted. He crept towards the curtained cubicle, seemingly the birthplace of the sound. Pulling the curtain across quickly he exposed a scene that would never allow him peaceful rest again. There above the coffin illuminated in the gentle low electric candle bulb, the slowly spinning body of the farmer, turning upon some invisible spit. He stood transfixed in terror with feet in treacle, body in an earthquake, a guttural growl which seemed to emanate from the very bowels of the earth filled the small chamber, he became aware of icy breath fanning the nape of his neck, it was followed, he would testify, by an erotic lick from a frozen tongue. The action galvanizes his body back, allowing his undignified exit from the chapel.

Although his wife had half convinced him it was all the result of the dozing and the bottle of Chardonnay they shared at dinner, it was a relieved undertaker that found nothing amiss the next morning.

The bishop had asked the family of the farmer to keep in touch and share any concerns they may have; he would be honoured to stay close to them during this spiritually demanding time. It was no surprise to him that a few weeks later, Elizabeth, the sister, sat before him in his office.

She tentatively began to tell him that she believed the house was still possessed, that the spirit of her brother was now imprisoned, trapped by the entity where he had sought relief. She saw no sign of ridicule from the bishop, just a deeper furrowing of the brow. She began her story.

A few days after the funeral she had entered her brother's cottage to begin the process of dispersal. While in his office sorting through various papers and bills she heard what sounded like a shuffling from the bedroom above. Heart racing, she slowly climbed the stairs armed with a shillelagh the Irish cudgel her brother had brought back from a stag weekend spent cavorting round the Curragh in Ireland's County Kildare.

Nearing the top she was able to peer through the open door of the master bedroom. The far wall had a picture of the family in happy times draped across an old Massey Ferguson tractor. Joy and love etched in each smiling face. In amazement she watched as tiny strips of wallpaper were peeled back revealing the dark emulsioned wall. Slowly words appeared. Sculpted from an invisible hand, three small beseeching words, profound words, words uttered by multitudes across the centuries, words fashioned from beyond the grave.

God help me.

She turned to flee but halfway up the stairs, something was coming, something unearthly, something leaching energy to gain form, heat was being stolen from her body, rapid cooling and terror leadened her being.

Forcing her feet to respond, she backed towards the bedroom. Slamming the door shut, reversing with pounding heart towards the old double bed, dread borne in the knowledge that the door would be no barrier.

Almost imperceptibly a few wisps of dark passed through the door like smoke from the forest campfire still drifting skyward in the early morning dew.

Through the door the substance rapidly increased its progress, filling the space between ceiling and floor.

She continued retreating, tripping and falling backwards onto the counterpane that covered the marital bed.

The forest smoke had taken shape, turning towards her was the giant form of a hooded monk.

The form advanced towards the mesmerized woman, eventually towering above her; she felt her legs being hoisted and parted.

She prayed. Beseeching the Lord to take this trial from her. The picture fell from the wall, the edges of the counterpane began to flap like some demented stingray.

The monk became distracted, the vice-like grip that contained her vanished. She vaulted from the bed, bolted for the door, slung it wide and was down the stairs and out, speeding away to seek sanctuary.

She told the bishop that she had felt her brother's spiritual presence in the bedroom and believed he had somehow intervened allowing her time to escape.

The bishop asked her to pray with him and told her that the church had special people who could deal with these situations, she must put her faith in the Christ. No matter how dark it seems, how black the outlook, Jesus had promised "I will always be with you…I am the light of the world, whoever follows me will never walk in darkness but will have the light of life".

She parted from the bishop deeply moved and comforted, impressed by his grasp of the practicalities of living in this world while governing his whole life by the requirements for the next.

The bishop, in the privacy of his office, reached for the phone and dialled the number of Michael Grogan. He arranged to meet Michael in the cathedral the next day.

The bishop poured a pint of tea into his Mickey Mouse mug, a lifelong idiosyncrasy, learned behaviour from his father, who was constantly plied with tea throughout his days ministering in the sweltering Tanzania.

'Watering holes, son, you've got to have watering holes, you've got to drink tea till you were aniseed.' Pint pots in various guises were pampered and cosseted, displayed like treasured trophies in the hospital cupboards and school shelves across his dad's piece of Africa. The heavy Mickey Mouse mug, a leaving present to his father from the school children of Impala, he held with as much reverence as any goblet containing the sacrament. It kept him close to the memory of his dad and the blissful days when the two would pedal out across the Serengeti/ savanna, stopping to gaze at the marvels unfolding before them.

'He gave us eyes to see his wonders, a heart full of seeds for love. Hands to lift up wounded souls, and Jesus to give us all a shove.'

He would always laugh, they would stand with one leg straddling the bikes the other firmly planted on the dusty track between them, his dad's arm around his shoulders.

They were golden days, coloured, no doubt, by the innocence of childhood, he would remain convinced throughout his life that through his child eyes he had glimpsed Eden.

He sat himself in the old worn leather chair, a chair he bought from a charity warehouse in Newmarket. At twenty-eight he had become the rector of Cheveley Church three miles outside the bustling racing town. Heady days conducting hatches, matches and dispatches.

Ministering to the racing and stud families that made up a fair proportion of the village, he had become interested in all the things racehorsey, which grew into a passion meaning the Bible and racing papers fared equal in his affections.

It was during his time in Cheveley the Right Reverend Jonathan Rumbold and his young wife Lesley met the Reverend Brian Grogan and his significant other half Jean, the rector of St Mary's Church in Newmarket.

Brian and Jean had visited the village fete with their present brood of foster children.

It was to prove the most profound meeting of his life. A

meeting that was to banish any lingering doubts about his path. A meeting that would strip him of all he thought he knew, spiritually behead him, drag him drawn and quartered through the streets of religion, bouncing him off every manufactured pillar until laid bare of all but pure faith, the door opened and he entered the Iceni.

Now, years later, he knew that the mantle that had been placed upon his shoulders would soon be lifted and placed upon another. A younger keeper, a keeper who, if the signs were to be believed, would witness the second coming.

The old leather cradled him in comfort, sips from the Disney mug spread their glow through his mortal frame.

He would send out the signal, they would come from the four corners. In the meantime he would contact Michael Grogan, adopted son of Brian and Jean, to deal with the Soham incarnation, it would be the "Last Test", confirmation that the young Newmarket man was who the bishop thought he was.

Michael Grogan had appeared wrapped in a sporting newspaper at the front door of the rectory at Newmarket's St. Mary's Church, barely a few hours old. The Grogans, responding to frantic knocking, found the bundle on the coconut welcome mat. Beside him under a small poppy cross a note which read "Mine always. Yours for life."

For a few days there was a major fuss as the authorities and the media put out appeals for the mother, all to no avail; she was never found.

The reverend and his wife were unable to have children of their own so had been fostering since shortly after their marriage. It was their greatest joy to see these young, often damaged, souls repair and blossom.

When it became clear that the mother would not be returning, the vicar and his wife applied to adopt. After a tortuous bureaucratic tennis match with the authorities the Grogans had a son, Michael.

Michael brought his adopted parents unbounded joy, from his first toddling steps he would dutifully follow, seemingly to relish the time spent on his mother's lap at various groups from the mothers and toddlers to the knitting and nattering.

Running around the churchyard hiding amongst the gravestones whilst his father pretended he couldn't find him was the most precious of times, the bond of love formed during those magical years would never be broken.

The Grogans were shattered when it was discovered that Michael had a degenerative heart problem that meant his life would be short. Medically there was little that could be done, if he reached adulthood then a transplant could be a possibility. The reverend and his wife tried in vain to put in place restrictions in order to limit the strain upon the growing boy's heart but the little fellow would have none of it, joining the rough and tumble of boy life at every available opportunity.

The first day at Holsworth Valley Nursery School, a short walk from the vicarage, the four-year-old Grogan was assigned his own carer, the six-year-old Ninal Prolly.

Ninal, a wiry petite blonde whose motherly skills were far in advance of her tender years, was assigned the task of looking after him.

Mrs. Wilsoncroft, the headmistress, instructed her to keep him safe from the rough boys.

It was a task she was well capable of performing, coming from a big Irish family living in Manderston Road on the Holsworth Valley estate. Her father Seamus, an Irish schoolboy boxing champion, fine jockey and now head lad and work rider for Hugo Botrill, one of the leading racehorse trainers in Newmarket, taught all his children the art governed by rules set out by the Marquess of Queensberry.

Ninal was never sure which skill was mastered first: boxing or walking. Tomboy to the core she could mix it with the best, football, climbing, fighting.

In the thirty a side soccer matches, that played out between jumpers and cardigans on the Manderston Road Green, she was one of the first picked, the four hour summer evening matches, whose team structure changed in complexity as combatants answering the "teatime" call, left and returned fortified by spam and jam sandwiches. As the daylight morphed into dusk, the dwindling throng, those most immune to the "bedtime" yell, would decide that next goal should be the winner and more often than not it was Ninal that slipped the ball past a flaying goalkeeper.

Ninal excelled in her duties. Normally just the dead eye stare was enough to deter the would-be bully. On occasions though one would misread the signals, or whose brain power was not advanced enough to believe the athletic sticks reputation. Their rapid education was made nursing a black eye or a fat lip.

The years passed; the two were almost inseparable. Ninal loved the rectory life helping Jean Grogan in the kitchen feeding the hordes who descended for various meetings, sorting through jumble, readying the Turner Hall next to the church for all sorts of functions from children's parties, public meetings, wedding receptions.

Sunday morning Ninal and the rest of the Prollys would attend the Catholic Church en masse for Mass.

Her parents had no problem with her joining the Grogans for evensong at the protestant high church of St Mary's.

Her dad would often say, 'As long as you are singing with Jesus, my angel, the song is not important.'

Michael loved life at the Prollys. Ninal's mother seemed to be forever on the end of a teapot fortifying the constant stream of neighbours. The house filled with children, joy and laughter. Ninal's four brothers, along with assorted friends, seemed to fill every available space. Cars, trains, skittles were the main obstacles to be negotiated for safe passage. Rolled up socks were the missiles of choice in the toy soldier battles. The highly polished stairs' banister, a product of pyjama bottoms speeding their way to the dinner table, was Michael's favourite.

Rapid descent by banister was a definite no-no at the rectory. The perpetrator could be met by a fearsome woman with folded arms and eyes like daggers who bore a striking resemblance to their kindly mother.

Experience had proved that to gain a little slack at bedtimes it was best to ensure "silent stare, statute lady" manifestations were rare. Sedate orderly descent down the oak staircase was the prudent choice.

In the summer of Michael's eighth year a street hard sunken steely-eyed urchin arrived for fostering from the Elephant and Castle area of London. He was woefully thin with skin of nut leather. He viewed the world as his enemy. At ten years old he had suffered more trauma that would normally taint a battalion of lives. His body gave witness through scars and cigarette burns to an existence no child should endure. Such was his appearance that later Michael caught sight of his mother weeping uncontrollably in her tearful husband's arms.

The young Oliver was to sleep in Michael's room.

Michael would wake to the muffled sounds of sobbing. Oliver would have his head buried in the pillow in an attempt to quiet the sorrow that would nightly overtake him. The eight-year-old would slip silently from his bed and begin to rub between the shoulder blades of the skin and bones from the streets of London.

The first few nights were met with a flaying arm, gradually the comforting hand became accepted, over time the demons that overwhelmed the boy visited less frequently, peaceful sleep became the norm.

During these episodes not a word was spoken,

Oliver never spoke of his early years. Later, as he made his way in the world as a jockey, he would tell the hungry media that he was born at ten.

The culinary side of life at the rectory took a major boost after the arrival of Oliver. Cakes, scones and jam, treacle tart, spotted dick, jam roly-poly, steamed puddings all with lashings of cream and custard. It was not until Oliver had some flesh between his bones and skin that the bounty began to dry up and the heaven-sent goodies only appeared at the weekends, prompting Michael to ask his chuckling parents if they could get another skinny boy from London.

After more torturous bureaucratic tennis Oliver and Michael became siblings. If ever an advert were needed for the benefits of nurture, Oliver was it, he became a rose from the briar. Above average diligent scholar, polite and unassuming. It was the sports field where he would excel. The culinary delights of the rectory were turned into hard toned muscle, coupled with natural athleticism, an iron determination to succeed saw him represent his school and county in running and rugby, soccer and squash.

The only bug in the butter was Ninal's reluctance to share her minder duties. A few minor skirmishes and time's soothing balm smoothed the young girl's ruffled feathers allowing Michael's new brother access to the outside of Ninal's inner circle of friends.

Oliver, like Michael, loved life at the Prollys. The unrestrained pursuit of enterprise and adventure received thick encouragement, a little grime was not to deter adventure. Punctured bikes would be upturned in the hall. Instruments to rectify, spoons, glue and rubber patches lay beneath, while the practicing surgeon's friend had arrived and tree climbing had been prioritized.

Seamus Prolly was completely oblivious to the din that filled his home, he could watch racing or sleep under the sporting paper without any perceivable recognition that he was living in the midst of a child driven tornado.

His only visible concession to the mayhem was the small wooden cabinet beside his chair, inside he would place his cup and saucer safe from aerial attack by sock missile.

Seamus, himself one of thirteen, had grown up on the Curragh in Ireland. Surrounded by horses, life had been tough, rugged and blissful. His father had been a horse dealer, selling Irish stores and ponies wherever there were a few shillings to be turned. Seamus believed he was taught to ride in the womb. He honed his racing skills on the beaches and carnivals of Ireland where pony racing thrived and the notion of "a punt" was woven into the fabric of the Irish soul, only bowing in reverence to the Virgin Mary and the tricolor.

A failed punt could mean a sparse table. Incentive enough to brand the uncompromising ferocity in Seamus Prolly's desire to win.

Skill, determination and talent saw him rise from pony racing star to champion apprentice in the hallowed world of flat racing. Increased difficulty maintaining an abnormally low body weight saw him shift codes to ride over hurdles and fences where the additional weight horses were set to carry prescribed a kinder regime for the stomach.

A tranquil appetite was trumped by a battered body. A body pummelled into the ground regularly to ensure a lengthy career.

Seamus would freely admit that the biggest gamble of his life had been as an eighteen-year-old. He assessed his odds of capturing the prize to be in excess of ten thousand to one when he walked his trembling frame towards Grace Percel at the County Fair.

Daughter of the local butcher and prettiest girl in all of Kildare. He swore he nearly fainted when she accepted his invitation to accompany him to the local dance.

Two years later they were married at the small Catholic church in Newbridge on the Curragh. Ten years later, after four boys, Ninal was born, the mirror image of her mother.

The early years of their marriage saw Seamus consuming increasing amounts of alcohol, seeking solace from the immense pressure faced by young sportsmen.

Saturday in early October. The young couple had dropped the first two Prolly offspring at Grace's parents, grateful for the short respite, a rare chance to accompany her husband to the racecourse to watch her jockey husband in gainful employment.

Returning from racing, the first signs of winter's icy

28

fingers caressing the fields, heading into Newbridge to collect their little toddling people.

Seamus insisted they stopped for a couple of jars in the pub a short distance from his in-laws' house. Grace preferred to continue, desperate not to overstep the generosity of her parents, potentially jeopardizing an invaluable benefit to the Prolly household.

An altercation ensued, which left Grace to walk the remainder of the journey.

Seamus sat in the pub looking at the liquid that had become so dominant in his life. His wife's parting words whispered in his ears. 'Please don't condemn me to a life where my husband is lost to the contents of a bottle.'

He'd only wanted a couple of beers after a long day, she couldn't condemn him for that. Surely every man had a right and yes, he did have a beer before work that morning, so what? It was not illegal, several lads had tinnies.

He sat in the half gloom of the pub, realization dawning that he was being drawn into a sea of grief where he would drown whilst those around him who loved him were yelling from the beach.

Jim, the valet, rearranging several beers in Seamus's racing bag to accommodate his riding paraphernalia, had looked him in the eye and, devoid of his usual joviality, said, 'You don't choose alcohol Seamus, it chooses you.' That cryptic message, baffling at that time now became crystal. A Damascus moment when the realization struck, the same realization that had struck everyone else who cared for him long ago.

An hour passed in a minute, a silent prayer for the strength he knew he did not possess.

He rose from the bar stool, lifted the glass in salute, brought it to his lips and kissed the glass with the passion of a lover sailing away never to return, tears dripped from his chin mirroring the droplets of condensation which wove their weary drunken paths down the glass, finally falling to the floor and oblivion. He placed the honey siren back onto the shiny mahogany bar, turned, walked through the door and into the first day of the rest of his life.

In the garden of his in-laws he cried and hugged his wife; she cried and hugged her husband, knowing the man she loved had wrestled and faced down his demon. He would be pursued every day whilst he walked upon the earth. She knew with help, with love and with God he would stay in the sunshine. Years later he confided in the Grogan boys.

You are never cured, you are always a recovering alcoholic, you are always gasping for one drink but you know a thousand will never be enough. 'It's like walking along the beach in the sweltering heat, the cool blue ocean is inviting you in, should you dip a toe you will drown.'

He rarely missed his weekly AA meetings; a brotherhood who understood the enemy's stealth and ruthless determination to reclaim its own.

A few years, many more winners, some cash in the bank, two more nappy dangling Prollys and Ninal on the way, saw Seamus accept the position as work rider and second head lad to Hugo Bottril's powerful Newmarket stables situated behind the beautiful flint cottages of Exeter Road.

Hugo presented head lad Robert "Jock" MacGregor, a granite Glaswegian, fashioned from a long line of shipbuilders, who had broken the mound, his interest drawn more to the ponies pulling the steel than the ships it became.

Jock, almost thirty years Seamus Prolly's senior, was desperate to retire and redirect his devotions to his ailing wife and his enviable flock of racing pigeons.

His passage to his present hallowed position mirrored Seamus's, a body painfully maneuvered, the result of too many high impact collisions with unyielding ground.

A brain, perceptive and rapid, honed on steeplechasing's myriad of battlefields, where sportsmen meet to unbridle the passion that mostly lies restrained, where big men cry tears of jumping jack joy or sobbing sorrow unhindered by the critical eye. The last stronghold for the horse, where it still clings to the ancient Celtic soul, a spirit that gave its willing sinew to feed and change mankind's destiny.

Jock was as fair as he was tough; maintaining the highest standard was all he required. Jock and Seamus became firm friends. A friendship born of mutual admiration.

Eighteen months later Jock was able to retire in peace, knowing that the working shrine to the majesty of the horse would be maintained if not enhanced.

Hugo Bottril's training establishment prospered under the stewardship of Seamus. Hugo's main attribute and the hardest to achieve was to get the horses in the first place. He was excellent with the media, accepting high praise for his training achievements with beguiling modesty, always deflecting any praise back to his excellent team of staff. He was fully aware that no part of the hands-on job could he do to an acceptable standard. His gift was to recognize and nurture talent in others, one which he shared with Seamus.

None of Seamus's sons seemed to have inherited anything but a mild interest in the horse. It was Ninal who would trip round the stables behind her father.

Over time she became admirably proficient. By the age of twelve she had progressed from riding the pony to cantering the quiet racehorse.

Oliver had now moved from the outer of the inner circle, to the inner of the inner circle of Ninal's friends when Seamus took both Grogan boys along with his daughter to Sunday evening stables prior to them all disappearing for evensong.

It set the course for Oliver's life: the affinity shared with the horse was instantly recognizable. Seamus, aware of the boy's troubled childhood, wondered if the dam of suppressed love burst in the presence of the horse. Oliver was simply besotted, grooming, stroking at every opportunity.

Oliver idolized Seamus, always referring to him as "Mr. Prolly". The next few years saw the boy from the Elephant and Castle rise from wobbling on the pony to slick work rider. The pair could often be seen in chess-like posture while Seamus explained some intricacy.

Before his sixteenth birthday, both Seamus and Hugo Botrill believed the boy to be a prodigy. At sixteen he was able to ride as an amateur; he quickly started to notch up the winners. Hugo increasingly began to farmer these types of races knowing that a lack of ability in the equine could be offset by the talent of his young jockey.

At eighteen he had turned professional and, like his mentor, had become champion apprentice. Trainers loved his riding style, only employing the whip as the last implement in the toolbox. When in the drive position his bottom hovered less than an inch from the saddle, his heels with vice-like grip dug the animal's ribcage, his head low, vision confined between his partner's ears, his hands and arms would pump along the horse's neck, pushing the head down, demanding extra effort and commitment.

Oliver Grogan's was the rising star of the weighing room.

Constantly Seamus's catchphrases would be ringing in his head. "At the two-furlong pole the race is only half over." "Switched 'em off and they will switch on." "Keep low for the dough the wind is your enemy." "Racehorses don't read the newspapers. The form book is a work of fiction, read the race not the form." "Give your fellow jockey the miles to Mars but not an inch on the racecourse."

Seamus often spoke about the grey area where most racehorses live. The black area contains horses that are so gifted that a modest talent will win with them. The white area were horses completely devoid of any type of ability, requiring divine intervention for the handler to take the spoils. Good trainers and jockeys will come a long way down into the grey area instilling belief and desire into the horse. Great trainers and jockeys achieved the pinnacle of their respective careers and got horses to run above themselves.

At twenty-one Oliver had a string of major victories behind him. He had cemented himself into the echelons of the sought after, although, like his mentor, switching riding codes was inevitable to retain his sanity. In keeping with the gifted he soon perfected the art of riding over the obstacles placed daily before the National Hunt jockey. Although success had entered his jockey life earlier than most he was acutely aware he had been blessed, the greatest of his blessings, his adopted family and the bond he shared with the Prollys, especially Ninal. It surprised the racing community that he would not race ride on Sundays, dedicating that day entirely to God and his family.

Every breath, every heartbeat, every straining muscle convinced him that he had been plucked from a dreadful place, welcomed and adored by his adopted family for some purpose, that purpose as yet unclear but somewhere in the divine order of things the focal point of his deliverance had at its core his brother, Michael.

At seventeen Oliver had asked Michael if he had any notions of a romantic link-up with Ninal. Michael had laughed and said, 'He loved her dearly as a sister.' If Oliver had any romantic intentions toward Ninal he had better get a move on because she had turned from the skinny beanpole tomboy into a long legged curvy creature that was turning heads and craning necks.

It was a nervous tongue-tied Oliver with feathers for saliva that asked Ninal to the cinema. Five years later it was a trembling, stomach-churning, powder-mouthed Oliver who asked Mr. Prolly if he could please marry his daughter.

High June in front of the pavilion on Newmarket's Severals, an expanse of dream-manicured lawns. Ninal and Oliver were married. The invitation had read "bring a brolly it's all outdoors." Rain to them was joyful weather. When caught and drenched riding out across Newmarket's rolling grasslands it filled the senses, stroked the soul awake, and switched on a dormant giggle button.

The Brollies would be unemployed, the day woke with nothing but lonesome cotton-wool clouds, drifting yachts on an upturned Mediterranean Sea.

The extended families of Seamus and Grace seemed to have drained Ireland of half its population. Pubs and hotels along Newmarket's famous high street working on maximum throttle to service the generous spirit of the Irish in party mode. The wedding, scheduled for six thirty p.m., gave time for Oliver's weighing room friends to make the thirty-minute journey from Huntingdon races.

The wedding would be unusual on several fronts. The bride and groom would wear green, the color that most symbolized their lives. Ninal, fiercely proud of her Irish roots, land of fable, poets and song, the emerald jewel of the Atlantic. The small piece of God's earth, its contribution to mankind far outweighing its physical presence. Ninal felt a strong connection with the earth and the green canvas on which stood its masterpieces. She saw merit in her father's theory that the invading hordes from the east pushed the ancient Celts into Wales, Scotland, Ireland and the West Country. These were earth people who lived with the earth not simply on it. They had an affinity with the natural world and all its mysteries 'Is it any wonder,' Seamus would say, 'that many of the world's great horse people have Celtic ancestry.'

Oliver's overriding memory of his first day of the Grogans was when Ninal, Michael and several other scruffy urchins placed him on a bicycle, with the lead rider, ball tucked under his arm, led his small platoon of the Manderston Road mob to the free side of Newmarket's Rowley Mile racecourse. Oliver was mesmerized, staring agog at the biggest expanse of mown grass in the world, listening gobsmacked to the thunder that roared down the racecourse, transfixed watching a palette of galloping colour, bobbing heads, straining for supremacy. Spellbound as the huge concrete totem erupted to a cacophony of released emotion, rising in unconducted crescendo to die quickly in disappointment or slowly in delight at a red and white lolly stick. Green for Oliver with its myriad of hues were the shoulders where other colours stood to shine.

After the ceremony, a relay of seafood emblemed white vans brought fish and chips from the plentiful fish bars that served the town and placed them upon the tables commandeered, along with small chairs, from the convent and Fairstead House schools that abut the Severals.

In front of the pavilion, on a temporary dancefloor, a ceilidh band played late into the night. The highlight was when Ninal and Oliver took to the floor and performed a slick display of Irish dancing.

Ninal's mother, Grace, had set up an Irish dance school at the Astley Club shortly after the family's arrival in England. A celebrated dancer herself with a serene teaching style, the school quickly grew to being one of the foremost cultural exponents of Irish dance in the country. When a long line of her students appeared from behind the pavilion onto the dancefloor, arms interlocked in trellis formation, their feet an intricate blur, the roar of applause filled the Suffolk town.

The most unusual part of the proceedings was that Michael would conduct the ceremony; the bishop had fast-tracked him through all the usual procedures. His explanation to the raised eyebrows was that Michael had not been called to God but sent by him.

It was a beautiful wedding. Oliver and Ninal exchanged vows, rings and apple trees. Two "James Grieves" eaters would be planted in the orchard at St Mary's Rectory where Michael, Oliver and Ninal had spent the happiest of times.

Laughing, Michael had said, 'When I am called home, spread my ashes around the roots. I'll be happy to know I live within your trees.'

Michael had defied the medical profession and lived well

past his life expectancy, baffling the doctors who puzzled as to how his defective heart could sustain life.

Oliver and Ninal knew that no matter what, wherever Michael went they would follow. Their entwined souls knew he was here for a reason, he would stay until that challenge had been met.

The newly-weds had recently felt a gentle blow of unease wafting through the faces of some senior ecclesiastical types. Wandering if this was the gathering storm that somehow Michael would have to face, little did they know the gathering storm would become a raging tempest.

Those closest to Michael knew very early that he had special talents, or that was what they were referred to as. Michael's adopted mother, Jean, was forever shooing an array of birds and wild animals away from his pram which seemed to have a magnetic attraction for them when baby Michael was placed in some shady spot for his afternoon siesta.

As a toddler he would accompany his father as he ministered to the spiritual needs of the patients at Newmarket Hospital. Michael enjoyed sitting on the bed, holding the hands of the patients. Those whose smile had abandoned them would be beaming with joy as he climbed down the bed rail and on to the next ascent. 'Good things happen when this little fellow's about.' Dr. Brady, the hospital's senior physician told the vicar.

Holdsworth Valley School's academic reputation soared during the Michael years. Visiting inspectors, eager to unlock the secrets, noted a serenity that fostered diligence and application, manifesting itself in achievement, extremely unusual for a primary school whose hinterland housed some of the poorest in society. The head teacher, Mrs. Wilsoncroft, was singled out for much praise; she herself believed the transformation had begun the day a little boy from the rectory joined the nursery.

Stories permeated the staffroom of a boy who could read seemingly without ever being taught, who wrote and painted with astonishing accuracy. The assistant headmistress, Mrs. Gorham, whilst patrolling the playground, witnessed Michael fall onto the tarmac, wiping away the blood and grit from his hands and knees. She was adamant that no puncture wounds could be found.

Whilst supervising the music lesson, with tambourine and triangle in full throng, a young thrush flew into the windowpane, falling immediately. Mrs. Wilsoncroft saw the unfortunate bird lying motionless, head skewed unnaturally. The headmistress would remove the dead bird during playtime.

Arriving at the side of the building a few minutes after the bell had rung she was astonished to find Michael sitting on the ground, the bird nestled in his hand. He smiled at her, stroked the thrush's head, then released the bird; it soared away into the heavens. She never repeated the incident to any member of staff, only confiding in Father Ramsey in the confessional box, believing she had witnessed something incredible, if not a miracle performed by the hands of a small boy.

Growing up Michael could often be seen talking to himself. When challenged as to who his imaginary friend was he would reply, 'I'm talking to God.'

In the early days his father would say, 'Oh you're praying.'

Michael would reply, 'No we are talking, can you not hear him?'

One summer evening Brian Grogan and his wife Jean were barbecuing the evening meal in the garden of the rectory a hundred yards from the purple flint clad high church of St Mary's nestled in the centre of Newmarket. Their guests and good friends, the Reverend Jonathan Rumbold and his wife Lesley from the parish of Cheveley.

Lesley took over the cooking duties, to allow Brian and Jonathan to ambling the garden, also enabling her a more intimate chat with her great friend Jean on subjects of great interest that the male of the species were not equipped with the mental abilities to comprehend.

The two clergymen strolled the grounds, biting into the long rolls filled with sausage and bacon, smothered in red and brown sauce, a thin line of yellow mustard augmenting the relish, leaning forward to allow unfettered access to the ground for any drippings, therefore avoiding the wrath of their washing fairies.

Jonathan pointed out that Michael had pulled away from the marauding horde of urchins charging about, pretending to be cowboys, Indians or aliens; he was sitting on an old tree stump chatting away in earnest to himself.

Brian replied, 'Michael tells me he is talking to God and I'm not so sure he isn't.'

The two men watched the young boy gesticulate as though emphasizing some point before slipping off the log and heading for the two washing fairies who had produced ice cream.

Walking past the two curates, Michael said, 'Mr. Jonathan sir, God says you are going to be a bishop.'

The Right Reverend Jonathan Rumbold stood dumbfounded.

That very afternoon he had received notice that he had been nominated for that position.

Michael continued to astonish with his growing, causing profound changes in a few, others visited the Bible, even confirmed atheists felt the bedrock of their faith crumbling.

As a boy he began giving Bible readings from the marble pulpit in St Mary's Church, causing a welcome light-hearted merriment to the small congregation, a faint squeaky voice reading some obscure passage from Revelations emanating from behind a pillar carved from Mount Vesuvius.

Time saw a head appear above the pulpit, the congregation had grown with the Bible passages now forming the skeleton of the reading. He became an orator at Catholic church much to the same response. Methodist, Baptist, gospel chapels, all became venues for his readings. Michael became a sought-after speaker amongst the Christian community. He generated a tranquillity of spirit, manifesting itself in swollen congregations, especially among the young who connected more readily with his modern style of delivering God's message.

To the casual observer, Michael could well have been a rock star. The boy had grown into a handsome young man, his soft brown hair, fashionably lapping his collar, his Wedgewood eyes piercing and bright. Around his five feet, ten inch lean frame was often draped a black leather jacket, faded worn blue jeans slipped over the top of various cowboy boots completed the illusion.

In his early twenties he would have been a match for any emerging pop star judging by the queues that formed to listen to him speak.

Hierarchy of the various strands of Christianity eagerly

embraced him hoping he would nail his colours to their particular brand. He often repeated that he was the least religious person he knew, he served only God.

He received donations for his services, after taking out his living expenses for the week he gave the rest to Save the Children, thankful that the money would bring sunshine and hope to blighted lives.

Michael enjoyed being out and about especially at night with Oliver and Ninal. If Oliver wasn't battling the scales then they would enjoy the various pubs and curry houses that dot Newmarket's high street. If food was off the agenda for Oliver then dancing in the nightclubs was the sole pastime.

After one late night stint the three stepped out of the nightclub along with dozens of other revellers to find a crowd had formed.

In the middle of the street, brandishing a broken bottle and threatening to decapitate anyone who ventured near him, was a tall, gaunt youngster of West Indian origin. Several police officers surrounded him forming a cordon. Oliver said he recognized the lad as one of Ron Shetland's. His nickname was Bingo on account of his penchant for the game. Oliver was extremely surprised as Bingo was always mild mannered and pleasant when Oliver visited the yard.

Oliver turned to embrace Ninal and before he could react Michael pushed through the cordon and was walking towards Bingo. Oliver and Ninal rushed after him but were prevented by the law enforcement officers, nearly being detained at Her Majesty's pleasure themselves. Bingo turned to face Michael with wild in his eye, the jagged edges of the bottle thrust towards the advancing throat.

The astonished crowd fell silent; Michael was chanting in

some obscure language. Bingo's countenance changed dramatically. He placed the bottle on the ground and knelt before Michael who placed his hands upon Bingo's plaited locks and continued to chant. Those close observers testify they saw something rise out of the young stable lad's body and fade into the night.

Bingo was duly arrested and came before the court. The judge decided, in view of so many good character references and never having troubled the judicial system before, he would be given community service.

Michael was berated by his brother for putting himself in danger and had the situation not calmed so quickly he was sure himself and Ninal would have been residing at a secure place designed to house those who had displeased Her Majesty's officers.

Michael laughed and insisted he was never in any danger and teased his brother with his most annoying catchphrase, 'Oh ye of little faith.'

Michael came to the attention of the chief constable after more instances where he had intervened, calming the situation and bringing peaceful resolution. He accepted a position on the team of negotiators, quickly becoming the bobbies' choice for the speed he could achieve the desired outcome. Threatened suicides, domestic sieges, gang stand-offs. Officers reported the powder keg of tension drained in his presence, potential dynamite situations ended with hugs and handshakes.

Jonathan Rumbold had made an excellent bishop. The bond between the Rumbolds and the Grogans grew ever stronger as the years melted away. Jonathan had watched Michael's spiritual development ever since the boy had told him in the rectory gardens that God had called him to be a leader of the church.

As time's train chugged on, the bishop became more convinced that Michael had been sent for a purpose. That purpose would soon be at hand.

The bishop called Michael to deal with the Soham incarnation as his final task before he introduced him to the Iceni.

And so it was that Michael found himself on the edge of the lonely fens in the dim hall of an old farmhouse; the only light struggled to gain entry through dingy windows, the lightbulbs removed to retain the preferred darkness of its present occupier. Michael edged forward, past the kitchen to the two reception rooms either side of the hallway, the only sound the gentle squeak of oak floorboards scraping the side of loose nails. In the left hand dining room the walls were clothed in family photographs. Neat children in school uniform, chocolate-smudged faces of toddlers surrounded by sandcastles with Hunstanton busy tide foaming in the offing. Two portraits of old, content couples stared at the camera.

A soulful springer spaniel lay prostrate, pear drop eyes hung in mournful countenance of one whose soul has been snatched by the cameraman.

Michael, having examined the photographs, then walked towards the opposite lounge, unaware that each picture in turn began to blister, each portrait contorting to form a hideous grotesque caricature. Michael became aware of the familiar temperature drop. Whatever would be stalking him was leaching energy in preparation for the onslaught. He circled the lounge, saw the pentagram and various paraphernalia of devil worship. His breath now was freezing fog. Knowing it would be walking in his tracks he re-entered the hallway, heading for the staircase. At its base the front door erupted in a crescendo of straining bolts, locks and hinges. Oliver and Ninal, realizing Michael had entered the house and locked himself in, were trying to gain entry; the door had withstood the first battering. Michael began climbing the stairs, his body now shivering with the cold, his limbs struggling to function. He entered the master bedroom. There in the long mirror beside the bed he saw his reflection. Standing behind and towering above him was a hooded monk. The manifestation moved towards him, he felt its glacial breath fan his neck as though in preparation for some satanic sexual gratification.

The retching stench, a blend of maggot and bowel, burned at Michael's nostrils. An irresistible force began to bend Michael across the bed. In the mirror Michael caught sight of the incarnation's huge phallus, its fleshless hand grasping the base, directing the damaging tool in preparation for the act of sodomy.

'Abaddon, Apollyon, Asmodeus,' Michael commanded. Instantly the pressure bearing on Michael disappeared. He stood and turned to face his adversary whose head, with reptilian movement, oscillated like a bewildered dinosaur, looking from where the unseen spear had been dispatched. Michael was aware that the main entrance door had been breached, commotion and shouting were racing up the stairs, to fall silent at their first encounter with a disciple of the Diabolical.

A guttural growl, borne from the bowels of hell, grew like a thousand tormented bulls whose stampede burst out of the manifestation's mouth into the confines of the bedroom, the structure shook to the foundations, furniture danced, the bed lifted and tipped. The family photo span from the wall to land

44

face-down upon the bucking counterpane.

The spectra of the monk's habit faded, the demented form that was left would defy any human description: a meld of goat head, skinned fighting bull torso, giant donkey phallus and legs.

It stooped before springing into the air, hovering with its lipless mouth almost touching Michael's.

Michael saw from the corner of his eye his terrified brother being prevented by Ninal from attempting a rescue.

The din had reached an excruciating crescendo when Michael lifted his hand.

'I command you to silence.'

Instantly the room stopped shaking, the furniture fell back into place, the manifestation descended to stand before Michael.

Not a decibel of sound was brought forth to trouble the human ear, not a ticking of a clock or creaking of a board, a tapping of twig on pane or distant purr of combustion engine. All was as the grave.

Michael spoke, 'I command you, Malak, to give up the soul of Martin. Martin I ask you to pray with me to ask your father in heaven for redemption and deliverance. Together we will ask him to lift this burden from you, to cast out this evil.

'There is one religion, the religion of love. One language, the language of the heart. One race, the human race. One God, he is the god of love.

'You were hurt and he tried to hold you. You ran into the dark. He holds the eternal flame for you now to light your way.

'To love another person, Martin, is to see the face of God. See those faces of your family now and pray with me.'

Michael began the Lord's Prayer.

With each word the spectre twitched, each line completed, the beast became less opaque, the substance that held the terror together was evaporating. At its core and taking form was the young farmer, Martin, his hands clasped together in prayer, his mouth moving inaudibly.

As the evaporation continued, a faint chanting of the Lord's Prayer could be heard in stereo with Michael's incantation. 'Deliver us from evil, for thine is the Kingdom, the power and the glory.'

The room began to warm and brighten, shafts of sunlight pierced the windows, flecks of dust danced in the corridors of the beams, a crystal tinkle rose from the window as though an invisible hand had tapped an invisible rim.

A burst of light filled the window space, temporarily blinding the observers.

Returning sight saw the chuckling, giggling Bernadette, Ben and Amy Green standing at the foot of the bed, beckoning the soul of their father to join them.

Freed from oppression, a joyful spirit joined the hilarity. Scenes of undiluted bliss filled the watchers' eyes, dancing and hugging, skipping and kissing.

Michael turned towards Oliver and Ninal who had moved into the doorway, both had rivulets of tears weaving their descent towards the carpet.

The reunited family moved towards the window. Bernadette suddenly floated back over the bed, gathering the stricken picture she replaced it on the wall.

Re-joining the rapture of her family, the Greens turned as one, waving their goodbyes. Golden light once again bathed the room and the souls of the farmer and his family were gone.

There is more joy in heaven when one lost soul is found.

Michael looked at his own family who were hugging. Eye diamonds' destinations had changed from carpet to shoulders. Michael smiled, 'There are no tears in heaven.'

On the drive back to Newmarket in Oliver's beloved Jaguar, Michael phoned the bishop and told him, 'Another one bites the dust.' Those close to him knew he had a penchant for phrases from the Bible, quotations from poetry or snatches from songs. It was a beguiling idiosyncrasy that his brother used as a tease in the constant brotherly banter.

'You must sit up all night studying one-liners to have such a vast array of alternative speak on the tip of your tongue,' Oliver taunted.

'Sleep is just the door beyond which the spirit can soar,' Michael replied.

Ninal, so familiar with this daily ritual, knew it masked a bond that would only be broken by death, a death that she felt sure would soon embrace her brother-in-law and friend who had toddled into Holsworth Valley Primary School those many years ago, for she had seen him stagger in the confrontation. What blood was being pumped from his failing heart had drained, he had become pallid and weak. How would Oliver cope, a rough tough jump jockey on the outside, a sentimental marshmallow with no shield to the arrows fired by those in distress on the inside?

Any report on the suffering of the planet's children could brine his eyes in the beat of a bee's wing. His family was everything; his brother, the world.

The trip back to Newmarket was unusually quiet as Oliver and Ninal were inwardly digesting the world they were entering. Over the years both had realized they were here for a purpose; Oliver knew, whatever it was, it was upon them.

Ninal felt sure that something of vast magnitude was about to unfold, although she could not for the life imagine what might be involved, although she was certain Michael was at its core.

Michael's thoughts were centred on the Eccles cakes, Belgium and Chelsea buns that could be mined from the cake shop in the middle of Newmarket High Street; these were the cakes and buns that all cakes and buns had to be judged against –they were poetry for the taste buds.

Michael suggested a plan for him to be dropped across the road from the shrine where the delicacies were created, procure a bag full, while his brother drove the remainder of the High Street then circling the green where the statue of Elizabeth the queen denotes her devotion to racehorses, returning to pick his brother up before heading to Warren Hill.

The plan worked to perfection – Oliver arriving for the rendezvous just as his brother exited the temple of the pastries. Michael jumped in the car – a pit stop that would have not attracted much criticism from the aficionados of Formula One car racing.

Parking the car alongside Moulton Road, the trio ambled the three hundred yards to the pinnacle of Warren Hill. As iconic a piece of revered racing turf as ever existed to the riders who daily plied their magic along its courses, anonymous to all those looking into racing's aquarium, without exception the hill that all the greats that have passed through Newmarket's academy, both equine and human, famous or anonymous, have indelibly printed in their hearts.

They sat down on the antique turf, feasting the stomach with a gastric delight, while feeding the eyes on the view, the delicate shades of green, untainted by much concrete blight, the unbroken horizon where sky and land touch in a closed eyelid, a rare and wonderful sight, bequeathed almost daily to those blessed to sit atop the racehorse. Michael, Oliver and Ninal were regular observers of the majesty, spending spare moments sitting cross-legged or prone, in restful admiration or asleep.

Warren Hill, Newmarket's iconic landmark, a place of such serenity, stillness and spirituality. Where horsemen have honed the muscle and sinew of some of the greatest racehorses, where Archer, Donague, Piggott took the art of the jockey, blended it with sorcery and magic, creating a flowing flying wonder that missile glides the gentle grass, lifting horses to unicorns and men to gods.

Ancient trees stand at its summit like sentinels jealously guarding the tranquillity, peering out across the flat lands where Ely's cathedral pierces the fenland's eastern skies.

Out towards the south and Cambridge, with its Gog Magog Hill standing in ancient repose, a silent witness to the quantum leaps born, nurtured and gifted to mankind's intellectual evolution by this most elegant of English cites, a fervent bubble of enlightenment, constrained only by the limits of imagination.

The north and east, England's villages. The Suffolk of painters Constable and Gainsborough, of reed thatch, blue sky and yellow corn. Where hedgerows sing, bursting with the song of the finch, summer skies twitter with the lark, hovering high, marking the strut of the stately pheasant below.

The conversation somewhat distorted by the content of the bags.

Oliver, never having experienced Michael's work before, was disturbed; prior to this he had believed rational explanation would prevail. Ninal, more sensory, felt a sense of foreboding creeping into her consciousness, she could pin no distinct beginning. like the rhythmic change of season arriving and departing by stealth. Ninal felt they had been drawn deeper into Michael's world for a reason and that reason was almost upon them.

Their regular perch, the southerly end of the trees, which gives way to the gentle slope of a side hill which runs down to the valley road that takes the traveller to the village of Ashley and beyond into the heartland of England's green and gorgeous wonderland.

They sat beside the concrete Ordnance Survey pyramid that denotes a two foot height superiority over the sister hill that rises the other side of the valley where the mighty Arab-owned studs propagate the lifeblood of the racing industry.

After several quiet moments watching the loping motion of a hare meandering its carefree path, Ninal broke the serenity.

'Several things conspired today and I believe for some reason we were meant to witness the exorcism.'

Michael conceded that a set of circumstances prevailed which could not easily be explained or orchestrated. His train back from London to Ely had been delayed by almost two hours; he was due to meet the bishop at the cathedral, a pleasant half mile walk from the station. The bishop would accompany Michael before driving him back to Newmarket.

Michael had phoned the bishop to tell him of the delay. The bishop had been prepared to rearrange, although for the next few days the schedule was tight. Michael had suggested that Oliver and Ninal, who were in the adjacent village of Wicken visiting its famous Fen Nature Reserve, on account of Oliver having transgressed the rules of racing and been given an enforced one day holiday. Michael suggested that they might agree to collect the keys from St Andrew's, meet him at the house, wait outside while he performed his work, before ferrying him back to the bosom of his beloved parents. After a pause the bishop agreed that this might be the best course of action.

Sitting cross-legged on the soft manicured grass, gazing down the hallowed turf to its foot where sprawled beyond a tangle of suburbia where unimaginably wealthy lived cheek by jowl with those who dedicate their lives to racing's coalface where the monetary yardstick for success is a tiny flint terraced house and a small car. Oliver marvelled that each end of the racing's wealth spectrum, envy the other, the imagined joy that untold wealth bought, the peace and contentment that riding and caring for the noblest of creations bestowed upon its carers, their riches, two entwined spirits, passing through a time and place at speeds that no non-mechanical entity could come close. A spirit kingdom where only the lucky have entered

Through the ages this blessed spot has brought balm to the soul, for the multitudes who have sat looking out across the endless skies, accompanied in high summer by the twittering skylark motionlessly preaching its urgent sermon perched on the edge of the very heavens. The black gown of a frozen winter's night with a trillion sparkling sequins shimmering for attention, a wonderment the match of any earthly spectacle.

When the goodies from the cake shop had disappeared from sight, residing in the mostly mysterious inner workings of the human form, the three had assumed their regular position, prone on the green counterpane, the hill's elevation allowing effortless viewing of where Suffolk skies connect with the earth's curvature.

The male form, universally blessed with its ability to banish all types of self-proclaimed benign irrelevancies, able to drift happily into the realms of sleep almost at the closing of the eyes; the female of the species mostly having to deal with the practicalities of the oncoming day. Sleep would be denied until the plan had been formulated. Ninal could offer no descent when her mother would proclaim, 'They think it all happens by magic, food on the table, children packed off to school, laundry done, cupboards stocked, bills paid, house tidy and clean. We have to leave them to run the world, we are too busy looking after them.'

It always brought a smile to Ninal when her mother went on a rant about her beloved husband Seamus, who unwittingly had transgressed, producing a stick to the spoke, often a hitherto piece of laundry that somehow he hadn't declared, found walking around the house on its own almost unilaterally ten minutes after the last cycle of the weekly wash had finished.

The next day's plan formulated, Ninal was drifting into peaceful oblivion, the two representatives of the male species that fitted her mother's caricature were both well ahead. All physical energy diverted to the digestion process, her mother was convinced there was a hitherto undiscovered direct attachment from the stomach to the eyelids, an uncanny ability for the male to fill up the tank and almost immediately fall asleep.

As Ninal approached the gates of dream world, she became aware of her name being gently called. She sat up, effortlessly rose to her feet, walked in some sort of trance, the tranquil silence peppered only by the occasional opinion of squabbling crows. She stepped into the spinney of ancient trees, walking transfixed, heading for the small glade of rich, soft, mossy turf, where she knelt, her face tilted skywards, arms outstretched, palms facing down, her face in total rapture.

Oliver, vaguely aware that his wife had left the trio, remained unalarmed, knowing that tree wees were a staple for life as a rambler.

He was jolted back to the present with the realization her absence was far in advance of her normal duration for the tree wee.

Oliver entered the spinney to find her kneeling, hands outstretched, her face in total rapture, her hands clasping some invisible entity, mouthing silent prayer, her face ecstatic; she seemed to radiate an inner glow through every pore of her visible skin.

In bewildered panic Oliver called her name, he ran, wrapping his arms around his beloved wife, fearing she was suffering some sort of seizure, he hugged her as never before, holding her head as tightly to his chest as he could, until the woman he loved returned from wherever she had been to this little piece of heaven that is Warren Hill, the silent guardian that gazes down upon its precious charge, Newmarket town.

Oliver, a cascade of soothing words tumbling from his mouth, cradled her head, stroking her hair. She began to speak.

'They told me some amazing things,' she said.

'Who?' replied Oliver, 'Who told you amazing things?'

Ninal sat up and gave Oliver the stop fooling around husband stare.

'The two beautiful women standing in front of me holding my hands.'

Oliver stared at his wife, concern and fear etched in equal

measure across his worried face, in the most loving worried tone he could muster he said, 'Darling there was no one there.'

It was an ecstatic Ninal and a deeply concerned Oliver who reappeared from the woods, to be greeted by a prone Michael, a long strand of ryegrass protruding from the middle of his front teeth looking skyward.

It was Oliver who broke the silence.

'There is my brother chasing demons, my wife talking to people that don't exist telling her amazing things that she cannot remember, am I the only person rooted on this planet?'

Michael lifted his head from the grassy pillow.

'Here we have a man who sits atop half a ton of unpredictable horseflesh, urging its reluctant form to leap immovable objects, where any mistake is punished by pain and occasional death, the only sport where the closest followers are two ambulances, this sibling of mine is under the misguided impression that he is somehow rooted on this planet.'

With that piece of brotherly wisdom, Michael returned his cranium back onto the welcome softness of the verdant pillow.

'So, beloved sister-in-law and guardian of my frail form, spill the beans, what has been occurring the last few minutes of your precious life?'

'Well, frail brother-in-law or bane of my life, as I was explaining to this neanderthal husband of mine or better described as work in progress.

I heard my name being called. I had the most overwhelming, undeniable urge calling me into the woods. Each step seemed to fill me with a profound sense of love, everything more beautiful than I had ever seen. The plants seemed to radiate—'

Michael broke in, 'Mine eyes have seen the glory of the

54

coming of the Lord.'

Ninal continued, 'A small clearing seemed to be my destination. You prehistoric types may have (understandably, knowing the ridiculously small bladder I have been blessed with) thought it was the call of nature that beckoned me into the woods. In keeping with your past innumerable efforts, your assumptions were, as usual, totally wrong.'

'Dear sister-in-law, as you know from the female perspective, we only have two faults, everything we say, and everything we do.'

'Correct, dearest brother-in-law, the vast majority of the world's women find it extremely difficult to argue with you on that point.

'I shall reiterate the last few minutes' proceedings.

'I heard my name being gently called.'

Once again she paused. Michael rolled over, perched his head in the palm of his hand, his elbow anchored in the cozy turf, viewed his sister-in-law with an intense kindly smile, she continued her narrative.

'It was a magical sound, really musical but somehow not, I felt my body being lifted gently with little physical effort on my part, the ground seem to float beneath me although I saw my feet walking, being guided somehow into the woods, every step the world seemed to become more beautiful and brighter, every breath seemed to fill me with a greater sense of joy. I had the most overwhelming, undeniable urge calling me on, each moment magnifying a profound sense of love, everything more beautiful than I had ever seen, as though a veil had been lifted. I was seeing the world for the first time as the paradise it really is, the trees, the plants seem to radiate—'

Michael again broke in, 'My eyes have seen the glory of

the coming of the Lord.'

'There before me, in a small clearing, two of the most beautiful women I have ever seen, their beaming smiles and outstretched arms beckoned, I walked towards them and knelt, each took hold of an outstretched palm, gently and lovingly stroking the back of my hands they spoke, their words seem to flow into my very soul, my spirit seem to swell within me, they began to fade, still smiling, then the strong arms of that brutish brother of yours, the one standing over there looking out towards the Tattersalls auction ring, pretending not to be listening, the only other place I've ever felt the Euphoria that fills me. I knew these women were the two rocks upon which Jesus had built his missionary, Mary, his mother and Mary Magdalene, his wife, they spoke of the dangers now facing the temple of Jesus Christ.'

'I'm not sure everyone would agree that he was married,' Oliver said.

Michael piped up.

'It would be mighty unusual if he were not seeing as most were betrothed before they were twelve years of age, of all his miracles, staying free from the command of a boss lady would probably have been his greatest. Anyway most of the religious doctrines have been skewed for man's purpose not God's.

'The gift from God to prove his existence is love, who would not suffer agonies in place of those they loved. Sorry to interrupt with my two pennies worth non-blood relation.'

'That's okay,' Ninal replied. 'If I had two pence for every two pennyworth that I have endured over the years I would be a very rich woman.'

'You are a very rich lady,' Oliver said. 'You've got me. I must get the recipe for those Eccles cakes they are making down the town, got to be a fortune in them.' Their laughter brought normality back to the strangest of time.

Michael's mobile phone crashed the serenity, with its Suzi Quatro song *"Down in Devil Gate Drive"* ringtone. This blast always brought a smile to those that loved this devout man of God, to the raised eyebrows the reply was always the Devil's always had the best music.

The result of this phone conversation was an agreed meeting between them and the bishop at St Mary's Church that evening.

Oliver spent the rest of the day talking with his racing agent trying to finalize his riding plans for the upcoming race meeting at Ascot where valuable prizes were on offer.

Meanwhile the bishop had made all the necessary arrangements, gathering together the Iceni, all that remained was to enlighten the chosen.

The bishop had in place all the relevant centuries old procedures; his life-changing meeting at St Mary's Church with Michael and his two life companions was imminent.

For the first time, for a long time, he felt a stomach-churning nervousness; the end game could well be upon them. Of all the watches that had gone before, he was the one, the one who would see the fruition of the prophecies. For the longest time the bishop had had no doubts but there were safeguards, rules that had to be followed so that no danger could befall. The enemy was so devious that the slightest chink, the merest hint of an opening, two thousand years of dedication and sacrifice would have been wasted.

He had rehearsed this moment hundreds of times but now he felt the fright that multitudes endure before they take the stage, he was sure he would be guided, invisible hands holding him steadfast several times in his life he had known he was being carried, now, once again, he could feel the presence.

The bishop entered St Mary's Church, in slacks and cotton T-shirt, through the vestry door and slipped into the main body of the church. In the front pews sat Michael, his foster brother Oliver and Ninal, who brought some sobriety to the lives of the two frolicking brothers.

The bishop exchanged pleasantries with the three, sat himself down on the steps leading to the altar.

'If I were to tell you that this church is the most secure place in the world, that the monitoring equipment used is the most sophisticated known to mankind, that those who protect this holy place are among the most devout people ever to set foot on the planet. That they would happily endure any atrocities rather than give up their piece of the jigsaw, you may then realize that what I am about to say, should you decide to stay and listen will change your world and turn it on its head. You will leave this place with the knowledge that few have been blessed with.

'There is danger at every turn, the enemy we face is powerful, immensely powerful, this is not a battle between armies where power and influence ebb and flow, where empires can be destroyed, this is a battle much more profound; it will last for eternity, it is the battle for the soul of mankind.

'I ask you now,' said the bishop, 'to pray with me, ask for guidance whether you stay to face the dread or stand and walk away with my blessing.' The four prayed from the root of their souls, *Gethsemane Garden Prayer*, a prayer of mind and spirit where world and body became irrelevant.

'Amen,' from the bishop brought them back from

spirituality to reality, in answer to his invitation to leave all three remained seated.

'We must go back two thousand years to around the time of Christ, England was in flames, the Roman armies were being destroyed by Boadicea the Warrior Queen, the legionnaire garrisons at Colchester and St Albans had been routed, questions were being asked in Rome as to whether this Britannia should be abandoned as ungovernable, the Celtic nations were fierce and even the mighty Roman legions questioned whether the struggle to suppress these people was worth the heavy toll.

'Though the Roman armies were steeped in the science of war, the ancient Britons seemed to have a mystical quality, an affinity with nature, an uncanny ability to appear and disappear, they seemed to be part of the animal kingdom, not divorced from it, in tune with the poetry of the earth, worshipping the wonders before them. They seemed to be able to communicate with the animals, not through domination but mutual admiration.

'What astonished the onlookers was their ability with the horse and the ease of which the two became one, a new entity, a spiritual being elevating mankind to an unobtainable paradise raised upon the back of the equine man could see further, travel faster, longer, glimpsing a paradise that alone he could not have witnessed.

'The most feared of the Celts was the Iceni tribe from the area of Exning and Newmarket, governed by Boadicea and her band of ferocious women. Her father had been betrayed and killed by the Romans, her daughters raped, her revenge knew no limits, "Hell hath no fury like a woman scorned", as William Congreve once wrote. Boadicea poured down upon the Romans from a cauldron of boiling hate.

'Perhaps because of her ferocity the Roman high command decided that to avoid a domino effect throughout the empire they would have to subdue this woman and so massive reinforcements were sent. Commanders were recalled from Anglesey. This woman warrior had to be stopped at all costs. Perhaps because of her and the withdrawal of the Roman legions, to bolster the attack on East Anglia, the great equine strongholds of Ireland, Scotland, Wales, the West Country where the Latin influence had little chance to dilute were saved as troops withdrew down to London. Still today the world's great horsemen seem to have their roots firmly in the Celtic bloodline.

'Faced with overwhelming odds, her battle plans had to take a radical diversion. Historians argue that this was the first diversion into guerrilla warfare.

'The New Testament was not yet upon us; the Old Testament shows God intervening many times: the ark, the parting of the Red Sea, Sodom and Gomorrah.

'To the west of Boadicea's stronghold in the heather lands lay the modern-day village of Reach, beyond which the treacherous wetlands, now known as the Fens, a fearful land where the inhabitants appeared to walk on the water, we now know that they traversed the shallows on stilts but to the impressionable observer it was another wonder that these mysterious people possessed. The Roman general Tufano, afforded the task of trying to subdue, reported that they fought like the savage tiger, battalions of the finest gladiators would be needed to overwhelm.

'Women born to this harsh environment were fashioned over centuries to be strong and sinuous; their land and culture threatened made them, alongside the menfolk, fearsome adversaries.

'A gradual rise from the treacherous wetlands saw the boggy black soil change to free-draining chalk, prevailing warm westerlies dropped most of their moisture onto the beautiful granite mountains of Wales which left East Anglia vulnerable to drought, which in turn would lead to scorching summer, to fires which swept across the plains leaving it a treeless environment or a break in the land of trees, now more commonly referred to as the Brecklands. To the east, where the soil became richer and deeper, able to retain moisture in the warmest of summers, blackthorn, hawthorn abounded, with its rapid growth it is almost impenetrable, so, from the modern-day village of Woodditton, there would be little chance of forging a major offensive against Boadicea's Iceni.

'The ten miles between the villages was extremely vulnerable and a perfect portal for any invading Roman army. The numbers now being amassed left her little chance of success without supernatural intervention.

'Almost all the theories advanced by modern man to explain incredible ancient engineering feats are found to be deeply flawed under examination. Logrolling of thousands of two hundred tons of precision carved rock across sand, then hoisted hundreds of meters into the air is fanciable on many fronts; the pyramids are as much a mystery today as ever they were.

'To this day the huge dyke that stretches between the two villages that fringe the Brecklands remains a mystery, almost two thousand years of erosion, yet millions of tons of soil still stand as a fortress, an earth barrier to leaden the heart of the advancing Roman legions. Calpurnia, the Roman general, wrote in his journal, "The ground rises like a huge wave in front of us, this can only be the work of the gods. I am fearful of the days to come."

'The Iceni called the Romans the Devalians, who served only greed, suppressing and pillaging. The Devalians sent their plunder back to Rome; human splendour is mostly built upon the back of pillage. Today this tidal wave of earth is still known as the Devil's Dyke. The unconditioned critical eye can form no other conclusion that this soil tsunami could not have been built by human hands.

'The battles raged on, the Devalians, with their precision warfare honed in countless campaigns, suffered massive losses by the unpredictable and seemingly foolhardy tactics employed by their adversaries. Their tank-like formations, with battalions moving forward with shields above and to the side, like some huge metallic armadillo, were smashed aside by herds of galloping horses, pulling chariots of enraged women, wielding razor weapons, their spinning wheels home to long, brutal knives capable of slicing the human form in half.

'Eventually the dyke was breached; Boadicea's forces returned to defend the watery fens to the west and the blackthorn land to the east. The heather and Brecklands were left to the Devalians.

'The queen of the east was tracked to her village, now known as Exning, where all trace of her disappeared. She and her inner circle of fighting women vanished, herds of mildly grazing horses surrounded by fearsome chariots studded the landscape but the Iceni queen had gone.

'To this day the world does not know what became of the Iceni, but we do.'

The bishop paused for a moment, the three looked at one another.

Ninal said, 'What became of the Iceni?'

The bishop looked at all three and said, 'Really, this is the beginning of the story.

'The Iceni continues to this day. They serve the highest ideals of mankind, its roots today as then are in the spirituality of our world, this Eden that was gifted.

'We are fighting a war, not a war of man against man but man against the Devil, he is well armed, it may appear that he has the upper hand, we are surrounded by greed of unimaginable proportions. Where people, who will never experience the pangs of hunger, or understand the bliss of the giver, will endeavour to use any means at their disposal to circumvent the need to pay from their plenty into a fund dedicated to the common good.

'We see every sin warned of in every holy book being magnified, every danger to the soul of mankind being pampered. Yet we have a gift from God that cannot be explained through any of man's theorem, so powerful, so joyful, so wonderful that nothing in the Devil's armour can trump, the power of love, the wonder of children. What father would not gladly exchange places with his dying child, what mother would not starve so that her child could eat.

'The joy of the children jumping into the bomb crater filled with water from the fractured water main on the Syrian street, they know nothing of some power struggle stoked by some evil spirit, theirs is joy, bliss, a present from some unseen entity that adores mankind with the same fervour as any besotted parent.

'The most famous football international of all time was

between Britain and Germany. No one remembers the score or how many were in the teams, how big the pitch was or who refereed this amazing international.

'It was played between the warring trenches on the Western Front; they stopped the slaughter to celebrate the birth of the child. Christmas morning, 1914.

'As man tries to deny his spirituality the Devil's offerings seem to become more attractive, the millionaire in his lonely counting house, unsure if those around him love him or his money.

'The mother atop the funeral pyre while the flames consume her earthly remains, whose life of struggle to feed her many children now weeping uncontrollably for her departing spirit. Which of these leaves this life the richer? Love is the medicine for the soul.

'The Iceni is charged with keeping safe the writings of Jesus Christ.

'One thousand, five hundred years this has been its purpose. Protect the greatest treasure of mankind to secure its revelations until the eve of the second coming.

'In order to explain this truth and try to relieve some of the astonishment now adorning your faces, I must return to the disappearing of Boadicea by the river in Exning.

'The Iceni abandoned their horses and walked into the shallow river heading upstream, marching the half mile towards the first of the hills that circle the underground lake.

'The Iceni simply disappeared into the hillside through a secret entrance where one of the seven springs that overflow the lake to form the Exning river emerges.

'The river washed away any trace; coupled with the prevailing notion that these ancient Britons possessed supernatural powers, the Devalians hoped they had seen the last of these warriors.

'Unfortunately for them, Boadicea would torment them, mounting devastating attacks, causing heavy losses before once again disappearing into secret portals that give access to the great lake that sits under the modern town of Newmarket. It was a pattern to be repeated by all the Celtic nations.

'Romans considered this to be a barbaric way of conducting warfare, referring to the home nations simply as "The Barbarians."

'Four hundred years later, when the Romans finally decided that this Britannia was not worth the endeavour, the Iceni had adapted the ability to remain secret to such a degree that few knew of its existence, access to the lake of Newmarket known only to a few of the most devout who knew that man was only a destructive observer of some immense power, something that made the sun to shine, the grass to grow, the animals to give birth to miraculous offspring that would outlive the parent and give immortality to the species.

'They knew there were other powers at work that targeted only mankind, that displayed traits that were not in keeping, to kill for pleasure, to be untruthful, greed, manipulation.

'To seek power, to adorn the body with gold and silver, to try to elevate the human form into something it was not and could never be. There was a falsehood a difference in mankind, alongside the need to deceive, other paradoxical callings, the need to dance, sing, plan, create, stranger still embarrassment, shyness.

'With each passing generation the Iceni became less of a military force, more covert, seeking to influence in favour of mother earth, to curb the excess of man's lust for power.

'When stories of a man named Jesus, who had spoken of forgiveness, of a heaven and a hell, of a single God. He had spoken of evil and the battle for the souls of mankind; the man had performed miracles, he had healed the lame, the sick, raised the dead, walked on water, calmed the tempest.

'He endured a terrible death and still asked for man's forgiveness; after a few days he had walked away from the tomb to show that death could not hold what God had created.

'He had been taken back to the place called heaven, a place where all those who believed in him would be taken. The torture and deaths of those that had witnessed the Christ were so horrific that they could have been forgiven for denouncing him, yet none did, they faced their tormentors with love and compassion, even as their lives ebbed they asked for forgiveness.

'The Iceni were enthralled. Here was an embodiment of everything they believed, everything they knew to be true but could not explain.

'There was a cosmic battle being fought out in this paradise.

'And so the Iceni had a focus and were aware that their secrecy could well have a major role to play in the future.'

It was Ninal who intervened, 'Bishop what does this all have to do with us?'

'I am sorry,' said the Bishop, 'if this all seems a bit long-winded but it is important that you know the history behind it all. It will become clear I promise you.

'Wherever Christians appeared so did their adversaries; killing the believers became sport from colosseums to the countryside chase, they were persecuted, slaughtered for promoting love. The problem for the opposer: every one eradicated sprung the birth of many. The Iceni had long perfected the art of concealment and were able to protect large numbers of the persecuted.'

'How?' interrupted Ninal.

'The vast invisible lake which lays at the base of huge chalk cathedrals, which rise up to form a natural umbrella over the lake, it weaves around massive chalk pillars forming a bewildering honeycomb, a labyrinth of dazzling white caves and plateaus, with an ambient temperature, light streaming in from shafts leading to hollowed-out trees; a parallel existence could be achieved.'

'So,' said Ninal, 'if I have this right, people could hide in caves in this area almost undetected.'

'Sort of, yes,' said the bishop. 'Although hide is probably not the best description. Alternative living, free from harassment and persecution in today's modern speak, is probably more accurate. Let's not forget for well over a thousand years the Iceni has been adopting practices commonplace today.'

'So,' said Ninal 'where are these chalk cathedrals?'

The bishop replied, 'We are standing on the edge of the lake which runs under much of Newmarket. The chalk cathedrals then rise up to form the hills that surround the town's High Street.

'Warren, Long and Bury Hill, well known landmarks to the racing fraternity. Hamilton Hill, which rises from this church up along its mile long peak, known now as the Exning Road, descending to the seven springs where the lake overflows.

'To the east, the Duchers' Hill where the mighty Roman legions camped; unbeknown to them their elusive enemy was

67

living beneath them.

'So,' said the bishop, 'I plan to take you on a tour that few have ever witnessed. Are you ready for your magical mystery tour?'

All three nodded, rising in unison at the bishop's beckoning.

The party disappeared into the vestry.

Slowly the church began to fill with a stench, a stench synonymous with evil. A stench so vile that none catching the slightest whiff would be able to retain the contents of their stomach. In the pews shapes were forming, hideous shapes, half-beast, half-man.

In the vestry, cassocks were pushed aside by the bishop, some mechanism engaged, a door slid open; the small band vanished through the opening, the door sliding silently shut behind them just as the first wisps of dark matter began creeping under the solid oak vestry door.

The band descended the wide flint steps, the hard, coloured stone embedded into the chalk, worn smooth by centuries of devout feet. Everywhere as bright as a summer's day.

'We are able to facilitate this place with the latest technology, gone the old shafts of light coming from hollow trees, now it's fibre optic magnification through prisms, no visible signs for the curious to stumble upon, we can totally control the environment.'

A few yards from the bottom of the steps, unique boats abutted a brilliant white chalk jetty, craft a fusion of Viking ship, gondola and canoe sat silently and motionless on a glass waterway, eerie and beautiful, reflecting giant natural pillars left by some retreating ice age.

The water, free from any impurities, gave the viewer unimpeded vision into its depth which stretched beyond calculation. The bishop invited the three into the foremost vessel, pressed a concealed button that started a small motor which in turn drove the vessel slowly forward, with an ancient paddle His Holiness was able to steer.

'Tiny rechargeable litriac batteries,' he said, 'a thousand times smaller and more powerful than the lithium batteries, capable of powering this boat for twenty-four hours a day for over a year without recharging, incredible technology developed here in our laboratories.'

'Laboratories,' the three said, almost in unison.

'Yes, we run the foremost research institutions to be found anywhere in the world. All under Newmarket Heath.'

Oliver piped up.

'My brother's fighting demons, my wife's speaking with angels, I'm riding horses on the top of great cathedrals that house wonders. I think I need to lay down in a darkened room with a wet towel around my head until my senses regain some equilibrium.'

'Many of the most advanced technologies had been formulated in these chalk caverns,' the bishop explained. 'Over the centuries, not only clerics, but also scholars and visionaries, anyone under threat and needing sanctuary whose work a benefit to planet and mankind.'

The bishop's paddle was directing the boat skilfully between massive chalk pillars, the gentle bow wave reflecting some weird belly dance motion of the columns adding another strange dimension. As the voyage advanced the thick columns grew gradually taller, all three captivated and mesmerized by its beauty.

Oliver suggested, 'It's like a white palace from fairytale land.'

'It is one of the most beautiful things I've ever seen,' said Ninal.

Michael, strangely quiet, suddenly said, 'I know this place.' All three turned to look at him. The bishop, with a kindly smile, said Michael, 'I think you probably do.'

Awestruck would probably the best way to describe the next few minutes as the trio gazed at the wonders in front of them. It was Oliver who spoke first.

'If we were above ground, Bishop, where would we be?'

'We would be striding the centuries old, finely manicured lawns of Warren Hill, the highest point in East Anglia, two feet taller than sister Ducher Hill. In a straight line between here and Moscow there is no higher elevation.'

The next few minutes saw the three dumbstruck as the bishop gradually moved the craft northward, from time to time giving points of reference: Long Hill, Bury hill, the craft gliding effortlessly. The pillars became smaller, the ceiling drew closer.

'We are heading back towards the town,' the bishop said. Eventually, they came to a plateau where the water lapped.

They looked upon a half mile long boulevard, a pure white slab chalk caves peppered the walls.

'The ancients fashioned this walkway to give easy access to their underground homes and the portals to the world above. It runs underneath Newmarket's Bury Road which marks the edge of the lake, the caves you see are often used by some of the greatest minds of today. They are able to apply themselves unhindered by convention, not unlike the space shuttle where brains can be locked away in creative solitude.

'There can be a hundred living and working in these caves at any one time.'

Ninal, astonished, said, 'How does all this happen unnoticed?'

'Quite easily really,' said His Holiness. 'Most come and go by train. Let me explain.

'As I have said before, the Iceni is hugely influential, it reaches into the highest echelons. It simply had a train tunnel built that ran past a portal.

'Let me explain the mechanics. Newmarket is unique in many ways. Half a mile of the railway line that serves the town runs underground, this phenomenon on one of the largest flat plains goes largely unnoticed by the townsfolk. A special train runs from Cambridge on average six times a year. It is unscheduled, it normally runs at night to minimize any disruption to mainline services so the only people to board are those heading for the laboratories, normally for increments of two months.

'The windows are blacked out, the train might make several diversions in order to keep the location secret before entering the tunnel where its cargo of boffins disembark. The train that emerges from the tunnel, empty of its cargo, goes on its way. The townspeople are left unaware of what goes on under their feet.'

Meanwhile, back in the vestry, the cassocks lay strewn, candles lay smashed, goblets, robes and cups flew through the air, crashing into the vestry walls, tumbling to the floor before being launched again for another aerial display, propelled, it seemed, by some unseen foot.

The vicar of Saint Mary's, having been alerted by a pager that something was amiss in the church the temperature had dropped.

The heater had probably broken down. Now opening the west facing door with its view of the altar he turned and emptied the contents of his stomach, such was the potency of the vile stink tormenting his nostrils. Returning undaunted he entered the church. Had a pipe from the heating system broken and spilled pungent fluid?

Every fibre in his body began quivering, alarm. Sensors had picked up the dramatic drop in temperature, others the sulphurous, acrid vapor filling the air. The realization dawned, this was not the result of some damaged furnace but the manifestation spoken of by Jesus in his gospel, "In the last days The souls given freely to Satan, will vent their anger against my People and their houses, Fear not My spirit will be with you, The time is soon when I walk amongst you, My father has brought forth the bounty of the Earth to feed you, He hath brought water from the oceans to quench your thirst, He will bring forth all thy kin who sleep in their graves, there will be Great rejoicing."

The human guardian of Saint Mary's Church knew he needed to pray in the hope of preventing the destruction of God's house.

The core of his being told him the last days had begun, the great demonic army would soon be upon them.

Souls beyond redemption, the vilest of the vile, the most evil of the evil. Huge shapes began forming around as he walked towards the altar. Retching from his empty stomach, every therm being drained from his form. Dark wisps passing back through the vestry door and reforming into hideous spectres. He staggered forward, each step more difficult than the one before, all energy draining from him. His body was being assaulted, slaps and fingers probing his body, onwards towards the altar until movement became almost impossible.

Surrounded, he fell to his knees, pressing his hands together in prayer, the vicar reciting the only part of The Lord's Prayer that seemed appropriate, his failing energy allowing a barely audible chant.

'Deliver us from evil for thine is the kingdom the power and the glory for thine is the kingdom the power and the glory for thine is the kingdom the power and the glory.'

The vicar, his body sinking ever closer to the ground, his blood almost frozen, his chants no longer audible; the slaps seemed to have become kicks. Then, from the altar, the statue of Christ seemed to pulse and glow, the kicking stopped the spectre, grimacing, losing form, retreated into the shadows, the pungent, fetid air dissipated. The church returned to somewhere more normal, apart from a vestry vandalized and an exhausted vicar lying unconscious in front of the altar.

Meanwhile, a mile away by the edge of the underground lake, the bishop turned the craft, heading east-south-east, weaving a zigzag path through the mighty pillars.

'The next part of our story,' the bishop said, 'is the most significant, far and away the greatest challenge and the greatest honour bestowed on the Iceni. We must now travel back in time to The Crusades, to a time when the pagan world had embraced Christianity, or more accurately its version of Christianity.

'The first four hundred years of the last millennium, the holy lands were a battleground. The root of the problem, according to the warring factions, was God's covenant with Abraham where he basically promised to bring forth his son from Abraham's seed. The problem being Abraham's wife

Sarah told him at the age of seventy-five she was unable to conceive and he ought to lay with Hagar, handmaiden or second wife, possibly a daughter of the pharaohs, so Abraham becomes the father of Ishmael.

'When God asks him what he's done, Abraham replies, "My wife told me she could not become pregnant so I must lie with the handmaiden". God replies, "I told you your wife would become with child". At the age of ninety Sarah, Abraham's wife, gives birth to Isaac Now we have two lines emanating from Abraham: Ishmael, the oldest and son of Hagar the second wife, who is generally regarded as the father of the Arabs, and Isaac, youngest son whose mother, Sarah, is Abraham's first wife, the father of the Jews. God tells Abraham, "Because of your transgression I will put enmity between your two houses forever".

'The Jews and Arabs have been at loggerheads ever since. Completely at odds with the teachings of Jesus Christ, several popes and powerful people throughout Europe felt The Crusades were an honourable cause, over the centuries rivers of blood flowed, a fruitless endeavour to reclaim the holy land for their particular brand of God worship.

'One must ask who was the driving force behind this folly.

'For hundreds of years the Iceni realized there was only one enemy in the world; his power was immense, his ability to deceive mankind was unparalleled, a fallen angel, allowed free rein until the day of the second coming, most would only see his work or be seduced by his inducements, but some would meet the Devil himself.'

The craft glided effortlessly on, the curvature of the roof, descending to form a sheer wall, sank into the pristine waters of the lake. Behind jagged chalk pillars and almost out of sight,

74

the tiniest of gaps, the ceiling so low one would have to almost lay flat to pass through.

The bishop maneuvered the small vehicle gently into the gap, illuminating light on the front of the boat switched on automatically at the loss of brightness, asking the occupants to lie as flat as possible he guided the craft through this small canal.

'We are now under the Ashley Road leaving Side Hill and heading for Warren Hill's sister Dauchy Hill.'

Once again the roof of the massive cave began to rise with the contours of the hill; the labyrinth that lay before them mirrored the previous chamber.

'Unfortunately we can go no further; we must wait now. We have a meeting scheduled in half an hour, just long enough for me to fill you in on the rest of the story.

'The four hundred years of sporadic conflict saw long periods of peaceful coexistence, the cultural influences of the Arabic nations evident today in the explosion of magnificent architecture that blossomed across Europe during that period. Marriages and friendships fostered deep bonds.

'The Knights Templar and their Muslim counterparts, the Arabian Knights, enamoured by one another's horsemanship, would arrange contests where they would test each other's skills. Racing their best horses against each other, a bond was formed between the Iceni and devout Muslim brotherhood known as the Mohammedans. After much testing of one another's commitment to God, the Mohammedans confided that they had been for centuries custodians of Jesus Christ's writings and his artefacts, taking over from Christian group the descendants of the disciples who were finding it increasingly difficult to protect this bedrock of the faith from those who wished its destruction.

'Though they would not relinquish their commitment to guard these treasures a more secure fortress was being sought far from the turmoil of the holy lands.

'It was then that the Iceni offered their underground castle that had protected them for a millennium. After surveying and much planning it was agreed that the writings and artefacts of Jesus Christ would be moved and housed in the Ducher Hill under the full protection of the brotherhood of Muslims, in return the Iceni would have access to the writings of Jesus Christ, the most profound gospel in Christendom.

'Muslims, in the Koran, believed that their book was the work of God, written by a man who could neither read nor write and, like Moses, tried to decline the job. Advocates question that if God did not write this astonishing piece of literature who did? Critics of the Bible would often say it was a collection of works written by different authors at different times and put together by man, with books that did not fit the philosophy left out. The Apocrypha, a forgotten collection of works, some written by apostles suggesting that Christ was married, did not make the cut, yet it would be extremely unusual for a Jewish boy not to be betrothed at a very early age.

'Here was the original work, no arguments, no room for debate, no deletions or additions to suit man's interpretation, this was the written testimony of God's son. The two devout organizations, serving one God through different routes, worked hand in hand to bring precious cargo from the holy lands to its new home in the hill of Ducher and there it has stayed for hundreds of years.'

'How on earth can all this carry on unnoticed?' Oliver

said.

'Well,' said the bishop, 'remember the Knights Templar and the Arabian Knights, the break lands and heather lands, no tree, ideal for horse sports. Exning market, through disease, had now been moved up the hill to the new market catering for the travellers to and from East Anglian coastal ports. It became an important stopover point, with the added treat of horse sports to be enjoyed, so over time Newmarket became a playground for the rich and famous alongside its value as a market town so it is no surprise that fame and notoriety became diluted by familiarity, where the great and good were able to amble streets unhindered. King Charles the First said in Newmarket, "I can be an ordinary blade". Quite by chance its popularity now made it much easier for the Iceni.

'Devout kings practically made Newmarket their home; through their commitment to God they were invited to join the Iceni, able to read the Testament of Jesus Christ.

'Palaces built along the main street, large houses, a church, constructed along the Bury Road to hide the portals to the lake, churches linked by waterways, other lake doorways ingeniously hidden, hundreds ride the connecting bridleways between the two main racehorse training grounds known as the water course with not a drop visible, few question the strange name, fewer still know of the deep channel weaving its path beneath their horses' hooves. Today the Iceni are completely anonymous, their comings and goings totally lost in this bustling horse racing community.

'So Newmarket became the foil, horse sports disguising its real purpose, protecting mankind's greatest treasure.

'Hiding in the catacombs amongst hundreds of chalk caves, cradled in one of these underground cathedrals, its location known by very few, its contents sought by thousands, lies The Definitive Word of God through the gospel of Jesus Christ.'

'I am stunned and shocked,' said Oliver.

'Well there's something new,' said Michael. Ninal gave Michael a playful dig with her elbow.

'Why not just announcing to the world, let anybody read it then there's no argument,' Oliver said.

'Well brother of mine,' Michael replied, 'had you been paying any attention at Sunday school, or had read the Bible as diligently as you read any of the sporting papers, you will have known that the main argument between God and the fallen angel and his disciples was that man would never come to him of his own accord, it would appear that God has tried all sorts to get man to obey a few commandments. It would appear that God has given man ample time not necessarily to find the good souls but to weed out the evil, there are, and have been, millions of great souls. Spirits with very little sin on a worldwide scale; the Devil is losing the battle.

'People care more about each other, the environment, the planet than ever before, they rail against hunger, corruption, atrocities, abuse of any sort. The Devil has grubby little fingers in every pie, all the religions contain devout and wonderful spirits yet the Devil has his digits firmly embedded. There are lots of institutions that would seek to destroy this work in order to preserve their own creed built on deception, serving its own interests.'

'I think,' the bishop said, 'that we are expected.' The boat moved forwards through another intricate passage of chalk columns to another promenade, through the centre of which ran a cavern. Inside was a circular room, the chalk platform

78

raised above the lake with just enough room for the boat to complete a circle. Twelve seats, each intricately carved into the soft white rock, beautifully embroidered, round red cushions were placed on three of the chairs, the bishop said that upon which sits the blood of Christ, symbolic of the Iceni.

Just as he spoke, movement from a passage that ran between the eleventh and twelfth seat entered the chamber. Three figures emerged, either side of the central figure. Two icons of the racing authorities held their arms in military fashion in case the Regal Lady should need support. The three stared in disbelief.

'Defender of the faith,' the bishop said with just enough decibels for those now stood in the boat to hear him.

Once this devout lady was seated the others took their pews, beckoning those in the boat to sit. It was the bishop who spoke first.

'Sister and brothers Iceni this is Michael, who long ago I spoke of when the signs started to appear.

'I think he is the avenger that Jesus speaks of.'

Sir Leonard Seale, head of the jockey club's disciplinary committee, who Oliver knew from several encounters they had had at the Jockey Club interview rooms, a very fair man in Oliver's opinion, said, 'On his right hand he shall have his brother not of blood but joined of one soul, on his left hand a mighty warrior queen, gentle to the lamb as the mossy bed, a quaking earth and thundering tempest to the ungodly. She will be exalted, hold hands with the saints, be blessed and held high in the last day.'

'My thoughts exactly,' said the bishop. Sir Leonard Seale spoke next.

'My friends I think my brother Iceni here will have filled

79

you in on the bones of our organization. Maybe I can give you a little more detail. Everyone in the organization is a devout Christian, believing Christ was sent to save the world; each would gladly end their lives protecting the gospel according to Jesus Christ.

'It was known that he was a writer, his ministry started at the age of thirty, by which time he was a remarkable preacher and miracle worker. His ascension into heaven was at thirty-three, by which time he had already changed the world forever.

'He carried no sword yet he commands the greatest army, he had two weapons of mass destruction, two forces to brush aside anything that stood against them: love and peace, "turn the other cheek", as radical a philosophy that has ever been promoted. God so loved the world that he sent his only son. The earth will continue whatever we do, the kingdom of God will continue, the only thing that is at risk is whether mankind can continue. It is not a question of will man destroy himself but when.

'Jesus is called the Saviour for a reason. He will come again, there will be no more tears. Until that time it is our job to help keep the Scriptures hidden, the Muslim brotherhood, for hundreds of years has guarded the treasures impeccably which they are honoured to do. Believe in Jesus or GRL according to their holy book to be one of the great profits. They have no axe to grind, no hidden agenda, have not majored over some minor point and built a whole new religion.

'The Iceni have full access to the Scriptures, they compliment the Book of Revelations, making it clear what some of the abstract scripture means there is no doubt.

If the gospel were to be made public then the footings, many of the institutions professing to serve the Christ, would

80

crumble. It can only be revealed when the second coming is imminent God would like as many to return to him of their own free will.

'We believe from Jesus's writings that we are in the last generation. You will be invited to read the words of Christ, but to summarize, Christ tells us that when "those that lie asleep in their graves outnumber the living fifteen to one, I will once again come among you, when man living on the mountain can trumpet his brother who liveth under the sea then I shall soon be with you, when the flesh can be stripped from a man as he walked my time has come". We believe now that there have been fifteen people who have gone before, population reference bureau in Washington agrees. With mobile phones it is possible now to talk to anyone anywhere in the world, nuclear weapons can strip the flesh from a man as he walks, the most wicked and deadliest enemy of mankind is the tiny virus as with the modern computer there are those who derive satanic pleasure from destruction. All powers have, and continue to develop, test-tube viruses if released would devastate mankind leaving everything standing, nothing else affected, it is the ultimate weapon. If targeting can be achieved then the world is in peril. Myxomatosis in rabbits is the only virus known to be government backed, yet many in the virology community believe viruses such as AIDS to be man-made.

'During the Vietnam War it is believed that soldiers resting off the coast of Pattaya in Thailand from the conflict were given drugs as a preventative measure at controlling sexual disease. Hidden within those drugs was an attempt to doctor the make-up of a permanent chromosome to create offspring to change the male fertilized eggs to female. It went disastrously wrong and is hotly denied by the administration to have ever taken place. Thailand today, living and feeling like women are ladies who possess male genitalia, they can often trace family history to a liaison with an American servicemen.

'Only the naïve believe governments don't lie. That the powerful would not use any means to gain and stay in control. We believe that not only nuclear weapons but man-made viruses exist that would strip the human form of its flesh in seconds. Jesus tells us that the Devil will gather his forces, redoubling his efforts to capture as many souls as possible before his coming. "The serpent, knowing his days are short, will gather his own, there will be many manifestations, the seas will rise, great storms will bear down upon the people, the righteous heart will tremble crying out where are you Lord, they will lift their eyes to heaven crying Lord why hast thou forsaken me. The serpent will look for the Scriptures I leave to calm the heart of man in the last days. The Devil will seek to destroy it but I will send angels to the battle".

'I have read the gospel of Jesus Christ so many times I could recite it in my sleep along with many of the Iceni,' said Sir Leonard Seale. 'Iceni now stretch across the world; there is no hierarchy system, we are either brother or sister Iceni, our senior leaders determined normally by the length of service. The gospel of Jesus has been meticulously translated into English by a team of Iceni who specialize in this work.

'We are multidenominational, each belonging to his own branch of the Christian faith we all recognize within each segment. There are those that belong to the dark lord but the vast majority are good Christians. We are convinced now that we are in the last generation; we are also sure from the

82

happenings predicted in the gospel of Jesus, that the great battle is upon us. Increasingly the dark one shows his hand. There has been a huge upsurge in demonic appearances throughout the world.

'As you know, Michael, from your own experience, possession is at a level that is nearly unmanageable, last week alone around the globe we have reports of over thirty appearances of men with superhuman strength, all stripped naked, jumping from third and fourth floor windows having smashed their way through, landing on their feet, turning cars over, running along motorways, seemingly immune to pain, almost always attributed to drug abuse. These manifestations are seen in isolation, the magnitude of the phenomena diluted by distance. As you all know in our own area in the last year we have had five youngsters hanging themselves in the stables for no apparent reason all, blamed on a mixture of drugs, alcohol, depression and workload, yet the jockey club's own investigation showed that none of these could have been an attributing factor. Michael, strange as it seems in today's modern high-tech world, we believe that you have been sent to lead in the great battle to come.'

The cavern fell silent as the magnitude of what Sir Leonard Seale had said sunk in.

Presently Oliver, with his usual witty irreverence, Sort of Sir Lancelot of the spirit world.'

That, as usual, broke the ice and sent those present into giggles and chuckles.

'We really have no plan of action,' said Sir Leonard, 'as we have no idea what will unfold before us. We trust in our faith.

'Do you have any questions?'

'Only about a hundred,' said Ninal.

'And I've only about five hundred more,' said Oliver.

'Fire away,' said Sir Leonard.

'How do you communicate with each other?' Ninal asked.

'If you don't mind,' said Sir Leonard, 'I will ask my good friend and brother Iceni here to reply as he is much more au fait with the nuts and bolts of the day-to-day running of things.'

With that Sir Leonard sat down and John Wilsoncroft, husband of the much-respected headmistress at Houldsworth Valley School, who had observed and witnessed Michael's growing, took to his feet. As they all knew, John was one of the most respected racehorse trainers in Newmarket.

'Firstly,' said the racehorse trainer, 'may I welcome you into the brother and sisterhood of the Iceni.

'To answer your question we still communicate the same way today as we did four hundred years ago. Modern communications being what they are, and the ease of which they can be intercepted, we avoid modern technology wherever we can. We used a flag system developed for the Royal Navy used by Sir Francis Drake and Nelson, it served them well enough.

'Let me explain further. At the edge of the lake and our furthest portal the ancient Iceni placed what appeared to be a grave. Legend has grown that it was a gypsy grave placed at a crossroads which suits the Iceni fine.

'It is between Newmarket and Kentford and visible as one drives by. By placing flowers with different colors, nowadays teddy bears as well in different positions, messages can be sent to the "watchers" which is the modern speak for the Iceni.

'Nowadays pictures of the grave can be sent worldwide

instantly, only the trained observer can disseminate the message, to the casual onlooker is just a picture of a gypsy boy's grave from some old legends on the outskirts of Newmarket, never questioning the immaculate condition of this four hundred year-old grave.'

'How on earth,' said Oliver, 'can this organization remain secret after all this time?'

'Although it might appear,' the racehorse trainer said, 'in this modern era that the benign, superficial and celebrity are the main fodder for the average soul, it is not really the case. It is only a perception fostered by the media. Most are deeply spiritual and that spirituality can only be tapped in times of need.

'Let me explain further. During the Second World War at Bletchley Park ten thousand people worked deciphering codes; they were facing evil beyond imagination. Across the Channel hundreds of thousands were being gassed, others shot, bombs were raining down on London, innocents were being slaughtered everywhere. Ten thousand were sworn to secrecy; Hitler never found out about Bletchley Park.

'We know the depths of depravity we face, we know the inhumane acts one human can bestow upon another, they are called inhumane because they do not stem from the soul of a human.

'Every member of the Iceni has been invited to join, they have proven themselves worthy in their day-to-day lives. We have several racehorse trainers who are brother Iceni, they are well aware that they work in an industry where the temptations for deception are great. Where the ten pounds gained from under the table is worth more than ten pounds gained honestly.

'Where the talented racehorse trainer is eclipsed by the

alchemist. Where winning is more important than how you fought. Over the years it has been an important testing ground for Iceni, we have been blessed to count amongst our number many good people who couple their faith with the love of the racehorse.'

With that statement four individual buzzers interrupted the flow. Leonard jumped to his feet with the announcement that they had to leave immediately: there was some emergency that needed attending. Offering his arm to help sister Iceni to her feet, along with John Wilsoncroft they were out along the passage. The bishop, having silenced his beeper, quickly turned the craft around and headed full speed, swerving in and out of the columns, through the narrow passage with the low ceiling, the Ashley Road traffic passing above with no hint of the drama unfolding underneath. The bishop, now fully concentrating on steering, its occupants realized he'd never driven the craft at this speed, and hung onto the gunnel of the boat, not daring to speak lest they distracted the bishop from his task.

Eventually steering the boat to the jetty alongside the steps leading to the vestry at Saint Mary's Church, the bishop raced up the steps, followed by the three, connecting the mechanism to open the door and stepped into the vestry, closely followed by the trio. The scattered cassocks, the remnants of the acrid smell, the bishop, face ashen white, almost as pale as the chalk, unlocked the vestry door and strode into the church to find the vicar slumped leaning his back against one of the pews.

All four rushed to his side amidst all the commotion of concern the vicar spoke.

'I am fine, a bit beat up and battered that's all. Within a

short while others started to appear until the church was quite full. The throng contained Sir Leonard, John Wilsoncroft, plus a lady in a tight scarf.

The bishop took control of the situation and told the audience that he thought the crisis was over, he would be in touch, everyone should disperse.

Oliver and Michael knew several of the faces and exchanged pleasantries. Ninal, deeply worried, stayed close by her father-in-law. The cassocks were returned to their rightful place in the church, restored to something like normality, the vicar explained what had happened, as he regained consciousness he pressed the panic button on a device that all Iceni carry to be used only when encountering the dark one, it gives location, time and begins recording. The vicar explained that, never having had to use it before, he forgot to press it until he regained consciousness. The five sat together in the church while the vicar told them all he could remember.

Towards the end of his narrative he looked at Michael and said, 'As I was returning to consciousness I kept hearing a voice saying tell Michael, Agnes is coming. Anyway if it has any significance I have told you, Michael, Agnes is coming.'

'Probably one of his old flames,' Oliver said, 'coming to heap retribution on his philandering ways.'

'Come to think of it I don't think he's ever had an old flame, leave him alone, said Ninal. 'It's not the time to be pulling his leg, he's just never met the right girl, he will one day, you'll see, he will be more romantic than you, just thank your lucky stars that you were extremely lucky.' They all laughed, the situation lightened.

'Listen,' Michael said, 'if I put an advert in the paper for a wife the queue would stretch from here to Carlisle. You, dear brother, are extremely lucky to have married the only girl on the planet who finds you remotely attractive.'

So the banter continued as the five headed back to the rectory. The bishop, deeply worried, said, 'I think they may have found a portal.'

It was late in the evening when the bishop headed back to Ely. At Stuntney, the road dips into the Black Lands; the bishop looked up at the million twinkling stars.

'The county of endless skies,' he said to no one. A blinking cloudless ceiling, a source of wonder for every heart on the planet.

He recognized the stench from the church now filling the car; his stomach emptied before he had time to open the window. He saw the abomination manifesting itself; energy was leaving his body. The windows began icing. He tried to bring the car to an orderly stop but failed, the car slipped over the edge, resting half on the soft verge, half on the road.

The side panels started to implode as though the car was being crushed. The incarnation now almost fully formed, a limb, because it could not be called an arm, reached out and digits, not to be confused with fingers, were placed on the bishop's chest. Almost instantly the back of the chair collapsed; the bishop lay prone, his chest in agony. The thing lay upon him, its weight unbearable, deformed digits clasped his neck and began squeezing. Incapable of any defence, unable to utter a single word in prayer, the bishop looked his assailant in its demonic eyes and smiled and thought, I will fear no evil, today I meet my maker and I am thankful to you for sending me on my journey.

The image in front of him began to blur as his body slowly

began to give up its soul.

All of a sudden, the sound of breaking glass and the release of tension from round his neck brought the bishop's senses back from the brink, he saw a police baton smashing through the window and heard commands being uttered. The incarnation smashed its shoulder against the door which flew open and sprang from the vehicle. It stood, momentarily gazing at the two officers stood in front of it.

With two taser guns pointing, one also with radio, demanding immediate assistance.

It turned in the direction of Stuntney village, with a nithandatal type motion began a lollop. Both taser guns hit their mark, first one with no effect and then the other with the same end result.

The abomination continued its flight, running with huge lopes. Halfway up the Stuntney slope, it ran off the soft verge, straight in front of a supermarket van returning to its depot in Ely. The stunned driver, with no time to take any avoiding action, smashed straight into the body of the beast, sending it tumbling through the air landing in the middle of tarmacadam. Picking itself up, it headed into the trees. The police scrambled their helicopter and several police units, dogs and armed response officers filled the cordoned off area all to no avail; the manifestation had vanished. The thorough search revealed no trace whatsoever. In the debriefing the next morning, the ridicule, which is often the source of great mirth amongst police officers when colleagues recount mysterious happenings, was absent, such was the gravity of the two officers' testaments.

The condition of both the car and delivery van augmented the puzzle, it defied logic, that such a high speed collision, causing so much damage to the supermarket vehicle, somebody could get up and run away. Intensive enquiries revealed that there had been no escapes from either prison or from any mental institutions, no other reports came in to suggest any hypothesis that could throw any light on the situation.

The testaments of the two officers both gave such similar accounts minimize any risk of exaggeration or fatigue playing its part. The gist of their statements was that they had been returning to Ely station when they saw a car swerved, heading off the road, balancing precariously on the edge of a dyke. Reaching the scene the car was rocking. Believing the occupant was trying desperately to get out, strangely the doors were gradually imploding. the windows were icing. Believing there was some major mechanical fault with the air conditioning causing rapid freezing, believing the occupants' lives were in danger, unable to gain entry through the damaged door, one officer smashed the driver's window in order to gain access.

The statements read that they both saw an extremely large albino man, lying on top of another man, in the throes of throttling him. It seemed the albino man was gaining some sexual gratification from the act. The albino man was completely hairless, almost skeleton like. Both officers simultaneously pulled their taser guns, instantly realizing the gravity of the situation. The door flung open, the albino man sprang from the car with cat-like agility.

Ignoring warnings from the officers, the albino man then began to flee the scene. The first taser was deployed, which appeared to have no effect, the second taser was also deployed, again the same result. The man then made his escape. Both police officers found it difficult to explain the strangeness of his gait other than to say it was a loping style not unlike the gait of the yeti depicted by animators.

He ran straight in front of a vehicle in his attempt to get to the other side and, although the police officers both believed they had witnessed a fatal traffic accident, the man simply jumped up and disappeared into the woods. The official statement was that the bishop had been attacked on his way home from a routine visit to Newmarket. It was believed the assailant gained entry into the car and hid in the back, eventually making his attack between Stuntney and Ely.

'We have no more details other than to say the assailant is still at large, the advice to the public is to proceed with extreme caution; everything at our disposal will be used to apprehend this man at the earliest opportunity.'

The bishop was taken to Ely Hospital where he was allowed home after examination. He was badly shaken by the encounter and spent much of his time in prayer. The next few days were fairly uneventful, the bishop playing host to many concerned parishioners, friends, Christian colleagues; he was also visited by the Newmarket contingent and latest recruits to the Iceni. Oliver and Ninal got back to their riding and stable duties. The vicar once again focused his attention on his hatches matches and dispatches.

Several days later in the woods at the top of Stuntney Hill. Roger Paxton was sitting on his walking cane penning an article. The longtime resident of Stuntney, with his extensive historical knowledge, had been asked to write an article about Matthew Hopkins, the witch finder general during the British Civil War. What had sparked the interest from the magazine that was commissioning him, was the interest shown by its readers into the hairless albino man evading capture.

Roger sat on his stick, looking out across to the beautiful cathedral that pushed into the skyline giving comfort over the centuries to millions; he returned back to his work. Wrestling with the words, trying to keep boredom at bay, while keeping the article interesting, he was explaining that Matthew Hopkins, during the Cromwellian era, had been appointed to find those who had taken the mark of the Devil and to destroy them. During his reign of terror over five hundred men and women were hanged. Hangings at the top of Stuntney Hill were commonplace, the bodies were buried in the witches' graves. At the foot of the gallows, they could be overlooked and subdued by the power emanating from the great cathedral. The witch finder general's methods came in for a huge criticism, eventually being banned by parliamentary decree which brought an end to his thirty-six months of brutality. Two of his many methods which came in for strong criticism were his water test. Believing that witches had renounced Christ and therefore the water of the baptism would now repel them, they were tied to the chair, then thrown into a moat, if they floated it was proof that water was trying to repel them.

If they were to sink and drown then they were innocent of witchcraft and were in heaven.

All witches had the mark of the Devil, according to Hopkins. Most in reality were either warts or moles some and really the point of this article had no marks at all.

Hopkins would employ prickers, usually women, who would strip the poor unfortunate naked and shave them in order to find the hidden mark underneath the surface of the skin where they proceeded to push needles into the area. If the victim did not bleed, witchcraft was your employment, if the crimson flow erupted and one of Hopkins' hungry cats lapped at the nourishment, your fate was sealed, you had an appointment with the gallows.

Most of the stuff is laughable in today's modern world with our advanced knowledge of science and a broader view of the international world. We live in a society where myth and legend have become fairytales.

During the English Civil War people were living in a time when all around was mystery.

The sky, the earth, the only knowledge was coming from the church, all-powerful, the Bible written in a foreign language, undecipherable, so the church's hierarchy had total sway over the masses.

Some say, from fairly reliable accounts, that although Hopkins destroyed many innocent lives, there were some cases that unnerved Hopkins himself, often involving the clergy or those involved in the monastic life.

There is written documentation that states permission was granted for a large contingent of Cromwell's puritan army to arrest monks from the Swaffham Priory who were believed to be the agents of Satan.

It is said that the struggle to contain them was difficult as each seemed to have the strength of fifty men, they were hairless and skin so white, their robes offering no access to their body from the sun's rays. The prickers could find no blood and no blemishes were found anywhere on the body, all were taken to Stuntney Gallows where they were hung six at a time.

None had shown any sign of fear but continued as a choir to chant a guttural refrain. The priory monks were buried headfirst, along with all the other witches in the hope that if after death they began to dig it would be towards hell. Legend has it that the flesh of a godless creatures is not consumed by the grave.

The Bible tells us that Satan himself will be chained and locked away for a thousand years. His influence will remain, although personal appearances will be performed by tribute bands.

The writer added a little humour to lighten the mood. It is said that when Lucifer's confinement is over he will call his disciples from their graves. Trees now obscure the view. The cathedral can no longer cast its watchful restraining eye over the satanic graveyard.

He ended his article with, "Maybe Satan once again walked the earth, maybe he is calling for his troops." A little mystery to end the piece, which pleased him. He rested pen and notepad on his lap and looked out across the black fenland; it had been a strange morning. It was one of those days when he could do nothing right at home. His wife, Sylvia, was convinced he was walking with the wrong leg first, he was breathing out when he should be breathing in.

He was looking forward to the day when she retired and the pressures of work were not brought home.

He himself had recently retired as head of history at one of the local colleges, then the dog had refused point-blank to cross the Stuntney Road. Strange behaviour indeed from an animal who the casual observer would wonder, who was taking whom for a walk?

He had taken the dog home with the proviso that if the dog was sickening for something he would take him to the vets later. The hound at the moment appeared in rude health.

To compose the article he felt it would be beneficial to his mindset to cross over the A142 at Stuntney and sit at the site of the old gallows; the vibe would help set the scene for his piece.

From time to time he had been aware of a slight pungent aroma, simply putting it down to recent muckspreading on the farmland.

Both teachers, they had moved from London, their home for most of their lives, to Stuntney. It was blissful, just two miles to Ely Station then an hour on the train, they could be walking the platform at King's Cross.

Visiting friends would sit in their garden, their very own mini Eden, Henry would say, "You hear that?" Their friends from the metropolis would say, "Can't hear a thing." "Exactly." A contented smile, a sip from a glass of Chardonnay held out in salute, "What a wonderful world," the historian would say.

Henry thought as he gazed upon the scene, even today it was unusually quiet, not a bird or insect, just the drone of an occasional vehicle; the animal kingdom was absent. The pungent smell suddenly became so strong that he retched. Feeling a breath fan his neck he slowly turned, his legs buckled and almost gave way, his heart burst into life and pounded in his ears, he lost control of his bowels, his baggy trousers began to stain with his urine. The white albino giant stood before him.

The abomination reached out and grabbed the historian's throat, lifting him off the ground, turning him around; he felt his clothes being ripped off.

He felt himself being violated. His mind recorded the back of his neck being savaged before his windpipe and his life were pulled from their moorings.

The police once again had the area cordoned off. Helicopter, dogs, forensic experts, every means at their disposal was being employed. The dog handlers reported that their animals wouldn't work, cowering and whimpering.

Henry's wife had found him, he had left a note to say where he would be, in the unlikely event that he was not present for her return.

She had been hospitalized, such was the intensity of her shock. Speculation was mounting that somehow the police had not searched the area thoroughly and for the second time in a few days there had been a murder and attempted murder and the assailant must be hiding within the woods or somewhere close by.

The article being penned by the historian was somehow leaked to the press who were having a field day. The tabloid press had slogans such as "Satan's priest seeks revenge. Four hundred year-old satanic priest returns for vengeance".

The more factual press reported that the murder and attempted murder had been on or close to the Stuntney witches' burial ground of Matthew Hopkins, self-proclaimed witch finder general, who, within a few days of executing the Swaffham Priory monks, had mysteriously died at his home at the age of twenty-five. Those who saw his body are convinced he died of fright.

The chief constable was under tremendous pressure. How on earth, the press chided, can such a striking individual remain at large? The chief constable, at his press conference, said, 'These two incidents may not be related. We are looking into all angles. No stone is being left unturned. To make the assumption that both have the same perpetrator may lead us in the wrong direction. As I have said all avenues are being explored.'

The lead detective and his team were sure there was no link to the gay scene; there was no evidence that this had anything to do with the homosexual community. Thorough investigation showed Henry to be well liked, well respected, a well-loved, agnostic man enjoying a well-earned retirement.

Forensic was extremely puzzled that although the victim had been brutally raped there was no seminal fluid, no DNA trace of the assailant, no residue of saliva from the bite marks on the historian's neck. No evidence could be gleaned from the surrounding site.

The chief constable was so infuriated that some of his officers supplemented their income by leaking information to the press. It had to be stopped, he thought. It was criminality and a betrayal of trust, it made policing so much more difficult, it was an investigation for another day. The article written by the historian was a very interesting read but this sort of nonsense just got in the way of real policing; hocus-pocus and mumbo jumbo have been confined to the history books, scientific evidence was all that mattered. There was a rational explanation to everything; it was just that sometimes it was difficult to find.

It was the bishop's statement that confounded him the most. When asked if he knew the assailant he said he did and that he had met him a few times but always in different guises. When pressed further the holy man assured them that he knew he was in the presence of pure evil and knew that he had been in this position a few times.

He was a deeply committed follower of Christ, giver of life and light, and the promise of heaven and therefore he must acknowledge the existence of his opponent the dark lord Lucifer, commander of the dark and death and keeper of hell.

The chief constable was desperate to get this matter solved as quickly as possible: these high-profile cases always drew a lot of unwanted attention. City police always believed the rural guys couldn't investigate their way out of a supermarket, operations like this almost always cemented that opinion. There were so many puzzling aspects and no solid leads. The local community was in a state of perpetual fear; a murderer was on the loose who attacked at random. Extra patrols were deployed, a greater physical presence was generated in order to foster reassurance.

Michael, a few days after the murder, was heading towards Bury St Edmunds, contemplating the huge influence Iceni must have. Newmarket, with its bypass diverted by many miles in order that the road made no contact with the town.

Bury St Edmunds, a much larger metropolis; the planners carved its path right through the middle of this historic haven.

Just approaching the little church that sits amidst the mansions was a girl, arms frantically flagging, gesticulating for him to stop. Michael stopped, wound down his window, the girl bounced across the road, smiling a smile that would have lit up Regent Street in London.

'Hello,' she said, 'I am Agnes.'

Michael gazed at her, leaned across and opened the passenger door. The blonde-haired, blue-eyed beauty trampolined in, leaned across, kissed Michael on the cheek and said, 'Let's go soldier.'

Once he had tracked through the gears and the car was steadily progressing towards Bury St Edmunds,

Agnes slipped her hand inside Michael's. Besotted,

smitten, love at first sight, head over heels, all phrases suited his present condition.

She sat in the passenger seat, staring at him with the most glorious smile. He drove to Bury St Edmunds in a haze; she hugged his arm constantly while he completed his errands. She held his body and kissed his chin before they re-entered the car. He knew he had known her forever and yet they had only just met.

He dropped her off at the place he picked her up and arranged to meet her later that day, then headed back to the rectory, his head in the clouds.

Oliver, the vicar, Jean and Ninal sat around the table eating a sandwich lunch; Michael appeared in the kitchen.

Oliver remarked, 'You look as though you've found 5p by the look on your face.'

Michael told his audience all about his meeting with Agnes.

'The Agnes of my dream,' said the vicar.

'Not sure about that,' said Michael.

They were all exceedingly happy for him. All a bit strange and sudden, but there again nothing could be construed as normal in Michael's life. The vicar mentioned that the bishop had been in touch and wanted to find a mutually convenient time to introduce them to the book. A rendezvous was agreed, the table cleared and all disappeared to attend to the wonderfully mundane.

The chief constable was getting no further forward, nothing was progressing the case, the scientific guys privy to the most elaborate techniques were totally mystified, it was the first case investigated were the assailant left no trace. Uppermost in the mind of the chief constable was another attack was almost inevitable. The quicker this perpetrator was off the streets the better.

He didn't have to wait long the police car, parked just off the 142 on the edge of the burial site, was being dragged away from the road with its two officers screaming down the radios for assistance. Before either had any idea of what was happening the car had been turned over and was being dragged away from the road, the two officers dangling upside down in their seat belts, incapable of deploying any resistance to the eternal credit and professionalism they were trying to give as an accurate description of events, they were being dragged by what appeared to be a naked form. Only the lower part of the body was visible. It seemed to have incredible strength, walking forward Neanderthal like, with one long arm draped to its side, the other pulling the vehicle. It suddenly stopped, strode to the back of the vehicle and lifted it vertically. The front of the vehicle slipped into a trough; the officers were struggling with the seat belts dangling forward over the dash and the steering wheel. They could hear the sirens blaring as they felt the first tingle of heat. Their screams drowned out the sound of the approaching cacophony.

The flames first licked at the bottom of the wedged car, quickly turning into an inferno by the fuel cascading down the vehicle, the screams from the stricken, augmented then overtook by the roar and ferocity of the burning. The few minutes it took for the area to be swarming with police, the fire had consumed everything, just a few dancing embers remained at the base. Both passenger and driver doors had sprung open. To the open mind it could have been construed that the vehicle had become a burning reversed crucifix .

Every emergency vehicle in East Anglia, it seemed, had

parked adjacent to the site, closing the A142 completely, the area swarming with police. Helicopters hovered above with searchlights scanning the area, long hoses running the hundred yards from roadside to the stricken vehicle remained unemployed; the senior officer, assured from the charred remains that life was extinct, needed the crime scene intact.

He was confident that the assailant would soon be in custody with little or no chance of evading capture. With the manpower, aerial power, times of response, he had no chance of fleeing the area. As night wore on and into the early morning daylight, confidence that the police would have their man was evaporating; by lunchtime it had gone.

The Stuntney witches' burial area had been searched three times: not a trace of the assailant. The later editions of the tabloid press had on their front covers a distant view of the car in satanic posture. The chief constable was at his wits end. What more could he do? What stone had he left unturned? Always in the back of his mind was the piece that had been written by the historian; he would go once again and see the bishop.

Michael picked Agnes up later that afternoon. She greeted him with the same dazzling smile, once again leant across kissing his cheek. They drove along the road to where it divided, taking the right-hand fork. About two miles along the road they turned left into a lane that marked the end of Newmarket's racehorse training grounds, the very edge of the underground lake.

Michael drove the fifty yards to the small unofficial soft verge unofficial parking area which racehorse trainers and dog walkers have used for decades. The pair walked back hand in hand to see the boy's grave.

Michael noted the positions of teddy bears, the flowers, their colour and positions. Then they turned and walked back and out onto the great expanse of heathland. Michael knew from the conversations with the bishop this was where they hauled the pure drinking water from the lake below. For hundreds of years it was used to supply the hamlets of Kennett and Kentford while the residents of Newmarket took their water from a well half a mile closer to the town. Today still referred to as Waterhaul and Well Bottom. Hand in hand they walked across the plains, mile after mile of neatly trimmed grass, a haven for training the racehorse and exercising dogs. They walked a mile down to where the horses cross the hallowed turf.

The tree filled hollows are where the ancients dug the chalk and crushed it, burning it in great kilns to create quicklime. Quicklime was desperately needed to cover the bodies of plague victims. East Anglia lost almost fifty per cent of its population to the Black Death; this part of the heath is still called the Limekilns today. Agnes hardly spoke, continually smiling and hugging his arm; Michael in a constant state of déjà vu.

They walked and walked. Agnes, slipping off her ancient looking sandals, said, 'You know, I like to walk barefoot to be in contact with the earth.' Michael knew it to be true, although how he knew he couldn't say.

Michael gazed out across this piece of paradise and said, 'One day this glory will shift into the control of the developer.'

He continued, 'It was inconceivable to those living in the bubble of the racing industry that one day their sport will be confined to the history books. It was well known in the high echelons of those charged with the governance of the sport, the pressure they were under, they knew their sport only continued with the backing of the public. Which was fast waning with each new generation who saw the sport as nothing more than animal cruelty, a pastime only for the benefit and gratification of the elite who have never seen a wage slip.

'Owners of the racecourses where the games were played were becoming more interested in the value of the real estate. The sights of the abolitionists were already turning towards the racing of horses.'

Michael sighed and said, 'One day these wonders will be no more.' They walked from Waterhaul down through the Llmekilns and back again. They hugged beside the car. Michael knew this woman was his other ninety per cent. He kissed her forehead, she kissed his chin.

'We got a job to do, my darling, and when it's over…' she left the sentence unfinished. The brilliance of her smile and the twinkling of her eye Michael threw his head back and laughed.

Michael returned Agnes to her spot before heading back to the rectory. The bishop was to pick the contingent up early the next morning, to head to the lake, to its inner sanctum, to read its precious secrets. Ninal and Oliver were over for dinner. Jean was preparing a hotpot followed by spotted dick and custard.

'Obviously beloved brother is not having to ride at his lightest in the foreseeable future,' Michael said.

Oliver replied, 'Beloved brother I have an enforced holiday on account of the stewards deciding my efforts to persuade my reluctant partner in a valuable horse's race at Newbury were in the main too vigorous, I pointed out that the conversation we had during the race that maybe if he tried a little harder he could give some respite to his beleaguered owners who monthly face incredible bills in order for him to enjoy his pharaoh-like status. Alas, dearest stewards, my attempt at mediation fell on ears of wax.

'I took the view, maybe mistakenly, that to an animal dining on the finest equine cuisine in the known universe, dangling a carrot from a fishing rod was unlikely to initiate the required reaction. Therefore I pursued the course of action for which, contrary to popular belief, I am not paid film stars' wages. For which my constant companions are two ambulances.

'I employed the first of the long-established stratagem of stick and carrot; having won the race by a short head I now stand before you awaiting my conviction. The sentence passed is five days in the sin bin.

'So, loved up brother of mine, we have five days in which to chase as many goblins and ghoulies as you want.'

Michael said, 'That fills me with so much confidence knowing that my wing man is your good self.'

And so the banter continued over dinner while Ninal and Jean would steer the conversation surreptitiously back to Agnes, appearing to be nonchalant about his new-found romance, yet eager to glean as much information about the beautiful Agnes as possible.

'So where does Agnes come from?'

'I don't know,' Michael replied.

'How old is she?' Jean asked.

'I don't know,' Michael replied.

'Where is she living at the moment? Has she invited you to meet her parents? Are they still alive?'

'I don't know, no she hasn't, and I don't know,' replied Michael. 'We just arrange to meet at a convenient time for us both and I pick her up.' The quizzing was only interrupted by mouthfuls of Jean's glorious hotpot, which relegated the world and all its happenings into second place.

The constant adulation heaped upon Jean from all who tasted her food, the source of the wizardry seemed not to stem from any cookbook.

'I just used to watch my mum in the kitchen, she would always tell me the main ingredient in your cooking is love. Baking is for the scientist, cooking for the artists.'

Oliver so often deprived himself of food in order to pursue his chosen career. Finishing the last crumbs of spotted dick, the custard bowl hardly needed washing, such was his endeavour in recovering any residue from its sides. He leant back in his chair, contentment oozing from the tip of his toenails to the uppermost hair follicle on his head.

'So,' he said, 'we know the name of this damsel who has, against all expectations, captured the dicky heart of this strange, weird, wonderful brother of mine. Alas, we don't know where she comes from, we don't know how old she is, we don't know where she lives. We do know she can't be attracted to his money because he hasn't got any. She can't be attracted to his good looks, as far as I can see they don't exist. So, after this much enlightened meal the wonderful Agnes remains a mystery.'

The assembly chuckled at his fairly accurate resume of the situation, although Michael took exception to the reference about his looks, believing that when he looked in the mirror he saw a stunning example of manhood.

The next morning Bishop Jonathan Rumbold and his wife, Lesley, pulled into the rectory of St Mary's Church. A hundred yards or so from its entrance, already waiting with a steaming mug of his favourite tea, was his best friend, fellow Iceni and vicar of St Mary's Church the Right Reverend Brian Grogan. Jean and Lesley, with a pot of tea disappeared into the conservatory to have a girly natter whilst the boys got to grips with the heavy stuff, after reassuring each other that neither had suffered any long-term effects from their encounters.

The bishop and the reverend spoke at length as to their interpretation of the recent events, the bishop convinced by the Stuntney happening that this generation would see the second coming; all around him he could see the evidence spoken of in the gospel according to Jesus Christ. He quoted the passage from the gospel. 'And the serpent shall call forth his warriors and they shall rise from their tomb walking mighty upon the earth. The lambs will tremble and cry with one voice, "O lord why hast thou forsaken us". The shepherd shall weep for his flock. The wolves who walk among the sheep will throw off their false garments crying, "I have deceived many and will be exulted high amongst the priests of Satan". Multitudes that live that day will not sleep in their graves when I return to gather my flock.'

He thought that the Stuntney man would never be caught; he would tell the chief constable that in their forthcoming meeting.

He saw corruption everywhere, greed permeating every pore of society.

He saw corporations devoid of any social or moral conscience, whose feign for caring for planet and its population were mere sales techniques, who wield power over government to such an extent that undefendable laws, written before police forces, in the time of the musket, sit solidly in a constitution whose founding fathers would probably be ashamed that their amendment has not been amended.

It is probably the greatest insight into the power that sits behind the faceless few who truly run the planet that the instruments that spray mass murder have dominion over the graves of the innocent.

Brian nodded in agreement, interjecting from time to time with his own thoughts. 'It seems the only sin today is to get caught.'

With that piece of clerical wisdom the door opened. Michael, Oliver and Ninal appeared, fresh from riding the first lot of horses.

Jean and Lesley returned from the conservatory, taking the helm of the breakfast conveyor belt. Tea, butter and jam, the weekday staple began to fill the old wooden table. Oliver, his nose buried deep in the racing paper, giving a running commentary on the events of yesterday in the horse racing world and the likely outcome of today's contests.

To the vast majority of breakfasts this information would be the best cure for insomnia but to this table bringing the night's fasting to an end and welcoming the adventures of the new day without the morning fix of news from the great horse racing family would be akin to the teenage world losing their mobile phones and social media: unthinkable.

After a loaf of bread, half a pound of butter and a pot of jam had been decimated the group of clergy and horse people took their leave, bidding farewell to the two clerics' wives, and headed through the ample grounds of the rectory, across the road and into the disused graveyard, past crooked granite headstones with sentiments long since blurred by decades of climatic baking and battering.

The vicar opened the old oak door of St Mary's Church.

The smell that had lingered in the church since the vicar's encounter had been replaced by delicate scent wafting through the flower-filled church, their perfumed heads working overtime to rid the space of any hint of the incarnation.

It was a bishop full of trepidation that pushed aside the cassocks and entered through the secret door, leading the group of Christ's people to his gospel.

The most powerful piece of literature ever penned. Years of painstaking research by those in pursuit of an explanation for universe, life, mankind and planet, devoid of any input from a spiritual being, gone in the beat of a bumblebee wing.

Exposed those that have bent their religion to serve themselves. The pomp and pageantry the jewelled towering celestial structures used to elevate, subdue, convince and dominate, felled by a single passage from the hand that never held a sword, who walked on the sea, quelled the hurricane, gave life back to the dead. Those that never saw him pour scorn upon the deeds, those that witnessed the miracles, suffered agonizing deaths rather than denounce him.

The bishop was certain now that the hiding place of the gospel had been discovered. How, he could not tell. The secrecy surrounding the lake and its community was as tight as any on the planet, knowledge of the gospels known only to a few.

Those who would seek its destruction and those whose lives mattered little in the endeavour to preserve the truth for its revelation prior to the second coming. Its whereabouts housed in an unfathomable web of tiny canals whose spaghetti fingers feed Newmarket's underground lake, stretching to the clay beds of Bedford. The navigational skill required, passed from one Iceni watcher to the next.

The only other plausible explanation was that somehow the Muslim brotherhood had been compromised, yet these were the most devout holy soldiers, masquerading as stable staff, guarding the land portal hidden close to the crest of the Devalians hill. The face, for the world, an Arab owned racehorse farm breeding the next generation of racecourse athletes. The real reason to honour a centuries old pledge to guard the most sacred artefact of the Christian faith, the gospel of Jesus Christ. Only the devout in the highest echelons of the Muslim faith were privy to this oath, forged through the deep mutual respect of warrior kings and caliphs, who realized there was more that bonded than divided.

The foot soldiers and commanders knew only that they guarded a treasure of great significance, should the need arise they would defend until their eyes closed and opened in paradise. Every instinct, every bone, every corpuscle spoke to him, this was not the source of the tear.

There must be another explanation, for the life of him he could not think of any shield that was not impregnable. Yet he was sure that the Devil would be released from his thousand years in chains, the writings of Jesus Christ gave clarity to the Book of Revelation. He could quote the gospel word for word. "In the days before his chains fall away the deceiver will call forth his disciples from their graves to cast the last word to the four winds, they will rise, the hearts of man will tremble and cry with one voice 'we have forgotten you Lord we beseech you do not forget us'. The men who can smite the world with a finger will fall upon their knees and pray for deliverance.

"Man before he lay his head" will speak and see his brother even though he dwell in a far off place. In the morning will have only his kin for comfort.

"The great houses filled with the fruits of the world will crumble, laid bare by the hands of the hungry. Those that lay with the money lenders and grow fat in their counting house will see their gold disappear into the air like the mountain mists. All will turn towards the heavens, they shall cry, 'We are deceived'. Man will dwell in Gethsemane. I will weep for the suffering, each will beseech my father, 'Take this trial from me'.

"My time is not yet; the heavens will be silent. Those ordained to serve mankind will have their noble heart strengthened; they will stand proud before the forces of the Devil".

The bishop led the way down the ancient steps to the lake's edge, to board the craft that would carry the occupants on a journey far beyond the distance to the gospel.

The conversation subdued, compressed with the weight and enormity of the moment. The bishop skilfully guiding the craft, his mind alternating between analytical evaluation and prayer. He was as convinced as he could be that the release of Satan from his thousand year confinement was imminent. His interpretation of the Christ's testament was those whose souls have been freely given to the deceiver, would be called, not in isolation where their incarnation could be disputed but en masse, bringing dread to the world.

He knew his encounter at Stuntney was with a soulless from beyond the grave, he had felt the intervention of the Holy Spirit for his deliverance, it had been for a reason. That reason, he felt, was in this craft speeding its way to the gospel of Jesus Christ.

He knew from a parishioner, who moved in the highest

halls of the banking system, that the house of cards was on the verge of collapse, that the perception of wealth was just that, a perception. My house, my car, my assets are worth X. It was a simple juggling act, where suits traded complex pieces of paper in the hope that the masses would not require the return of their deposits; it was an incredibly risky system that had been lucky to have lasted so long, his parishioner in a moral dilemma trying to balance his faith with the shenanigans being played out in the money shrines.

The gods of the imagined gold mountain knew the bottom card was about to tumble. The collapse of banks, credit cards, cheques all rendered useless, meant millions left unable to feed their families, food stores, unable to operate, would be ransacked, anarchy would reign, governments and companies, unable to pay their way, overwhelmed. Riot and chaos would be the staple. The Internet rendered useless, either by intent or consequence, would magnify the collapse. He felt the prophecies of the gospel were upon us. He had traversed these waterways countless times, never before with such a feeling of dread.

Back in Ely police station the chief constable stood before a crowded room of elite detectives drafted from almost every police force in the country a fair swathe of his fellow senior policemen had asked to attend leaving their various counties in the care of others. All sympathized with his plight, realizing that there but for the grace of God go me.

The sleepless nights, the pressure from ministers, media, the self-doubt, the crippling realization that this case was beyond the capabilities of a small regional force a humbling experience.

The fear that they had missed something so blindingly obvious that his life of devotion to the law and order of his beloved country would be swept aside by his unwanted honourable resignation.

To trundle along and receive the grateful recognition of a job well done by his community to end his days having spent his retirement sat beside the slow deep River Ouse, fishing for roach, bream, pike and perch now seemed an unattainable daydream scarred by his inability to apprehend a triple murderer.

The priority now was to put all personal ambition, fear of ridicule, behind him and concentrate on the capture of the perpetrator of these diabolical crimes.

Just before he began to speak one of the wits in the room looked around the crammed room of elite lawmen and said, 'great day to be a villain.' The room erupted with laughter which broke the tension.

The chief constable gave an in-depth account of everything that had been done, each avenue explored, each painstakingly meticulous research of global incidences that had any similarities.

After a considerable time, the floor was opened for discussion. The fear of the chief constable, that the blindingly obvious would be pointed out in a career ending moment, did not occur.

Just the opposite. Apart from the predicted questions like, although no DNA was found was the testing equipment faulty, the questioner was assured that three separate institutes had been used to verify the results. After some discussion nobody could add any useful avenue that had not already been explored.

The chief constable of Devon and Cornwall, Gary Pritchard, stood to speak. He had the reputation of being a bobby's bobby, a plain speaking, belt and braces man, started on the beat, escorted youngsters caught relieving orchards of their apples home to their grateful parents with his finger and thumb strategically placed to elevate one ear a good four inches above the other. With the stark warning all bank robbers start by stealing apples, he would leave the apprentice villain to the wrath of the parents, a greater deterrent than anything he could devise at the station.

'This may sound a bit off the wall, especially to the younger guys, but have you considered a supernatural angle to this?'

There wasn't as much amusement as one might expect from this top bobby's statement.

'When I joined up the older coppers swore there had been a murder in the church where no human hand had been involved. The vicar had been performing an exorcism of a small girl in the village; apparently she had extraordinary strength.

'When in a state of possession she was six and could pull trees from out of the ground. They found her dead the morning after the exorcism. Two days later they found the vicar rammed into the church's old chimney, every bone in his body broken from the force exerted. They had to dismantle the chimney to get the body out. The similarities in the cases are the suspects.

'In our case two drunks, sharing a bottle of sherry in the cemetery, swear they saw a giant hairless being come out of the ground feet first and lope towards the church. We have revisited the case on several occasions; it still remains as much a mystery today as it did then. Those who worked the case are convinced there is no logical explanation. The two drunks never change their story; both embraced a life of sobriety.'

Ely's chief constable remained quiet, then, as the room hushed to complete silence, he spoke in an audible whisper.

'I had a long and frank discussion with the bishop of this diocese last evening., the one whose attempted murder began this series of events.

'He is convinced that we are dealing with forces of great power, demonic in origin. He showed me scripture, that I must confess I didn't know existed, about the Devil being locked in chains for a thousand years before being released, thereafter he would wreak havoc on the world. The power of man would be like a candle in a hurricane, his disciples would return from their graves while the righteous would remain asleep.

'The bishop spoke of Stuntney Hill having been used as a gallows for witches and any practicing devil worshipers; they were buried head first in holes as opposed to conventional graves in the hope that if they returned from death they would dig towards hell. Such was the belief of the day.'

The policeman said in conclusion that he was concentrating on all conventional lines of enquires and thanked all his colleagues for their input and continued support, adding as a footnote that he had been much taken by the bishop who had sown a considerable seed in the mind of the chief constable.

'I hope for all our sakes the holy man is wrong. If,' he added, 'we could keep the notion that a rational explanation may not be the answer from the press then we may be able to contain the widespread emotion to fear and not panic.'

The chief constable knew that with lucrative inducement

on offer it was unlikely to get past the evening papers.

The small craft had weaved its way from St Mary's Church under the portal for the Catholic church following the path of the ancient underground river that fed the palatial cavern housing the lake where daily hundreds of racehorses practiced the art of racing.

Heading down the aptly named watercourse across the Severals, into the giant natural cathedrals of Long Hill and its sister Warren, down under the Side Hill stud where, once again, the occupants of the small craft crouched almost flat to secure passage under the Ashley Road into the splendour of the Devalian Hill, the most secret and sacred of the natural cathedrals. The bishop returned from the darkness of his thoughts to marvel. No matter how often he saw this natural beauty the raging furnace of his faith was blown to inferno by the spiritual bellows of its glory.

The bishop rested the craft gently against the flat chalk jetty, in the cavern where Ninal, Michael and Oliver had first met with the Iceni's "defenders of the faith", ascending a precision crafted spiral staircase, the white calcium risers embedded with split blue/black flint bringing longevity with jewelled grace.

The staircase gave way to a cavern as pristine as it was spherical, the floor again filled with the flint that graced the chalk lands. Three more staircases left the room heading skyward. Immediately opposite the boat party was a glass door surrounded by a marble frame that was itself decorated with tiny chips of the most exquisite flint. The structure could have stood unashamedly beside any masterpiece gifted to mankind.

Beside the staircases and door were sentries, elite Muslim

soldiers, proud, devout men of honour and dedication delivering on the promise of centuries past. The door opened, out stepped the head guard: a lean, sinewy man, skin tight across his features, testament to hours of physical strain maintaining a state of readiness should the need arise.

He bowed low then held his hand out, the bishop shook it warmly, they exchanged genuine enquiries into the other's wellbeing. Years of professional contact had cemented deep respect for the other's spirituality.

The guard held four teddy bears in his hand, placed and taken from the gypsy boy's grave the night before, the ancient enzymes that had served the Iceni long before the air shrunk the communication world to the size of a pea.

The Muslim soldier studied each of the bishop's party, making occasional reference to one of the teddies, after satisfying himself that the information revealed matched, entrance to the room was invited.

The room contained three other soldiers glued to screen, each nodded a brief welcome before returning to their vigil.

'State of the art surveillance,' the bishop explained, 'on a par with any organization.' The bishop placed his face and hands for inspection in a scanner that stood beside a metallic door, more functional than ornate, a few seconds later the heavy metal door opened, guided by powerful cogs and hydraulics. The Christians entered, the Muslim guard remained outside, his mission completed. Whatever was in the room he cared not, he and his men would guard it till paradise.

The room, a perfect round, the ceiling a perfect dome, hewn from the purest chalk, once again blue/black jewelled flint bedecked the floor to add longevity, exquisite in its simplicity. In the room's centre a solid round chalk structure rose to stand four feet above the base atop a two inch thick polished crystal glass top. At the furthest point from the door, now firmly closed behind them, an altar cut in the same medium and precision. His Holiness knelt on one of the silk white cushions placed before the altar, the others followed suit. He prayed in silence along with the others; he gave thanks for being blessed among men to read the words of Jesus Christ.

To feel the spirit of his Lord constantly beside him, to feel the Holy Ghost lift his soul to rapture.

Those wonderful days with his earthly father, cycling and gazing out across the African Serengeti, to the spiritual poetry of man and horse galloping out of the early mists on Newmarket's ancient heath.

'If God made anything better,' Humphrey Bottril the racehorse trainer had said, 'then he kept it for himself.' Such was the joy that God bestowed upon man when he raised the veil. He knew through his life he had been lifted and carried.

Lifted when he stumbled, and carried when grief had rendered him immobile. He was in no doubt that, although he presided over his father's funeral, he did not conduct it, strong arms had held him steadfast as wave after wave of despair engulfed.

To the world the service had been spiritually profound, moving and professional. The bishop knew it was Christ who held him, it was Christ who had come to take the joyful spirit of his dad home.

Michael broke the silence with 'Our father which art in heaven hallowed be thy name,' the rest joined. The bishop, convinced that this young man had been sent in readiness for the days to come, once again marvelled at the delivery of the prayer that Jesus had taught his disciples.

Michael always spoke as though he had a direct line, a view the bishop had since the days of garden parties at St Mary's vicarage in the days of yore.

Brian Grogan, vicar of St Mary's, knelt between his adopted sons, his beloved daughter-in-law, Ninal, knelt beside Oliver, her husband.

The clergyman prayed with an earnest for their safe passage through the ordeal that he felt sure was almost upon them; he believed, along with the bishop, plus the rest of the Iceni, that the conditions for the release of Satan had almost been fulfilled.

Mankind's darkest days were in front of him.

The bishop rose, took several leather-bound books resting on the altar spreading them on the glass top of the chalk table. The books had inscribed on the thick red hide the gospel of Jesus Christ.

He invited the party to read, explaining that these were copies of the original writings that were sealed in an airtight case under the altar. The transcripts had been translated and placed in book form.

Each page in the gospel had a photo of Jesus's original work, then the translation; any ambiguity was added for the reader's interpretation.

The next few hours were spent in silence and profound reverence as each spiritually fed on the written word of Jesus Christ; it was the last supper for the devout. No room for doubt, the word giving clarity to the Book of Revelation.

It was a sombre and chaste group that left the chamber. It was an active and pumped room that greeted the emerging readers. The chief Muslim guard confided in the bishop that security had been breached, a tracking device had been detected sending a signal from this area they were about to destroy it through electro tsunami.

The Muslim guard explained that the technology was so old as to be almost obsolete. The technique for its destruction was simple. The next time it operated and the signal transmitted it would be intercepted and sent back magnified in intensity until the device exploded.

At that moment Oliver let out a cry of pain, the top of his head seemed to pop. blood began to run down his hair in rivulets. Ninal cradled his head, her tears running in unison with her husband's blood. The Muslim brotherhood leaped into well practiced action, clinical and precise, gears and rams pulsated as the hideaway went into lockdown, monitors showed Arab stablehands running towards their assigned positions, ready to defend and enter paradise in exercising their real role.

Anxiety replaced shock as the group surrounded Oliver. The head guard, satisfied that lockdown was in place, pushed his way through the worried group armed with an array of medical equipment. Oliver, protesting his wellbeing, was sitting in a chair while the guard, obviously well trained in matters medical, examined the injury.

He extracted a tiny flat microchip from under a flap of skin that had been torn from the scalp by the force of vibration. This device is from the age of the dinosaurs, probably been carrying this around for over twenty years. It is powered by a minute battery that is recharged by the body's heat similar to those used by the space program to send information back to earth as they explore distant astral bodies. The guard meticulously cleaned the area, replacing the flap, injecting anaesthetic before expertly stitching the wound. A further injection of antibiotic and Oliver was returned to somewhere near normal.

The guard could not see how a device, planted over twenty years, could have any bearing on their assignment and when Oliver volunteered that it must have been planted when he was in care, the Muslim soldier was more convinced. All governments have used children who are in care for experiments, they are easy food for programs that walk on the dark side, from lobotomy, sterilisation, drugs of all hues have been administered to the vulnerable and children in governmental care head that list. The official secrets act is the greatest cloak afforded the ungodly.

The bishop was not so sure. He knew that the Cheltenham listening centre had computers that monitored every word and signal that entered the airways, that phrases and formulas would trigger redirection of information to interested parties. Whether the device planted in Oliver's head was to target the Iceni or a random experiment carried out on the vulnerable under the guise of the greater good remained debatable. Someone, somewhere, would be listening, for what reason would remain a mystery.

Oliver, who never spoke of his early years, confided, as they sailed the craft back to St Mary's, that terrible things happened in those places supposed to give sanctuary. In the main he had managed to blank their memory. Ninal knew: they returned regularly in the depth of the night; he would wake screaming, wet with sweat, shaking and terrified. He had never spoken of the horrors invading his sleep until now.

Oliver said, 'There were white coats forever injecting something, in order to study the effect. Electric shocks administered regularly, intentionally altering the mind in order

120

to justify intervention with the scalpel.

'Men of the cloth, nightly checking the boys to make sure they had removed their underwear, simply an excuse to grope, would climb in the bed to keep the boys warm. Care homes were simply a magnet for paedophiles, sexually perverted, who would adopt any cloak of disguise to stalk their prey.

'Nuns tying young girls in sacks and tossing them in the lake, dragging them out half drowned as a punishment for bed wetting. Acts of such horror that to the God-fearing normal these crimes seemed so outrageous they must be figments of the imagination, yet I was there.

'Still today I cannot utter the words of the acts of depravity enacted upon me, only my brothers and sisters who stood with me at the doors of hell can truly understand. Someone cutting the scalp to insert a device was a flurry of snow in a demonic avalanche.

'My only comfort is to know that God promised that revenge is his. The perpetrators will one day stand before him to answer for their atrocities.'

The craft remained quiet as its occupants tried to imagine the horror of his suffering. The two clergymen knew he had had a troubled first few years but had blossomed into the fine young man he had become in the bosom of his adopted family. Ninal cradled his arm as though she would never let it go, Michael placed his hand between Oliver's shoulder blades and gave it a genial rub a, well-practiced gesture that spoke more than words could ever say.

The two clergymen sat in silence, each pondering the latest developments. How could such a small, prehistoric device in the world of superfast surveillance have any impact? How could those that planted it have any knowledge of the gospel of Jesus Christ? How could they even suspect its existence? Surely its developers can only have had tracking in their minds, tracking of criminal terrorists.

The bishop had heard that tracking devices were in action that would only send a signal should the device find itself in uncharted spaces, useful to the military to plot underground bunkers that might house missile launchers or underground command centers. Tracking devices that are so small that they could be administered by a drone no bigger than a mosquito.

Not for the first time, the Bishop thought, science fiction had become reality.

What would be the outcome? Surely, in this modern world of microscopic surveillance, it was inconceivable that the military eye of various nations did not know of the hidden lake and caves that lay beneath the facade of the horse racing town of Newmarket.

The age-old method of flowers, artefacts, toys and teddies, placed in a myriad of positions on the grave of a gypsy boy, had undoubtedly kept the secret of the gospel safe.

Those receiving intelligence that a hitherto unknown cavern had been identified would, the bishop hoped, just assume that it was all part of the same complex and pay it little heed.

In a cave deep inside Mount Zagros, northern Iraq, a monitor bleeped; an arrowed icon descended on the screen. Eventually the bleeping stopped indicating that the signal had been lost or destroyed, A number appeared beside the icon, cross referencing the number the operative could see it was a signal indicating that it was close to its target.

In keeping with the space age technology that allowed space probes to analyses the surface of far off planets years after launch, the microchip had picked up the chemical make-up of papyrus and vellum or parchment. It had woken and sent its whereabouts to the cave in the mountain.

Had the icon indicated the British Museum, or other such places, he would have dismissed it as irrelevant but the arrow, pointing to a sparsely populated hill in a hitherto unknown underground cave, gave rise to a degree of interest. Coupled with the fact of its disappearance gave rise to the notion that it could have been destroyed which meant the information should be sent for further investigation much further up the hierarchy.

The Nephilim Yazidis warrior sent a coded message, then returned to monitor his screen.

The Nephilim Yazidis, widely despised by both Muslims and Christians alike for having at the centre of their faith "Melex Taus", the Peacock Angel, fallen from grace. The champion of eternal life, the flesh of the peacock does not degenerate after death.

Melex Taus believed by theologians of the Muslim and Christian faith to be the Devil himself leading a rebellion against God's will in heaven.

The Nephilim Yazidis believe themselves to be direct descendants of the fallen Angel.

Genesis 6:1-4

"When people began to multiply on the Earth and daughters were born unto them. The sons of God saw they were fair and they took wives for themselves of all that they chose.

Then the Lord said, 'My spirit shall not abide in mortals forever, for they are flesh. Their days shall be one hundred and twenty years. The Nephilim were on the Earth in those days and also afterwards when the sons of God went into the daughters of humans and bore children unto them. These were the heroes, that were of old, warriors of renown."

The Nephilim Yazidis, the most secret of this secret religion, believed their ancestors were the Nephilim, the legends of Greek mythology and ancient writings of giants– of Atlas, Hercules, Goliath– huge, powerful beings that walked the earth.

"The Lord said unto Moses, 'Send the men to spy out the land of Canaan which I am giving to the Israelites', so they went up and spied the land and they told him yet the people who live on this land are strong and the towns are fortified and very large and besides we saw the descendants of Anakites.

So they brought to the Israelites an unfavourable report of the land they had spied out saying, 'The land that we have gone through as spies is the land that devours its inhabitants, all its people we saw in it are a giant size, there we saw the Nephilim (The Anakites come from the Nephilim.) and to ourselves we seemed like grasshoppers and so it seemed to them.'"

In essence the Nephilim Yazidis believe that God made Melex in his own image from celestial stardust and instructed him to bow before none but God himself. Later when God instructed Melex to prostrate himself before Adam he refused saying, 'You made me from a piece of heaven I will not bow down to Adam made of dust.'

God, according to the Nephilim Yazidis scriptures, was so pleased that Melex obeyed his original commandment that he gave him the earth along with six other archangels.

Melex argued with God that man should "tread his own path through the celestial heavens," Gods image, "would build by his own hand, guided through his own sorcery, will ascend the heavenly ladder."

Melex proposed that the strong would inherit the heavens; the meek would be left behind. Corruption, greed, envy, worship of gold, were all much more value to the ascent of the sons of Adam.

Nephilim Yazidis believed that almost all the world lived by their creed yet professed allegiance to the god of Abraham.

All governments were corrupt. The accumulation of gold and more gold drove most of mankind.

Envy stoked the fires of accumulation. Plenty was never enough. Men slaughtered other men on a daily basis, all justified their actions because they had the god of Abraham on their side.

The rest of the world despised, hated and feared Nephilim Yazidis.

Nephilim Yazidis believed they were the rightful descendants of the lord of the earth and would continue with his work.

They were as fervent in their beliefs as they had ever been. All of their scriptures were stacking.

"Man will see his adversary through the eye of an eagle and smite him with a finger".

"The seas shall come ashore and swallow the people, while man eats and watches at his table in a far land".

"Man will sleep on the table while his heart is ripped from him, another heart from one who has given up his ghost will be placed in his chest, he shall be as new".

All these beliefs, and many more, were laid down in a time when they were incredible, impossible, unbelievable. Yet drone warfare, tsunami, transplants, watching events unfold on screens, has slipped from astonishing to normal.

Melex, Satan, Lucifer, The Devil, The Peacock Angel, whatever other name he has been assigned spoke to his disciples saying, 'Enjoy the flesh for one day you will be parted, the journey to the heavens will have begun, I shall be among you.'

The Peacock Angel's followers were convinced they were in the final days. According to their sources, work in many of the laboratories around the world was fast advancing, whereby the brain and mind of a subject (much like the DNA code) had almost been unravelled. The complex electrical signals and pulses that emanate throughout the brain that gives the human species unfettered access to the most complex and powerful computer known to mankind will be unlocked.

Once the mind of a man can be transferred to a computer then the frailties of the body will no longer be a hindrance.

The magic and sorcery referred to in the ancient Nephilim Yazidis' text was now understood to be science.

What wonders that now live in the realms of fantasy will one day be as common as the mobile phone, satellites, Facebook. Much of the world's young live their lives in the altered reality of cyberspace.

Dark energy, dark matter, fills the universe, so powerful it makes nuclear energy seem like a wet match. The double slit experiment, the common man's glimpse at quantum physics.

Black holes with such a degree of gravity that it pulls light and time backwards. A universe expanding faster than the speed of light.

A universe that can be crushed with such an unimaginable pressure that its matter could be enclosed in a space no bigger than a stock cube.

Brilliant minds and intellects that can trace the universe's existence back to a millionth of a second after the Big Bang.

All these wonders eventually lost to the sons of Adam through the decay of the flesh. Nephilim Yazidis scholars had predicted all of these things in the language of the times.

"The time will come upon the sorcerers, all will be as one, immortal, and stand at the doorway of the heavens which will be opened unto them and great bounties will be bestowed upon them.

"Oh my people let no man stand in front of the sorcerers, smite them, cast them to the wolves, they will confine you as a song bird in a cage."

The high priest of Nephilim Yazidis stared at the message on the screen. His heart beat faster than at any time in recent years. Could this be what he had waited for almost all of his adult life?

The resting place of the gospel of Jesus Christ.

They knew of its existence and had been close to capturing it and destroying it those centuries ago but it had been whisked away almost from under their noses. They believed, in that time, that Christ's people were beginning to fracture and splinter into different sects. Those closest to the gospel decided to put it under the protection of the Mohammedans, who had escorted it, they believed, to England with the Crusaders. No amount of coercion or torture had loosened those ancient warriors' tongues. The trail, for centuries, had simply gone cold.

Many schemes had been embarked upon to locate the sacred: book all had suffered the same fate and had failed.

The Peacock Angel's people believed they were one step

behind in the race to monitor modern cyberspace and those protecting the gospel were always at the cutting edge. It was almost inconceivable that a scheme put together almost two decades prior had borne fruit.

The plan had been to implant microchips into the scalps of homeless children under the care of the local authorities. They were simply flotsam on the seas of humanity.

A telescopic distance down the list of priorities. Sent to the four corners of the earth, used and abused for almost any purpose from drug trials, slavery to electric shock treatment.

But some would find themselves in vicarages where good people, through love, would try to repair the damage.

Nephilim Yazidis served only their lord of darkness; they cared nothing for the individual. They had supported the work of the Nazis' high command with its many experiments on humankind, they had helped disperse, hide and protect those involved in the medical experiments, integrating them into different societies. Those whose belief in scientific advance at any cost was undaunted.

All countries have their own spies and agents, a world that sits below the world of mock respectability.

Nephilim Yazidis would be a match for the Israeli Mossad in its ability to orchestrate a plan.

So the scheme was hatched and implemented, so children destined for vicarages, anaesthetized and space age microchips placed in the scalp that would only wake and send a signal in the presence of predetermined elements.

The experiment had borne no fruit apart from a few occasions when the map had pinpointed the British Museum.

The Peacock Angel's people had checked the source in the hope that the real work of Jesus Christ was masquerading.

They had satisfied themselves that the tree was not hiding in the forest. Expectation was that the gospel was hiding somewhere in a church in England.

Time passed, any hope of the bullseye being struck diminished, joining the ranks of many such schemes that had failed to deliver.

The Devil's worshippers were, along with many other religions, desperate that the gospel should never surface.

They believed that it gave an in-depth account of the meeting in the Judean desert between the Devil and Jesus, where the Devil suffered humiliation and defeat; all the powers at his disposal were thwarted.

Jesus could not be shaken, insisting that man could not enter into the heavens by his own hand, that while the Devil ruled the earth, he would never conquer the power of love Whatever the Devil put in his way, Jesus would conquer with love. The corruption of man and the corruption of the flesh will pass like night into day.

Nephilim Yazidis thought that if they could destroy the gospel of Jesus Christ that would buy them extra time which would allow the scientific community to develop the transfer of a man's mind into a computer, tapping into the uncharted depths of the human brain. A brain far outstripping any evolutionary influence, over endowed, capable of feats, quantum leaps in advance of anything it would encounter in one lifetime.

All the signs were in place, from reports around the world, of gathering storm clouds, of pestilence and chemicals that could wipe man from the earth, corruption and greed at the highest level, slaughter of the innocent. Rampant gluttony. The

Devil's influence was at its most powerful: now was the time for his physical return.

Melex Taus' chief earthly warrior sent out the signal that the site was to be investigated. If, as he suspected, there was a high probability that they had found the quarry, he would call on the dark lord for assistance. Knowing that the protection of this work by Jesus's own hand was almost certain to have divine protection, the power to overcome would surely only be provided by the fallen angel himself.

Paul "the pen" Pattison's phone rang out. He was just heading for the pub close to his flat in the borough of Hackney, one of London's less fashionable districts.

'Are you heading for the pub?' the voice asked.

'Yes just going there now,' Paul replied, see you in a few minutes then, the caller hung up.

A twinge of excitement ran through Paul "the pen" Patterson. This informant from the boys in blue was almost always a great source of information.

Paul Patterson, or "the pen" as he was affectionately known, was one of the most renowned investigative journalists in the business. His list of informants was impressive, from senior policeman to judges, some high-profile criminals, many politicians would use his services. Paul paid good money and never referred to anyone by their names, he had nicknames for everyone. Paul was meeting Officer Dibble of the cartoon tom cat fame.

Officer Dibble had provided Paul with some wonderful leads in the past. Paul, a freelance, knew how to play the system, how to squeeze the last drop out of a story.

He always carried a thousand pounds in fifty pound notes

in a little brown envelope. Speed and timing were of the essence: whatever the story was it needed to breakfast. The informant needed to be back in his usual surroundings with no more contact till the dust had settled. The thousand pounds was often enough to keep the creditors at bay until a suitable amount of time had elapsed and a more lucrative payout could be arranged.

Paul's favourite meeting place was his local pub and Irish style bar. The top room had curtained bays where parties of up to six could eat and drink more intimately. Paul would nightly sit in the middle bay, eating a wholesome man-size dinner with two pints of Irish stout, typing his latest piece on his laptop. His flat was his sleeping quarters, the pub his home.

He had full view of the door that opened into the snug. When Officer Dibble came in he would order a drink and sit in the cubicle next door, an age-old practice that never put the two together; most of his informants popped in occasionally for a drink so the pub appeared to be a regular haunt.

The practice had served him well for over thirty years. Paul slipped the brown envelope unseen through the curtain that separated the top half of the cubicles. Paul listened intently to the narrative.

'This could be a good earner,' Paul said.

Officer Dibble finished his beer and headed for the door. Paul pulled out his mobile phone and started the bidding process.

Next morning one of the leading tabloid papers had as their headline, "Rural Bobby suspects the Devil for unsolved murders". Whatever next, goblins suspected of robbing the Brentwood post office. The piece went on to vilify the local constabulary, casting them as incompetent buffoons.

The chief constable had been surprised it had got past the evening papers. The problem now was the world's media attention would be drawn to such an unusual storyline.

Paul "the pen" Pattison had been in Stuntney village most of the morning, knocking on doors, trying to gather as much information as he could. This story had legs and the possibility of a serious amount of cash being directed his way. The world's media were gathering, big vans with satellites were appearing all along the road.

Paul was convinced that somewhere someone knew something about something. It was probably some satanic cult living in this small community of Stuntney, hiding a fugitive. If he could just get an angle this story could run and run.

Those residents that would open the door to him without shutting it almost immediately were very scared indeed. It was a strange one, most people close to the centre of an incident were normally only too happy to help in the hope of gaining their fifteen minutes of fame in newspaper or TV.

Paul thought, as the light was fading and doors were even more reluctant to open, he would head across the road and ferret about amongst the trees on the site of the old gallows and burial grounds.

The local bobbies were fine when it came to standing at the bottom of the hill and jumping out on unsuspecting motorists pointing a speed gun but this sort of stuff was surely well above their heads. Paul was convinced they would have missed something.

The pressman circumvented the dwindling throng of TV people. Most had finished with their presenters, now heading off like storm chasers hoping to gain the best vantage point for the next breaking tornado.

He walked past the sole police car with two armed officers sitting surveying the scene. He nonchalantly nodded a greeting and gave the impression that he was heading for his car, parked over the brow of the hill another quarter mile towards the town of Soham. Ducking across the road into a long strip of sweetcorn planted for the camouflage and concealment of the pheasant, he walked well past the spinney containing the burial ground, turned left and hoped that in the growing gloom he could not be seen. Once at the back and out of sight of any observers, Paul headed to the ancient woodland. Once inside the cauldron of tapes and ropes he began his search: something unusual, something that was easily missed. If this was a satanic ritual site then there would be carvings, probably high on the trunks of the trees, completely missed by those fingertip searching the ground.

Using the tiniest of torches attached to his keys, with the light almost gone he meticulously began examined one tree after another, following its trunk from the ground up.

There would surely be some satanic carving somewhere, if he could get a picture of it he could build a story around it.

It didn't have to be true as long as it would sell newspapers: the local plods were sure to have missed something.

The pencil-thin beam of light picked out each crevice and contour, each segment of bark the subject of detailed scrutiny, meticulous in a gradual ascent, metronomic in its weaving. Two meters from the base, the beam of illumination stopped abruptly, its guide aware of the presence stood beside.

Paul was suddenly gripped with fear; an uncontrollable terror, a tidal wave of hitherto unimaginable fright. Moving the beam past the tree and into the face of the long dead. A face that rendered the feet encased the bowels uncontrolled, the voice inaudible.

In that moment the investigative journalist knew that his cynical view of the world was wrong; he had believed that power and money were its only driving force. He now knew he was woefully mistaken; he had laughed to scorn the notion that there were higher combatants at work, they were figments of the deluded.

Paul knew that if given another chance he would pursue a different course. He knew that chance would not come; he knew, as the massive digits grasped his windpipe in readiness for its severance, would not allow his Damascus moment any time to blossom. He knew the pain induced by his pen far outweighed any benefit he had brought to his fellow man.

It was a troubled soul that left the confines of Paul's body.

As Paul's soul departed, distant wailing of police vehicles broke the mournful silence of the dark Cambridgeshire evening.

The throb of helicopter blades approaching augmented the police symphony. The two armed policemen had seen a pinprick of light in the spinney.

Following instructions to call for backup before investigating any occurrence, the full arsenal available to the constabulary was dispatched.

Within minutes two helicopters circled the ancient burial ground. Powerful beams scoured the area. Heat seeking equipment had pinpointed what appeared to be a person hanging upside down, high in the tree canopy, heat rapidly leaving the body indicating a corpse.

A haggard chief constable was fast on the scene; a cordon set up.

Helicopters had searched all the farmland between Stuntney, Ely and the surrounding area.

The heat seeking equipment had identified every fox, deer, horse and pony: nothing untoward lurked. Special armed units were on their way.

They would seal the area until first light leaving no escape route. The chief constable hoped in his heart of hearts the perpetrator of these dreadful events had taken his own life.

Dawn broke. A ring of armed units entered the spinney, inching forward, eventually meeting under the tree where dangled the dead pressman, some four meters from the ground. His windpipe hung like a drunk's tie in front of his upturned face. His foot seemed to have been rammed solid into the V between two branches. Several officers were retching in the bushes; hardened bobbies ashen-faced.

All the senior officers could offer no explanation; suicide out of the question. Lifting a body to such a height, leaving no trace of a climb, bordering on the impossible. All in the full glare of the world's media.

Once again the assailant had left the scene with no trace.

The media was again swiftly into action. Those that had left quickly returned. The story was now grabbing headlines all around the world.

The red tops all about ghosts and ghouls. More level-headed trying to fathom out the reason why the assailant was able to baffle the police, many hinting that the lack of experience in these matters by the local force was the main reason the case had not advanced.

The police quickly understood the victim's name,

establishing that he was a leading investigative journalist and surmised that he had sneaked into the area hoping to uncover a story. Certainly found what he was looking for. Unfortunately he didn't live to tell the tale and not much about the corpse gave any indication as to who the murderer was.

Why had the murderer returned; had he left something as yet undiscovered? That was what baffled the senior officers on the case. Why was he not hundreds, if not thousands, of miles away?

The only logical answer was that, as he was so distinguishable, he must be in hiding locality, probably in the village of Stuntney. Being shielded, probably, by a family member.

It was not unknown in these parts, in times gone by, to lock an embarrassing member of the family away in an attic room or somewhere where the general public would never see them. Only very close members of the family would be aware of their existence, such was the stigma attached to those that were different.

Yet no one in the village seemed to have a profile that could, in any way, fit the scenario. Credit card statements, bank statements, doctors' records, mobile phone usage, all had been checked to see if anyone was claiming benefit for someone who apparently didn't live there; food bills that didn't match with the occupancy, medications prescribed that didn't fit. Nothing seemed to be untoward or out of order.

The mystery seemed to deepen with every passing hour.

Atop the Ducher Hill, the Muslim brotherhood were in lockdown, in readiness for what they fully expected: an assault from some hostile force. They did not share the bishop's hope that the signal from the probe had gone unnoticed.

They were convinced those with the guile to set up the program were stealthy adversaries.

Years of waiting would be followed by an expeditionary force. A team of the highly trained and ruthless. There would be no early encounter in the unlikely event that they would be convinced that the outward appearance of a respected racehorse breeding operation would suffice.

The high security surrounding the breeding stud had long been accepted as necessary because it housed many Arab potentates.

Now it would be invaluable. The main security gate which housed all the normal surveillance paraphernalia was also fed to the secret bunker guarding the gospel which also housed the most sophisticated surveillance equipment from satellite imagery to striro pulse radiography. A rabbit could not exit its hole without the information being fed back to the bunker.

Eighteen hours after the signal had been sent, the brotherhood commander watched as six slipped from the back of the Range Rover which momentarily slowed and stopped beside the hedge that borders the Duchess Drive.

The small band of Nephilim Yazidis melted into the thin belt of beech trees that enclosed the horse stud, the gathering dusk affording them anonymity from all but the Muslim brotherhood.

With precision and stealth, they headed directly for the coordinates the signal had sent.

Directly underneath the highest point of the Develian hill the commander watched, fully aware that should he stop their progress, then the game was up: whatever they were guarding, the opposition would know it had found its quarry.

He also knew that he was charged with guarding, at all costs, what happened after that was up to the powers that be. The six posed no problem but what came after, only Allah knew.

The Peacock Angels people made swift progress, teeth firmly grasping eight inch stiletto blades should the assassin's tool be required it would be instantly available.

Reaching the coordinates they found three stables; two housed expectant equine mothers. The middle one empty.

The head of the group positioned his men with a series of well-practiced hand movements.

Around the perimeter of the stable block before entering the empty stall. Bags of horse feed were stacked on wooden pallets against the walls. Buckets from which to feed stacked neatly, various types of additives: honey, molasses, cider vinegar, vitamin supplements, perched on adjacent shelving. Nothing that could remotely connect this stable with the most profound piece of literature bestowed upon mankind.

The Nephilim Yazidis soldier worked with dexterity, diligence and a determination to discover the secrets held within this 3.5 square meter equine home. Each centimetre of the walls examined; the ceiling, the same attention. He began to move feed on the hand pump pallet truck to expose the floor.

In the furthest corner from the door he found a small metal ring. A brush with his hand to remove the dust exposed a trap door.

His fingers grasped the ring. He began to pull, it would be the last physical action of his life, the electric current that passed through his body stunned and immobilized him. Nanoseconds later crossbow bolts slammed into the vertebrae of his associates just below the scull affording them easy deaths, not so their leader. The agile Muslim warrior that ascended the steps of the open trapdoor, adorned in black balaclava, body suit and trainers to match, opened the mouth of his stricken adversary and, with pliers, began to pull his back molars out, until he found the one containing the cyanide capsule, the escape route for the captured.

The Peacock Angel's soldier lay strapped onto the interrogation table, his body in agony from the electric used to stun him, his jaw aflame with pain.

He knew the process well: gone were the days of torture. No need, the truth drugs available left no room for resistance.

He would tell them everything; these people were good. To stun him then remove his escape, this was as good as it got. He also knew, once he was drained of information, his end would be swift. These were soldiers of the highest calibre, not sadists who took pleasure in killing. He would be afforded an honourable soldier's death: quick and as painless as possible.

He felt the hypodermic needle enter his vein, he told them everything, he looked into the eyes of the Muslim warrior as he dropped the retrieved capsule back into the mouth of his adversary, his eyes thanked his fellow Samurai as he bit into the death capsule with what remained of his teeth.

His body was placed beside his compatriots in a pre-dug horse grave in the cemetery in the centre of the stud devoted to the outstanding racehorses that had given great service. The small digger kept on site quickly erased any trace of the Nephilim Yazidis' visit.

The bishop received the coded message that the holiest of sites had been visited.

All was well but a more determined effort would be expected soon. His worst fears were realized, Nephilim

Yazidis were behind it, the Peacock Angel's devoted followers.

These were not the usual satanic cult that blossomed then faded in the same manner, more intent on fostering fantasy than any deep-rooted devotion.

These, it was said, were Lucifers people, direct descendants of the fallen angels, saved from Noah's flood by the deceiver himself, placed safe on the top of Cheekha Dar mountain in northern Iraq, an undiluted demonic bloodline, discouraged from any relationships outside the religion; they lived separately for centuries. Those that came into contact with them said they possessed strange powers. Some could levitate, some could walk on burning coals, many professed to be more than one hundred and fifty years old. Illness and injury seemed not to play a part in their lives.

Those that left the Cheekha Dar mountain, although never to be allowed to re-join, were encouraged to remain in contact and form part of a global order.

It had been put forward, that those around the world who seemed to have been born with incredible abilities that far exceeded explanation: four-year-old children composing and playing complex musical pieces on the piano, six-year-old mathematicians whose understanding of the cosmos is beyond comprehension.

Psychokinesis, a minuscule number of people who move objects simply by the power of thought.

Telaesthesia, used widely by the military, people who can see and read documents from a great distance.

Students of genealogy who studied these people, often called geniuses prodigy gifted, have traced their ancestry back to northern Iraq where the trail always went cold.

The most notable despots in the history of humankind

were, in modern speak, psychopaths unable to feel empathy, guilt, remorse or shame, no emotion towards the slaughtered.

Never more blatantly demonstrated than Adolf Hitler and his band of Nazis, whose blind determination to destroy the Jewish race in perfect unison with Nephilim Yazidis theology.

The bishop knew the theory, the battle lines for the soul of mankind had been drawn up at the time of the flood. Noah, and subsequently God's people, the Israelites, had been set down on Mount Ararat.

The Nephilim offspring Yazidis had been set down upon the summit of Cheekha Dar three hundred miles away. The two had been in battle ever since. God had sent prophets to show the way.

The lines that emanated from Abraham. One he sent Jesus, the other Muhammad, in more recent times Bahai. The basis for man's salvation, the Ten Commandments.

The Peacock Angel saw no merit in any of these.

"Thou shall not kill".

Killing was necessary, to cull the weak who only filled the earth with dross; a burden in the advance to the galaxies.

"Thou shall not steal".

Stealing was absolutely necessary, a shortcut to power, be it land, peoples, information, it was a prerequisite, employed in every corridor, a universal practice.

"Remember the sabbath day and keep it holy". God's creed.

"Thou shall not waste thy days in idle contemplation".

The Devil's people saw the seventh day as a day wasted in the advance of science.

"Thou shall not commit adultery".

No sin for Peacock Angel followers.

"Keep the seed abundant, leave not a barren womb".
"Spread thy lord's seed where ere it can be sown".

The bishop knew well the creed, everything in complete opposition to the commandments laid down by the God of Abraham, the seven deadly sins, non-existent and encouraged in the Nephilim Yazidis' law.

The bishop's own personal nemesis was gluttony, he would freely admit the Devil had the upper hand.

"Feed upon the bounty of the earth; fill thy body with its harvest". An instruction from the old Nephilim texts. He often joked in his sermons that the laws on gluttony were put in place long before apple crumble and custard had been invented.

His Holiness the bishop knelt in deep prayer before the altar in Ely Cathedral. He had to act quickly: should they run and hide or should they stand their ground? Was this the moment foretold by Jesus's own hand?

The deceiver shall send his armies, they will rend the heart of man, fear not and have faith for the word will not touch the hand of the unjust, I am the light of the world; those who believe and live in me will not die they will see the heavens open, those that sleep in my name, I will call forth. There will be great rejoicing; there will be no more tears, if it were not so I would not tell it. My father in heaven hath beseeched it.

The priesthood of Nephilim Yazidis convened; the gospel of the Christ had been found. No other conclusion could explain the loss of six of its elite military soldiers sent on a reconnaissance mission to check the signal's validity. They could only have been met by a force as highly trained as themselves, soldiers driven to the highest levels of readiness and professionalism by religious fervour. Only two elite military fitted, the Israelis' Mossad or the Muslim brotherhood. It was inconceivable that Mossad's relatively modern force, with no prior known connection with the gospel, could be in any way involved. Whereas the ancient order of the brotherhood was known to have become guardian of the gospel, the passage of time would not have diminished their devotion to the solemn oath undertaken millennia ago.

The Arab racehorse stud farm was the perfect ruse for the concealment; now it had been pinpointed it would be subject to the most stringent surveillance.

Ancient rituals to call upon their dark lord for assistance would be enacted, not only in the remote caverns of Mount Cheekha Dar, but in secret destinations across the globe. The Peacock Angel's seed, through Nephilim Yazidis, had spread into every sphere. People began to resemble the Nephilim, the young often standing head and shoulders above their parents and totems of athletic achievements fall and replaced on pendulum regularity.

The independent observer would conclude that the creed of the dark lord was far more prevalent than anything written or done by any of God's prophets.

The Malak faithful included among their number a fair proportion of the world's most eminent scientists, people who had grown their scientific reputations by producing theory after theory of how life had begun, how one species morphed into another. It was spoken of with such conviction that the vast majority believed that somehow a primeval soup had developed into the most complex piece of living matter, the brain, able to perform incredible feats.

Keeping its host safe from a hostile environment. Monitoring tens of thousands of signals every second, responding instantly to calls for it needing to repair itself, able to fight organisms that would destroy it, learn how to defeat them. Miracle upon miracle able to reproduce itself, miracle upon miracle upon miracle, and perhaps the most astonishing, the most bewildering the most unfathomable that by a process of baffling complexity it is able to reproduce itself younger.

The scientific path that enthused the young academic vanguard, believing that solutions to the perpetual chicken and egg conundrum, lay just over the hill.

Ely Cathedral could be seen on the far horizon, its spire piercing the fenland sky. Michael's thoughts drifted to the different world being played out underneath his feet: the underground lake, the rivers that fed it. The seven springs and the Exning river it fed, the portals to the secret world mostly covered by churches or manor houses, the townsfolk unaware that the water they used came from the lake, pumped and monitored from a secret location hiding in full view on the edge of the Rowley Mile training grounds manned and maintained by the Iceni, the secret portal at Waterhaul only yards from the "boy's grave" used by the Iceni to send its messages,

Well Bottom, the doorway Iceni "dog walkers" used to reach the Waterhaul portal.

Michael and the bishop sat in his office. They were as close to being father and son as two people who were not related could be.

A pile of strawberry jam sandwiches awaited Michael's attention. The pair sat either side of the low table like opponents in a chess game, the hill of sweet-filled delights eroding with each passing minute.

Michael's passion for jam, especially whole fruit varieties, kept in corners of kitchen cupboards in various locations, its shelves occupied, supporting the weight of a variety of jars used to house the mostly home-made delights.

The bishop had a grand source in the form of a Mrs. Tweed, a long-time widow of the diocese who, as well as tending to the cathedral a few hours a week, kept the most delightful cottage garden, with a raised caged strawberry bed. A few pots of the bounty it produced found their way into the pantry of the bishop. Subsequently, one of the main beneficiaries for the sweetest of red berries from the blackest of fenland soil was Michael, whose world stopped and conversation paused, should he bite into a sweet berry, that would require his full attention.

After the decimation of the pile of strawberry jam sandwiches and Michael returned from taste bud heaven, His Holiness knew now was the time to commence his narrative. Years of experience had taught him that Michael was unable to mentally digest any other train of thought while his taste buds were besotted with sugar and berry.

After enjoying the spectacle of Michael returning from the rapture of the last mouthful, the bishop began explaining that he had been in constant communication with the chief constable about the Stuntney incident and that the man was at his wits end; all avenues of logical investigation had been exhausted. He had come around to the view that the bishop had been right, the instigator and perpetrator of these atrocities was not of this world.

'He believes he is out of his depth. I have asked him to meet with you if you are okay with that.' Michael replied he would be happy to help in any way he could.

'He should be here shortly,' the bishop replied.

The last of the jam sandwiches long disappeared with the same degree of intensity as the first. The pot of tea drained, the conversation drifted across various topics.

The bishop's wife popped her head around the door to say the chief constable had arrived. He was shown in; his hand shook warmly by the pair of God's men.

The policeman said he had come in plain clothes as not to draw attention to himself, he was being hounded by the press constantly and did not want to feed the fire.

The policeman listened intently to Michael, the bishop interjecting from time to time to add more clarity. Any scepticism that would have been present before Stuntney had totally vanished.

Michael said that there had been a rebellion in heaven. That Malak, one of the leading angels, had argued with God that his most prized creation, mankind, who he had made in his own image, would never obey him. He would be easily tempted that man would turn away from a righteous path and pursue his own gods: gold, power, subjection of others.

God had given Malak, or Satan, the Devil, the dark lord, Lucifer or many of the names bestowed upon him by people of the earth, license to do whatever he could to deceive, the only condition that he could not engage his own might against God's creation, he could enchant, respond when called, reward his own with earthly treasure, bring forth the ungodly.

God had installed into his creation a sense of conscience, the ability to choose between right and wrong, no other creation had he given this gift.

Mankind would be tested, only those who had denied

146

Satan would receive the blessing of heaven. God had promised to double the good deeds and half the bad on the day of judgment. God had sent prophets to the world, all had at their centre the one God, they differed in theology but the core belief in a supreme, loving being. The one binding factor is man's conscience. Man's individual choices.

Michael explained to the policemen that God's presence could be seen and felt in everything on the planet, also Satan's work was endemic wherever man had placed his hand.

God had set the Devil a time after which he would return and claim his own.

The battle for the soul of mankind was nearing its end; the signs foretold in the religious books and teachings were being played out across the globe.

More precise details of Armageddon or Judgement Day were kept in secure locations well away from general view.

The Vatican, for instance, holds many ancient documents that it has acquired over the centuries, kept in lockdown, not for any purpose other than to keep its contents secret. If these old transcripts were open to the masses, the Catholic Church's power over its people would be further eroded.

The devil, Michael explained, was in a difficult position in the celestial chess game, although he appeared to be in control of everything, the vast majority on the planet still lived a righteous existence; the more he showed his hand the more it alienated the masses. It was a time when concern for the planet had never been greater. Man was reaching out to those that share the planet like never before. Humankind was caring for his brothers and sisters in catastrophe with astonishing charity and compassion.

The power of the few, either religious or governmental,

was being eroded by the computer superhighway, true power lay in the ability to control the data. No longer was it as simple as locking uncomfortable manuscripts in dusty vaults. Increasingly the question is, "why do you need to keep this information from me?"

The cloak of national security is seen as, "I don't want you to know of the dirty deeds". The powerful elite were under intense scrutiny from the godly masses.

The tide of humanity and the collective consciousness were blooming into an unstoppable force. Moving against the evil that dominates.

Time was running out, the tide was turning. All that was left was a last assault, consolidate the gains he had.

The chief constable listened growing a realization that what Michael was saying made so much sense. From his own experience, he knew when he was first married, questions like is it naturally grown without the use of chemicals, is it damaging the environment, is it fair trade, is it sustainable, never was a topic of discussion.

Today every product bought had to undergo strict examination from him and his wife.

The head policeman discussed in fine detail where the case was, the measures he had taken. He explained that in reality they were no further forward than day one.

The perpetrator seemed to be able to appear at will and then disappear into the ether, he seemed to have strength well in advance of the normal, he was so distinctive yet so elusive, more in common with the mythical Big Foot or Abominable Snowman than of human origin.

'The bishop has told me of your special talents so I'm here to ask for your assistance.'

'I don't think there would be too much trouble putting this one to bed but I fear you will never have a suspect in custody. I am of the opinion that this is a celestial hors d'oeuvres for what is to come.'

The beginning of the end game.

Plans were made to meet at Stuntney burial ground the next evening, Michael said that he would need to be in complete control and no interference under any circumstance.

The policeman needed certain procedures in place to preserve his job. He would need marksmen in case things went wrong, helicopters in the vicinity. The bishop felt he was the target for the manifestation and ought to be there; traffic could be diverted through Stuntney allowing the road to be closed.

The meeting broke up at about three thirty, the policeman arranging to collect His Holiness from the cathedral at five thirty for the rendezvous with Michael at six o'clock.

On the way back home, after all the arrangements had been put in place, the policeman found himself praying and hoping this would be the last of the matter; he was surprised how spiritually affected he had been by the meeting.

As he walked into his house he sought the arms of his loving wife; they hugged with a fervour long forgotten. He loved this woman with his whole being. She had been his sanctuary, cocooning him since the day they met. She had given him their children, the most precious blessings. He seemed to have a new perspective: given the opportunity to be anywhere in the world the place he would choose would be where he stood.

The tears ran in rivulets down his cheeks onto her shoulders. She knew if she watched him cry he would be embarrassed, so she pushed her head deeper into his chest, hugged him harder until the sobs subsided.

'I've got a nice piece of smoked haddock for your tea with some mashed Maris Piper potatoes fresh from off the fen. I made some of that parsley butter you love.'

'Thank you,' her husband said, 'I love you, you know, I probably don't tell you enough, you and the kids are my everything.' He kissed her forehead and headed for the shower.

He was a very good policeman, an even better father and a wonderful husband, she knew she had been blessed to have him by her side.

When he sat in front of his yellow fish, a knob of homemade parsley butter slowly melting on top of a hill of Maris Piper mash, the king of potatoes grown in the black fen within walking distance of his home. If there was a better meal anywhere in the world he had never tasted it.

He put out his hand towards his wife, she took it and squeezed.

'Today,' he said, 'I met the most remarkable man I have ever met.'

She squeezed tighter. Rarely did he speak about his day, never did she question his work, she saw her role as providing a sanctuary; shutting the door meant closing the world outside off.

Every day the outside had him he was Chief, Governor, Boss; when the front door closed he was Darling and Dad.

The kids had flown the nest pursuing their own dreams; she hoped that one day they would be blessed with grandchildren.

She looked over at her man, what a great grandad he would make.

He was temporarily transported from the moment, his

dancing tastebuds banished, all but the delight of the forkful of yellow fish topped off with fluffy mashed potatoes, glazed with the melted parsley butter. She wondered who got the most pleasure, her watching or him eating.

Upon returning from taste paradise and able to concentrate on the world around him he continued the narrative.

'During this investigation into the murders at Stuntney I have become more and more involved with the bishop who was the subject of the original attack. I have become drawn to him as a person, his humanity, his clarity of faith, he seems to ooze goodness, his spirit seems to touch you, it is very difficult to remain agnostic or atheist in his presence.

'Anyhow, when the bishop speaks his conversation is peppered with references to a Michael, he speaks with such reverence about this Michael that I have found myself intrigued by this Christian soul.

'The more comfortable I have become in the bishop's presence the more I have felt able to speak on a personal level.

'I felt bold enough to say, "Bishop, if I can be forthright and speak directly from my heart," he said.

"Oh if only everyone would".

"Bishop, I have found you to be the most spiritual person I have met, without the trappings of office anyone meeting you could come to no other conclusion that you were a man of God."

"Thank you," said His Holiness. "The wisest man I ever met, also doubled up as my father, said to me, 'son the only gospel most will ever read is you, let them read it well'."

"'Very profound, you have done your dad proud". The point I am trying to get across is that when you talk of Michael you speak with such reverence that it is hard for me to fathom how you could seem to be in awe of another Christian man."

'The bishop thought for a few long moments then replied, "It is because I am. He is in this world but not of this world. I think he's an angel sent from the boss, with a hotline direct to him. I am of the opinion that in the very near future the reason he is here will become apparent".'

The chief would have laughed out loud had these words been spoken by any other.

'The holy man continued to outline the history of Michael, how he had turned up at the front door of the rectory of his very dear friend only a few hours old with a note that read "Yours for life, mine forever".

'"Now he has a cult following especially among the young, he is packing churches and chapels of all denominations. To use a quote from John the Baptist, 'I am not good enough to tie his shoelaces'.

'Today,' said her devoted husband, 'I had a meeting with Michael and the bishop. I have never been so spiritually affected. I know through my days as a policeman I have stood in the presence of evil many times.

'Today I stood in the presence of God. At times I felt euphoric, goodness bled from every pore of the young man's body. The bishop's own kindness seemed to be magnified, at times there seemed to be an aura around the men in front of me, I had to use all of my training to try to stay rational, yet, strange as it may sound and in the face of extreme scepticism, I would testify that we were not alone, there was a presence, an entity, a powerful, benevolent force, hovering on the edge of visibility. The Holy Spirit, angelic host, I don't know how to describe it.'

The policeman put down his knife and fork, stretched both hands across the table to hold the soft, warm palms of the woman he loved. With the tears welling in his eyes he said, 'I think if he had asked me to leave everything behind and follow him, I would have gone.'

In all the years they had sailed life's seas in the boat of wedlock, through storms, doldrums, she had never seen him overwhelmed. She squeezed his hands, a signal that everything was fine, no matter what: she would follow him into the jaws of death if necessary.

Remembering her Sunday school days, the Bible stories of those who had met the Holy Ghost, the direction of their lives changed forever, they happily walked the rest of their days with God.

She brought his hands to her lips and kissed them; she knew without doubt that her husband had, this day, been blessed.

The rest of the meal was finished in silence, the policeman heading for the kitchen with the plates, the kettle fired into action, the teapot primed for its function, the tray loaded for its evening ritual of transporting the brown liquid nectar into the small conservatory.

They sat together, warm, content and extremely happy.

'We are all meeting again tomorrow evening at the Stuntney burial ground where Michael will perform some sort of exorcism which the bishop tells me is his speciality.'

'Isn't that dangerous,' said his wife, 'considering everything that has happened.'

Her husband replied, 'There has been a heavy police presence, and tomorrow there will be more with armed units in place, helicopters at the ready, if the assailant is of this world then he won't get to the burial ground, if not then apparently we have the best man for the job on hand so I wouldn't worry.'

Michael headed back to Newmarket, stopping briefly on the Landwade Road through Exning to check the racing results from Huntingdon. Oliver had ridden two winners and a second, his horse had fallen in the novice chase. Michael hoped his brother was in one piece, such were the daily worries of those living in the wake of national hunt jockeys.

Michael had, for some time, been aware of a growing fatigue in his body; the weakness of his heart was the unspoken concern of all who knew him. He often found those who loved him scanning his mortal vehicle for signs of its downhill trajectory.

He found little respite now from the physical struggle. He was sure his family had seen it but packed it at the back of the airing cupboard of conscious thought, hoping their minute observations were the fantasies of over concerned minds and not based in reality.

He was sure his time was short. Agnes had come to take him home, she was the other side of the same coin. They were an item, how he knew it he couldn't tell, every time he felt the veil lift to glimpse a distant past it slipped back.

All those around him, he adored, especially his adopted mother; she had heaped love on him since his earliest memories. She still called him her "bundle of rags by the front door".

He would pick Agnes up, they would go and walk some part of the heath before dropping her back. He would then head for the rectory, Oliver and Ninal would be there following the short trip home from Huntingdon races. He was giving a service at the Methodist church that evening, then he would have an extremely swift half pint in the Five Bells pub next door, along with most of congregation, before getting himself between the sheets at the earliest moment.

An overwhelming need for sleep engulfed him: he closed his eyes.

Such a joyous scene filled him, hosts of raptured faces, beckoning arms; he walked towards the sea of love, felt the ecstasy of the returning traveller. He wanted to be immersed in this ocean, half-remembered faces floating in and out of view. He wanted to stay, he was home. He looked at the montage, where was she? He searched, if he could find her he would stay. Where was she?

In the distance he heard a door open, the scene in front of him began to recede.

Michael opened his eyes and watched the form of his dream search climbing into the passenger seat beside him.

'Not yet, soldier, there is work to be done.

'You didn't pick me up so I knew I had to pick you up. We need to get through the next few days, then you can rest.'

A less fatigued soul might have asked how she had travelled the two miles, how she had known what was happening. Through half-closed eyes he half knew anyway.

She leaned across and kissed his cheek; it rejuvenated him, the feather touch of her pursed lips brought a tickle trail to the side of his ear and nose, in turn bringing a smile followed by a laugh. He turned the key, bringing man and machine back into full operational mode.

Michael drove through the narrow streets of Exning. On the edge of Lacy's Lane he parked, the pair walked through the horse tunnel, up the hill to the vast man-made green savannah. Miles of rich grass with its unpampered roots searching deep into the loam, centuries of struggle under the summer's burning suns blessed the horseman with its tangled mass of roots, the perfect shock absorbers for half ton of galloping horse.

Unlike its cousin, the racecourse itself, a lush green strip, pleasing to the eye, deceptive in execution.

Grasses unable to sustain without constant mollycoddling, root systems no longer than the thumb, a glorious green baize sitting on top of either slope or rock soil, unbroken for decades by the searching roots. The morning gallop on the ancient turf a good clean hoofprint,

In the afternoon race, the combatants look like they followed the muck spreader.

Sitting lonely in the middle, man's concrete totem to the racehorse, like some stricken alien spacecraft whose wrong turn resulted in its sad, soulless existence.

Three hundred and fifty-five days a year it stands empty. One day it is hoped that its stunning architectural beauty and significance will be recognized by the populous who will stand in awe, much like the towering tower blocks whose days in the architectural sun are still to come.

Michael told Agnes about his meeting with the chief constable; about the attempt at exorcism the next evening. To the left of where they stood Seven Springs Hill, still guarding the ancient portals to the lake where the Iceni disappeared and reappeared, bringing fear and carnage to the invading Roman legions. To the right, the waterworks, the modern portal to the lake. The pair walked out across these tough shades of green, every tread met with the same resistance so admired of those facing oppression: trodden, crushed, stood upon yet so deep-rooted and strong.

Michael recalled Oliver's father-in-law often said, "One day, this centuries old turf will be destroyed by some thirty-year-old schoolboy, who knows nothing but the classroom, persuading some other thirty-year-old, with a fistful of degrees, who heads the decision-making, having bypassed any physical work in the real world, elevated more by school and university than any semblance of talent, that they ought to have a watering system. In a few short years, the work of the centuries will be laid waste, turf will become lawn".

Michael smiled at Oliver's father-in-law's doom-ladened forecast for the racing industry.

"Kids who would be far better employed carrying on the traditions of their forefathers, stuck in universities learning useful nation building subjects such as media studies. Horsemen are on the edge of extinction, electricians, plumbers, carpenters, bricklayers, all endangered species.

"Most of those charged with improving the situation have never opened a wage packet or held a tool, the only qualifications to attain any meaningful position in racing's highest echelons is to have been an officer in the army".

Michael thought Ninal's father, Seamus, though an icon to all who knew him both on and off the horse, saw life with all its complexities with clear vision. For him there was little grey, you got up early, you worked hard to become as good as you could be, failure was no disgrace, not to give it your best shot was, to Seamus, a criminal offence.

If you were blessed with children they were the nucleus of life itself. You took on one of the two most important roles of mankind, you became dad, anyone falling short in that department should be cast into a pit of vipers.

Drug dealers were mass murderers. The fires of hell would be a blessed escape compared to the torment that Seamus felt should be heaped upon them. He was a great source of merriment for Michael.

He was sure his brother, Oliver, and Seamus, his mentor, spent hours working on their one-liners, in order to compete with him. It was, he felt, a vain attempt, he was simply the king of quips and quotes.

One of Michael's favourites was when Seamus proclaimed that he wouldn't be troubling the pope for a sainthood because all his Christian values vanished when he learned of children being harmed. "I would box the horns of the Devil himself; he'd have to put a toothbrush up his posterior to clean his teeth".

Michael walked back to the car arm in arm with Agnes, the growing fatigue in his limbs evident in the final hundred yards.

'If I can get through the next couple of days I'm going to have a good rest,' he said as he lowered himself into the driver's seat.

'I know you are, darling,' she said with a smile that would have lit the cosmos.

In the inner sanctum of the Zagros Mountains, a cave the match of any cathedral. It had a fair amount of the world's gold decorating the walls, in various effigies, mostly depicting a bull-headed creature enacting every conceivable position of fornication.

The faces of the women depicted were either in rapture or excruciating pain.

In the centre of the dome-shaped cathedral cave was a huge pentagon on the floor, each point of the demonic star had, on either side, images of the diabolical in various poses, all of a sexual nature. Nephilim, the fallen angel's disciples, flew through the mosaic, some dragged human women by the hair into the heavens, some appeared to have bound their captives with snakes.

As a work of art it rivalled anything in the Sistine Chapel. As a statement of history it was a perfect example of woman's struggle against inequality.

In the texts of Nephilim Yazidis, women were nothing more than incubators for the seed, when asked to defend their position their standard answer was what woman invented anything or moved mankind forward.

Six hundred and sixty-six throne chairs spiralled out in six rings; the high priest had led the procession of the Devil's cardinals. They had circled the pentagon six times chanting age-old incarnations as they gradually wound their way to their allotted thrones. So heavily draped in ornate garb that the casual observer may have wondered if there had been a competition between the opposing priesthoods to see who could dress their men in the most splendour.

As a descant to the high priests' beseeching, a bleating of goats echoed in the ceiling of the cathedral cave as the ensembled group chants reached a crescendo, the bleating stopped; a cage swung over the satanic star, quickly lowering to sit in the centre.

Six goats and their kids lay, still twitching as their lives ebbed, their blood from their severed throats spreading across the pentagon.

From deep in the bowels of the earth came a guttural roar,

unlike any sound that should emanate from the planet, like giant wounded hellhounds smashing through the gates to wreak havoc on an unsuspecting world. The sound grew in intensity, filling the space with a uniform trembling, a cacophony of terror to the unsuspecting.

These devotees were unfazed, they had waited their whole lives, or since their conversion, for this moment; countless had gone before, hoping in vain to see the return of the dark lord, the bull hoods they had over their heads keeping their eardrums from bursting.

The Devil's cathedral shook, winds swirled, their forms spinning like miniature tornados, beautiful faces appeared at the edges, turning grotesque, every nightmare that could be imagined was broadcast from these whirlwinds.

As quickly as it started; it stopped a stillness descended, a quiet, a total quiet, not the slightest movement would have been noted on a decibel counter.

In the centre of the pentagon, a figure stood. A huge entirety, a Goliath, four meters in height, one and a half meters wide, a hybrid of man and bull. Mythology and their artists must have had an insight into the make-up of the beast, for what stood before the host was recognizable from ancient impressions.

The flawless bronze body, half man, half bull, oozing immense strength, the six digits attached to, what for ease of description passed for arms, looked as though they could hurl boulders to the moon.

The beast turned slowly, surveying the devoted, its feet crushing the flattened cage and the bodies it contained, the sacrificial blood shooting from the already drained bodies.

As his gaze fell upon his people, they stood, began

chanting the ancient text, "The mighty will own the heavens, the Nephilim seed will rule the universe".

Once again the rumbling built from the core of the earth, building to its crescendo. Mini tornadoes filled the space. The cave shook, then stopped. The stillness returned.

The beast had gone, released into the world, the blood, bodies, and trampled flesh had disappeared.

All that remained was a tangled, crushed cage on the edge of the devil star, unrecognizable from its past life.

Michael, having dropped Agnes back at the usual spot, returned to the rectory to prepare for the evening's Bible meeting at the Methodist church. Oliver and Ninal had already arrived back from Huntingdon races. Liver and bacon almost ready to be devoured by the hungry host, it was one of the many favourite meals that Jean Grogan prepared for her horde.

The meal often reflected the degree of dedication Oliver had had in the previous few days in order to ride at the correct weights: the harder he had to work, the further to the top the favourite meal became. Liver and bacon was midway up the table of glories which meant that Oliver had probably only missed three meals in the last few days, had one sauna bath and had run no more than five miles.

The news playing on the TV in the background supplemented the chatter of the day's events.

One item captured the attention of the family. A massive earthquake had been recorded in north east Iraq; the epicentre had yet to be pinpointed. The magnitude of the quake had surpassed any in modern times, certainly an equal to the Chile disaster of 1960, suggesting serious structural damage, depending on the location it was likely there would be major loss of life.

Oliver and Ninal had decided that when his riding days were over, if they had not been blessed with children, they would like to join an emergency response team flying at a moment's notice to disaster zones around the world. They were actively pursuing skills that would be needed should the opportunity arise.

The rest of the family looked on in silent prayer, the vicar remembering the terrible loss of life an earthquake of lesser magnitude had brought in Kobe, Japan.

According to the news reports, governments had been alerted and were poised, ready to respond.

The day's events seemed to tumble down the hill of importance at the prospect of massive loss of life. It was a quiet, contemplative meal, free from the normal banter that ensued.

Michael excused himself and went to ready himself for his Methodists.

Reports were arriving post-haste at the White House, Kremlin, Downing Street, at headquarters of military nations throughout the world. Some nations were put on a war footing, most the highest state of emergency.

Every high-ranking military mind was heading for a bunker somewhere.

The reports that had the world in a state of panic revealed that this was not an earthquake, it had no collateral damage and no loss of life; the only conclusion was that someone had tested a bomb of such ferocity, the like of which had never been seen.

This was game-changing. The assembled might of the superpowers could not match the power exerted by this phenomenon.

The American president was pacing the floor, the assembled group was being augmented constantly by new arrivals, each adding nothing to the pot of knowledge.

'Now,' said the president. 'Let's get this straight and feel free to stop me if I haven't grasped the detail.

'My understanding is that I am the leader of the free world, I have at my disposal some of the greatest minds, both civil and military, I have more financial clout than any president ever.

'My overriding responsibility is to protect my people and the people of the world, who share our values, from the despots that abound.

'To that end we have, or so I am told, the most sophisticated surveillance technology updated constantly. I am told that a mouse can fart in the halls of power and we can analyse what he ate for breakfast.

'Am I right in assuming that someone has exploded a bomb underground, the like of which is well beyond our understanding, the power of which beyond our imagination?

'The people who have this technology are in an extremely strong negotiating position. Would I be wide of the mark if I made a stab in the dark and said our collective pants have been pulled down, our asses have been spanked, our bollocks have been exposed on a shovel and all because this great nation knew frik all about it?'

The packed room collective squirmed.

'Around the globe, as I speak, similar meetings will be in progress, our allies will be looking to me for some comfort; they will expect dossiers on what we know, what plans we have to nullify any threat.

'I shall reluctantly tell them the information thus far I will send them on the back of a postage stamp with a few excerpts from *Monty Python's Life of Brian* to brighten their day.

'The average hardworking American is generally happy to know that a few of their tax dollars find their way into the grubby pockets of the planet's unworthy, knowing that the information they provide keeps us prepared and them safe.

'When the press find out, and they surely will, having honed their espionage skills well in advance of their governments, that a device has been exploded that instantly demotes the United States of America from long-time leader in the arms race to a distant second. This bomb has the ability to sustain vibrations long past the point where solid ground would liquefy.

'We are looking into the abyss.

'If the information is correct, and all the reports concur, North America could sink into quicksand, the ground would swallow everything above it. Have a few moments, people, to digest.'

The president paced. The company thought, the reality dawned.

A nation lost, swallowed by the earth; homes, cities schools, skyscrapers, hospitals.

The terror realized: no easy death. Sinking into the ground to be covered with a slurry. Down, down, all the complex structures that form solid, broken.

The land, a sea of mud; underground bunkers, no defence, would sink miles to be incinerated by the mantle.

Each of those present began to realize this was the horror of all horrors. This was not a case of sending an army, the ensuing slaughter played out on screens while most went about their daily lives unaffected. This was different: this was apocalyptic.

After some time, the president spoke.

'As you have come to realize this could be checkmate if this technology is in advance of our understanding; we have no knowledge of it. It may well be under our feet and could be activated at any time. Not to overdramatize the situation, my friends, but America may not be here tomorrow.'

As the evening progressed the gloom lifted in the Reverend Grogan's rectory. The news channels were reporting no structural damage and no known casualties from the massive earthquake. Experts were rolled out, one after the other, explaining that very occasionally the energy from the quake was directed downwards into the mantle which absorbed the shock, leaving the earth's crust relatively unscathed, although as a caveat there was an increased risk of a volcanic eruption somewhere else.

Michael came back extremely tired from his evening. He was heartened by the news of no reported loss of life from the events in northern Iraq. He hugged everyone then went to bed.

Oliver and Ninal, having waited for his return, set off for their own piece of heaven on Lowther Street, less than one hundred yards from door to door.

When the coats, that had kept the evening chill at bay, were hanging in the hall, Ninal took her husband and hugged him close. She whispered in his ear as gently as she could, 'I think we are going to lose him soon you know.' Oliver hugged her and sobbed into her shoulder; she was voicing what he already knew, his brother was failing.

Oliver had many illuminati in his life and two shining

165

stars, one he was holding and one he was losing.

Ninal held him close and stroked his head while the sobs subsided.

'He will probably outlive us all,' Oliver said, kissing his wife's forehead before heading for the kitchen and the teapot, their nightly ritual before bed.

Next morning the heat had gone out of the story, no damage, no dead. The practiced concern of the media pantomime frontline had moved on, they now looked mortified at the prospect of the earth warming by .25 of a degree in the next fifty years.

The halls of power worldwide were in a state of panic. Opposing ideologues suspected each other of testing a new generation of weapon, having secretly been developing the technology against all antiproliferation treaties. Warlords were at each other's throats, each blaming the other for agreeing to the cessation of military leapfrogging which now rendered them impotent.

Every agent from every country was on the street, hundreds of thousands of hastily arranged meets. The steady plod of the vast world of espionage had burst forth like some diplomatic tsunami. Fine dining restaurants were reaping the bonanza, vintage wine sellers scouring the planet for more stock, opera houses experiencing unprecedented demand for tickets, high-end escort agencies unable to cope with demand.

The next evening the chief constable picked the bishop up and headed for their rendezvous with Michael. Six o'clock had been agreed so that the road could be closed and traffic diverted through Stuntney village in order to create the least disturbance as possible.

The pair passed through the Ely side road closures

manned by two uniformed officers; the chief saluted the men he knew well. They headed up the slope to the burial ground, a command vehicle parked on the verge, inside a full complement of operatives, scanning screens, donning headphones, microphones, all modern paraphernalia that is needed to combat the modern criminal.

Michael had not arrived. The pair decided to walk to the north end of the woods closest to where the old gallows had once stood. Three police marksmen were positioned, sat on bales of straw, a further line of straw bales formed a wall in front of them, their automatic weapons rested on top.

As the pair set off, the bishop's mobile phone rang. It was Michael. He had been stopped at the Newmarket end of the road block; the officers had orders that no one should be allowed into the area, could the chief have a word. The policeman spoke to his men and thanked them for their diligence, asked them to allow Michael access.

The two men walked on towards the armed officers. They enjoyed each other's company; the head policeman hoped that when this ordeal was over they might spend more time together as friends.

Everything that could be done had been done; police marksmen, north, south, east and west, enough manpower to quell a mini riot. Helicopter parked only moments away, if the assailant was of this world, and he put in an appearance, then there was no escape. If not of this realm, then,, according to the bishop they had the right man for the job.

The chief would check with the marksmen that everything was in place before returning for a briefing with Michael.

The duo arrived at the straw bales, the swat team assured the head policeman that they were ready for any eventuality;

scepticism never got in the way. Experience had taught that from the most benign situations turmoil could appear.

The chief constable thanked his men, the bishop blessed them, then turned to retrace their steps and meet Michael.

The furthest right of the armed response team pulled the sight of his weapon to his eye and fired a single shot, his two colleagues were almost instantly following suit. The two unarmed men turned towards the woods.

Loping towards them was the huge hairless frame.

The bullets from the guns aimed at the legs in the hope of immobilizing them had not worked.

One after the other, the officers flicked a switch on their weapons. Hundreds of bullets screamed out across the ancient burial ground, all to no effect: the brute kept coming. The officers, fearing loss of life, changed their remit from immobilization to elimination, their bullets now directed towards the torso.

The lead defence offered no resistance, the forward motion towards the group was not disrupted.

Within seconds the scene had transformed from tranquil serenity to murderous mayhem.

Breast radio communication filled the air as the swat team reported. Video footage from helmets sent to the astonished command vehicle, helicopter scrambled, chaos ensued.

In the heat of the moment the bishop knew it was him that the Devil's disciple wanted, it was his arrival that had triggered the resurrection. He walked towards the advancing creature.

'Although I walk in the valley of death I will fear no evil. For you walk beside me Lord all the days of my life. You brought light to my darkness, held me when I could not stand, carried me when I could not walk. Carry me now as I face my cross.'

The bishop met the hairless abomination a few strides from the straw bales. It stopped. The armed officers had ceased their attempt at intervention, now stood, mesmerized by what stood before them. This was a scene from science fiction, it should be played out in the safety of a movie screen.

A blur of activity surrounded, media drones, a helicopter circled, sirens screamed.

The two representatives of the opposing celestial forces stared into each other's eyes, the soulless, whose body had been robbed of its ability to decompose, lifted its bony fingers to the throat of the God soldier and began to squeeze. The first to react was the chief constable, he threw himself at the assailant with a ferocity he didn't know he possessed, he grappled with his whole being. He was joined by the swat team; they fought with an intensity not found in any training manual. Others arrived and joined the struggle, kicked, punches cascaded onto the soulless form all to no avail; the thing just threw them aside while continuing to hold the throat of the bishop.

Dizziness began to swell in front of the bishop's eyes. A blackness crept into his peripheral vision; he could hear his father singing *Onward Christian Soldiers*: his father loved that hymn.

He started singing.

'Onward Christian soldiers marching as to war with the cross of Jesus going on before Christ the royal master leads against the foe forward into battle see his banners go.'

The darkness began to encroach further.

'At the name of Jesus Satan's host doth flee on then Christian soldiers on to victory.

'Hell's foundations quiver at the sound of praise brothers lift your voices, loud your anthems raise.'

The bishop became aware that the darkness was receding; a voice had taken over from his father, it was Michael. The pressure left his throat with the digits that had squeezed it. As full consciousness returned he was aware that his assailant was backing towards the woods; advancing on him was Michael.

The hairless was gradually becoming invisible, its form disintegrating, until it had disappeared into the ether and another realm. Michael began to chant. The astonished onlookers saw the ground in various places begin to churn and crumble like oversized moles working their burrows. Then giant feet emerged, followed by more hairless beings, pushing themselves feet first from their ancient graves, they stood beside the ground that had entombed them these past centuries. Michael continued to chant. One by one these entities followed the fate of the original, until there were only two left. Michael suddenly sank to his knees; the onlookers believed he was praying: in truth he was dying. All strength had left him, his heart was struggling and was about to stop. His eyes closed to the world, a great peace descended into his being. It was the moment before sleep for the untroubled mind, a place of bliss and serenity.

A soft hand pushed itself gently into his armpit.

'Come on, soldier let's finish the job together.'

Michael opened his eyes. Once again the beautiful face of Agnes appeared, again she had sent a surge of strength through him. He rose, continued the exorcism until there were no more demons left. There were no more atheists left either. A spontaneous round of applause greeted the disappearance of the last entity.

Michael turned and walked back to where a huddle stood which contained both chief constable and chief holy man, who was insisting to the medics, who were surrounding and fussing, that he was fine.

The policeman, ever the professional, was orchestrating the crime scene of an attempted murder.

Michael looked around for Agnes but she had gone, she was a reluctant socialite, avoiding contact wherever possible; if they came upon another soul out walking she would hug his arm and not speak. The words of Seamus echoed in his head, bringing a smile to his tired face.

The first man who unravels the workings of the female mind will take his place in front of Einstein in the order of brilliant brains, such is the magnitude of the task that all of the geniuses that have gone before have unanimously agreed the task is beyond the understanding of man. Him outdoors, who has stood in front of her indoors, trying to explain why he is walking with the wrong leg first or breathing out when he should be breathing in, has never found a reason to disagree.

Both head men broke from the throng. Both knew their lives would continue because of his actions: he was the conduit for some immense power that cherished mankind.

An arm around the shoulder was all the policeman could offer as thanks, a gesture that conveyed more than the spoken word.

They guided Michael through the throng that had now gathered: medic, police, media who had swamped the area ignoring the police cordon, the whole episode captured on drone footage and relayed to news outlets around the world.

A frenzied media storm was being unleashed the footage was past astonishing. The drone operators were elevated in a few moments to the status of the millionaire.

Michael was being guided to the control vehicle, microphones thrust towards him. The chief constable was the first the realize the enormity of the situation and one of the priorities would be to keep Michael safe.

'Michael, we need to get you somewhere safe. If what just happened has been recorded by the media, and my suspicions are that it has, it will be the biggest media feed since 9/11.'

'What has gone before in this news pantomime has been only waves lapping the shore, there is a tsunami coming that none of us can escape, but we must protect you as best we can.'

Michael insisted that the best place for him was his home at the rectory.

The chief constable knew, from internal reports and documentation, what the experience of those damned by the superstar tag had to live through. Prisoners in their own homes, caged by the servants of the media moguls, the unacceptable posterior of the press, unfazed by any hurdles placed in front of them by the law.

Riches dangled for the scoop, the exclusive, the inside story, meant little protection for those who flew too high.

Those who sought the hands of the journal compilers, to elevate them above the normal, found they easily slipped through the fingers to the feet where they would be trampled into the mud.

The chief constable was in full crisis mode, delegating areas of responsibility to those under his commands. A fast car would be dispatched, taking Michael to the rectory, surveillance experts would be heading there in a few minutes. A constant high visibility police presence, new secure telephone numbers required within minutes. The nuts and bolts of a protection ring were surprisingly complex.

Across the world pictures were flashing again and again across TV screens of police fighting with an alien, zombies rising out of the ground. An exorcist dispatching them. Hollywood or Bollywood could not have done it better.

The president and his inner circle were once again locked in, coffee urns drained and regularly replaced, sleep banished or confined to head on the desk minutes. Reports abounded, operatives keen to justify their existence were filing them in unprecedented numbers. The president ask for everyone's attention for a few minutes. Professor Phillip Harman had just arrived from Mildenhall Air Base twenty miles north of Cambridge in England.

The president explained that the professor was the world's leading expert on advanced wave spectro realignment.

The professor gave a brief overview of his academic history. He had worked on spectro realignment for many years; Cambridge University was at the forefront of the present understanding.

'Spectro realignment had the potential to affect mankind more profoundly than the microchip.

'In its simplest form it has the ability to turn solid matter back to liquid.

'The planet is basically liquid: rocks spent millennia as liquid in the mantle before solidifying to form a relatively thin layer floating on top of oceans of its liquid form. Plants and animals are over ninety per cent water. What we perceive as solid is a complex configuration of cell walls that build up and support pressure far in advance of its own molecular strength, it is this configuration that commands the world we live in;

without it, mankind cannot survive.

'An egg, gentlemen, is the perfect practical example. If, when you go home, I ask you to take an egg, place a finger and thumb at either end and squeeze, you will not break the egg. Move the position to the girth of the egg and the slightest pressure breaks the egg. This is a good example of the configuration of the molecular strength, how it could have developed is a mystery; evolution could have had no part to play.

'Imagine scaffold. Poles and cross sections joined in such a way that it will support huge burdens. That is what a solid is. Shake those poles to destruction and the molecular strength returns to zero.

'Those who remember Bible studies will remember the soldiers marched around the walls of Jericho until they fell down. A biblical example of spectro realignment.

'If you make anything vibrate at the right frequency the scaffold will break. The molecular structure collapses.

'Cutting edge thinking, by some very eminent geologists, suggests that the earth is subjected to these forces fairly frequently. In geological terms, maybe every couple of million years, the tectonic plates move, not a few inches or yards, but many miles, sending such unimaginable shock waves, or spectro realignment. The solid ground liquefies, everything sinks to be covered and the life cycle of the earth begins again. There may be several stages to spectro realignment, much the same as their cousins, the earthquakes, where they are rated in degrees of intensity. It is thought that at the bottom of the scale the ground would soften enough to be unable to support the weight of large animals and may go some way to explaining the rapid disappearance of large species.

'The evidence thus far suggests this is a real possibility. At the high end of the scale the spectro realignment is so intense, everything is liquefied down to the mantle, which flows upward, forming new lands and mountains.

'Imagine if you would,' the professor said, 'an aircraft hangar full of watermelons. We could all scramble to the top and sit quite nicely, yet we are sitting on, predominantly, water, with very little matter supporting. If a giant blender was introduced, the molecular structure of the watermelons would be destroyed and we would all be swimming.

'At Cambridge we are working to harness this phenomenon. In medicine, if we could liquefy tumours, fats, bone, the possibilities are unimaginable. In construction, to be able to liquefy the rock, making tunnelling through mountains hours rather than years, opening the possibility of projects, unimaginable now becoming possible. Liquefying and remodelling granite boulders in the morning, granite houses by the afternoon: we are only limited by our imagination.'

The assembled throng sat in silence. the president spoke.

'Is it possible that there could be a military application?'

'I imagine there would be,' replied the professor. 'Though what it would be like I have no idea, the science is very much in the early stages. Any applications are several years away, that would be my best guesstimation.'

'Is it viable,' said the president, 'that somewhere else in the world, this work is more advanced?'

'It is of course possible,' said the professor. 'Although I would be amazed, the scientists working in this area are well known to each other; we regularly share advances, cross-border contact is commonplace, any breakthrough in any sphere is often built on small steps achieved by a global

175

community working together. The Nobel Prize is normally awarded to the head of the team whose final step broke through the clouds into the sunshine and immortality.'

The president asked the professor if he would be so kind as to read through a document and give his professional opinion.

The scientist was shown into a quiet room next to the main bunker to form an opinion on the dossier.

The president turned to his audience. 'Well people the mystery thickens. No stone has been unturned.

'Our people on the ground are in overdrive, other people's people are like headless chickens wondering why our people are running around like headless chickens. The headless chickens who run the headless chickens are arming every piece of military hardware expecting anything by anyone at any time.

'This headless chicken has spoken to other headless chickens and has assured them that this is nothing to do with us.

'We are working to make sure no one launches a pre-emptive strike.

'Everyone has everything pointing at everyone. The situation is as ludicrous as it is terrifying. It is the epitome of the fear of the unknown.

'The area of north Iraq is the home of many despots and crackpots; I kid you not, we have reports of a secret women's army intent on taking over the world from men, these women apparently believe the male of the species and his fragile moral standards do not render them fit enough to run a three-legged race let alone the world. They suggest that while tying the legs together men would still be looking for a way to cheat.

'Another pile of reports falls back on the age-old aliens staple, who are doing everything from repairing a stricken craft to sending bolts of energy to a mothership that has pulled into the forecourt of Earth for refilling before proceeding on its intergalactic travels.

'One report suggests that the Devil has been summoned from hell and Armageddon is upon us.

'On a rare positive note we have not received any demands from anyone, which, in the normal course of events, is strange in itself. History tells us, show your strength, to exact your demands, the atomic bomb at Hiroshima a prime example.'

The door to the small room opened; the professor was led back in. The president gestured for him to address the assembled.

'Well gentlemen, if what is in this document is correct—I must assume that to be the case, as there is so much supporting data—then I am in a state of shock and disbelief.

'The only analogy I can come up with at short notice is that I am training Olympic high jumpers, spending my life perfecting training techniques in order to optimize the chance of jumping a centimetre or two higher than ever before. I know, every other Olympic trainer in the athletic world, any advance is soon adopted and we move on. The advances are more often technical than untapped latent talent, there are many limiting external factors whose influence we have no control, gravity, thrust, et cetera.

'Then one day out of the blue there is indisputable evidence that someone can jump over the Eiffel Tower.

'This is an Eiffel Tower moment. If we are not in the world of fantasy then we are in the world of quantum, where the world as we know it and the laws we think govern it do not exist .

'It is the double split experiment transferred to spectro realignment. It is without explanation.'

The room was quiet while the information cud was chewed.

The president eventually spoke.

'The ten billion dollar question, as I see it, is, "Is this a weapon?"'

Professor Harman looked at his audience and spoke.

'In my opinion this cannot be a weapon.'

A collective relief spread across the faces of those assembled.

'There are many questions unanswered, one would be why is this area intact, it should be now resolidifying, having been reduced to its liquid form. If the energy released had been channelled downwards then a well would have been created down to the Earth's mantle, you would now be looking at a catastrophic eruption that would bring an end to mankind, seas would boil dry, earth temperature rise by thousands of degrees; it would indeed be hell on earth.

'The energy exerted in north Iraq is beyond our understanding. I firmly believe it is beyond the understanding of anyone alive today. I am of the opinion that, as regard to a weapon, you must look elsewhere for the explanation.'

A round of applause accompanied Professor Phillip Harman as he was escorted to the debriefing room before his supersonic flight back to England.

As the scientist was being escorted out, the segmented screen, at the direction of the commander-in-chief, flickered into life.

The assembled crowd watched astonished by the action that had been played out in England. It was rerun through three times before the president spoke.

'I think we may be entering a new era where we are not the dominant force.'

Michael sat with his family in the kitchen, watching the images that were being played on TV screens around the world.

Oliver said that he didn't think Leonardo DiCaprio had much to worry about. They all smiled. Michael said he thought he cut a very dashing figure; judging by the bedlam in the streets around the rectory he was already quite the film star.

It was true, the roads had become packed. Journalists were arriving by the minute, Fitzroy Street had restricted access, police either end to enforce. Teams of surveillance engineers were working in the grounds of the rectory to ensure no one could reach the house unobserved.

The family had been given new phone numbers, their old numbers redirected to answering machines which, as predicted, were ringing off the hook.

Any journalist worth their salt could discover a phone number in a very short period of time.

A mobile unit would be in the grounds of the rectory. Operations to keep the family, and Michael in particular, free from harassment were well under way.

The bishop and chief constable were also under siege. The holy man was arranging a thanksgiving service at the cathedral, his colleagues were doing the same in the diocese.

There had been an unprecedented upsurge in the need for spiritual food since Stuntney.

The bishop often pointed out that the perception was of a

church on its knees, yet there were more people in church on a Sunday than were in football stadiums on a Saturday.

This was unprecedented. This was Christmas times a thousand; the few services that had been held thus far, the congregation had been out the door.

Strategies unthinkable a few days ago now occupied the thoughts of the religious planners.

Quadrupling of services, rolling services, every dog collar dragooned into help. Retired clergy, lay preachers, everyone connected to the cloth, brought up to the front line.

More "grooms" had arrived at the Arab Devalian stud; in truth they were the elite of the elite of Arab forces, the Brotherhood, their skills honed in the hottest conflict zones of the Middle East. They bolstered the already impressive force guarding the gospel.

The Nephilim Yazidis forces were equal ready, keen to avenge their comrades. Every inch of the racehorse breeding operation was now known to Lucifer's men, their leaders, some of the most influential men on the planet, were awaiting orders from their high priests.

Nephilim Yazidis waited, the brotherhood waited, the president waited. Nothing made sense. The Iceni waited, whatever happened the gospel itself would be safe. Just like the Magna Carta, there were several copies.

Leaders of the superpowers were close to buttons that would destroy mankind; leaders of the Iceni were close to buttons that would change the course of man's journey to eternity, one press and the gospel of Jesus Christ would flood the Internet.

Glyn Kingston had worked for the British geological survey

team all of his adult life.

It was painstaking, enjoyable work. Nearing retirement, his thoughts often drifted to his caravan and travelling the Scotland that he loved.

Having finished his university days in Edinburgh, he had never left; he loved the place, never ventured to warmer climes, he did not want to spend a day away from this piece of paradise.

On closer examination it was probable why he loved his job. Scotland, to the geologist, was heaven: the mountains, the glens. the lochs. To hold a piece of Grampian granite in his hand whilst sitting beside a deep loch carved into the surrounding mountains by the receding ice age, his wife of forty years sitting beside him, he could think of nothing better. He would happily settle for this as heaven.

The seismograph on the desk beside him burst into life. He looked at it in disbelief. It monitored the hundred stations scattered around the British Isles; it normally recorded two earthquakes a week. Very few were capable of detection without technology. The screen was telling him there was an earthquake in East Anglia, north of Cambridge, bigger than anything ever recorded. The data was also sent to computers around the world, in the hope that over time a picture would emerge that may help predict earthquakes and hopefully save thousands of lives.

Glyn's first reaction a quick visual check of the equipment. Satisfied that nothing he could see was amiss, he put into action a procedure, practiced but never used, that would have his colleagues swarming back to the British Geological Survey station in Edinburgh.

Hotlines to government departments, emergency services

all activated.

The seismograph rang out again. The astonished geologist looked at the Richter scale: as big as the first. This was not an aftershock but a separate earthquake. People began arriving and huddled around screens.

The excitement in the seismic world had been palpable since events in northern Iraq, various theories advanced but none lasted past scrutiny.

A third time the seismograph needle went wild. Another separate earthquake of equal magnitude recorded, a triangle of equal distance between the epicentres.

The president sat with his closest advisers. He had aged ten years in a few days.

'What do we make of it, gentlemen, three more earthquakes, equal distance apart with magnitude that should have rendered the surrounding areas desolate yet no collateral damage. Those living a short distance away heard and felt nothing; those closest, dead or in a state of deep shock. What on earth is going on?

'Could it have anything to do with the incredible scenes we witnessed just a few miles away from these quakes?

'I have had two long and interesting telephone conversation with the bishop of Ely, the guy we saw nearly strangled in the drone footage.

'I found him to be level-headed and not evangelical at all. We were very candid, we spoke at length about the lake, about its importance to us as a secret research centre a stone's throw from West Row, the back door of our biggest airbase outside the U.S.

'The bishop told me of the Iceni, the women's army that

had so successfully held up the Roman legions, how they used the lake to disappear from view, he told me the organization still existed, charged with looking after ancient manuscripts.

'The Iceni were ancient Britons, Celts, in touch with the earth. Family was all-important, blending herbs for medication, preserving foods. As the centuries passed it began to meet and share ideas with other Celts, no physical enemy save the ongoing battle against inequality, it began schools, hospitals. Education for women and the poor was their highest goal. Eventually a group in Wales called themselves the Women's Institute. It has been a fantastic feeder organization for the Iceni.

'The ancient Iceni conversion to Christianity was swift.

'Legend has it they were hiding in the caves beside the lake, when Jesus, his mother Mary and his wife Mary Magdalene walked across the lake to them. Ancient texts of the Iceni speak of several encounters with the son of God and the women that served him, of his hand outstretched walking towards their camp, beseeching them to lay down their arms, embrace the love of God and to put their trust in him. He has great works for you to do.

'Today the organization, at its core, is deeply God-fearing.

'Some suggest its anthem *Jerusalem*, lyrics written by the poet Blake, was inspired by those early encounters. "And did those feet in ancient times walk upon England's mountains green".

'A second conversation with the bishop was a few moments ago, maybe of more relevance to us, I told him of the mystery of the earthquakes, I asked if he thought they could be in any way connected to the happenings at Stuntney.

'I tell you, gentlemen, he was very convincing. Until a

183

more plausible explanation exists it has to be considered.

'He is of the opinion that there has been a large increase in demonic activity in his area; he tells me it has always been a hotbed for devil worship.

'It goes back beyond the mists of time. "At its simplest," the bishop said, "is the city of Cambridge. As it grew as a seat of learning the intelligencer found it hard to accept the Bible. They saw it as promoting myth as facts, hurdle to learning, they saw man's hand in it everywhere. Why were some books left out? They couldn't accept the explanation, the compilers had their hands directed by God, they saw it more as 'it doesn't fit our doctrine so let's leave it out'

'Awkward questions about its origin. The loss in translation of meaning. The word 'maiden' somehow morphed into 'virgin'. Religious teaching met at every step with scepticism, it became increasingly difficult to advance the course of Christianity in Cambridge.

'"When a mighty cathedral was proposed for the centre of Cambridge it was a step too far for the learned men. The notion was dismissed.

'A compromise was struck. If the county must have a cathedral it would be built well away from Cambridge itself. The devout were offered a boggy outpost, the logistics of which meant moving heavy building materials across virtual swamp, where fever was rife, where people were sparse, where life was short.

'Undeterred the Christians built their magnificent building on an island at the very edge of the county in a village called Ely where it stands in all its splendour today.

'The bishop continued. "There was, and still is, a great swell of opinion against the tenants of Christianity, they became known as anti-Christians, or the Antichrist, a phrase coined in Cambridge, now changed from its original meaning to refer to the Devil himself.

The president found himself listening intently to the holy man.

'There has always been this conflict between proof and faith.

'Time advanced, Christianity grew, it became dangerous to be Antichrist, the spread of the Nephilim Yazidis, with their high intellect, found its way into the seats of learning. Their faith was much more in keeping with men of learning than the commandments of the Bible.

'Suspicion grew about anyone not serving God. The Antichrists solved the problem by serving God, but which God? the God of the Hebrews or the God of Nephilim Yazidis?

'Churches were built solely for the glorification of the dark lord, much of the congregation thought they were praying to a god of love and peace, the rest knew they were praying to a god who, through Eve, had brought the tree of knowledge, survival of the fittest. Evolution, the glorification of gold. Only the Latin academics knew these churches were filled with imagery and icons specifically banned in the Hebrew Bible.

The president joked.

'Yes there are more devils staring down in some of your churches, than are looking at me in the Senate.' The two men laughed.

'Priories, monasteries, abbeys, many have dubious patrons, judging by some of the practices that went on.

'The Iceni became "the defender of the faith" of Christianity, opposing the deceiver and his stronghold over Cambridge and its shire. Exning and its offspring, Newmarket, have been the bedrock of the Iceni stance.

'Today, counties are of little importance to people's lives but for centuries they were as important as countries are today. The few times that a proposal has been forwarded to straighten the boundary of Suffolk and move Exning and Newmarket under the umbrella of Cambridgeshire has been fiercely opposed.

'The county of Suffolk has a large clown's nose of Exning and Newmarket sticking into Cambridgeshire. Maybe if they could attach a thumb to the nose with wiggling fingers it would suit the Iceni better.

'"For where two or three are gathered in my name I am in the midst of them", Jesus had said.

'In the records of the Iceni, a spiritual wall of Jesus, was erected from Ely Cathedral to Cheveley church some twenty miles away. All the holy places are aligned to form a wall, each can be seen by the next in the chain; it is intriguing that without any modern technology every church along the route is in a perfectly straight line. Looking at the architecture and achievements, maybe the dark ages were not so dark.

'Queen Etheldreda, born in Exning and fifteenth defender of the faith, one of Iceni's most devout, spent much of her time travelling between the churches with her entourage in order to pray.

'Jesus had promised always to be with those that were praying in his name.

'Queen Etheldreda, or St Etheldreda as she became, prayed in the churches along the route in order to keep the wall strong with the Holy Spirit, and the devils from Cambridge at bay.

'When the Catholic church in Newmarket was moved to

186

its present site, it took twenty years in the planning, it was moving out of the chain.

'It was critical that the portals to the lake (that all the churches in the Newmarket enclave have) would never be suspected or found during demolition or construction.'

The president listened, gripped by the bishop's narrative.

'This area has always been a hotbed for conflict between the two rival religions.

The president said, 'Bishop you mentioned Nephilim Yazidis, that's the second time I have heard them mentioned recently.'

'Yes,' said the bishop. 'As you are well aware there are many groups or societies around the world who shun contact for a variety of reasons. Some it is political, many it is religious, they hope, by keeping themselves separate, they can preserve their doctrine.'

The bishop continued.

'Nephilim Yazidis is unique in that they worship the Devil.

'It tells us in the Bible that the Devil took with him his supporters, also that they took wives of the children of Adam. In a nutshell the offspring of this union became the Yazidis, half human and half fallen angel. The flood came, maybe some scholars believe it was the forming of the Mediterranean. The ice age was receding, the seas were rising, bursting through in the area we now call Gibraltar.

'Sorry,' said the bishop. 'I digress.'

'Just as God brought Noah to safety, so did the Devil,, and his angels the Yazidis, were set down in what today is Northern Iraq, where they remain to this day.

'In the past sixty or seventy years, as with all societies,

187

the young are not so easy to mind control, inasmuch that they bring new eyes to the world. They lift the veil on many fronts; they teach the older generations.

'It was the same for the Yazidis or the Nephilim Yazidis as they have become known. The young wanted to travel, fall in love with whoever, in the beginning they were excommunicated, but it caused such problems that they were allowed to communicate, visit, many stayed true to their religion.

'The outcome is that their doctrine and seed has spread throughout the world. If one takes an objective view, one could come to the conclusion that the way mankind runs the world is more in keeping with the god of Nephilim Yazidis than the father of Jesus.'

The president squirmed at this point, knowing what the bishop was saying was very close to the mark.

'In height, each generation seems to dwarf their parents.

'Some maintain that today the food is somehow better, yet most are eating the same staple as the generations that have gone before.

'If this phenomenon was true then domesticated animals would have increased in height: they have not.

'The manuscript that I am privy to tells how mankind will be tested, how faith and love will conquer greed.

'If one knows for certain that if you steal you will be shot, one does not steal. It is not the heart that has rejected the temptation but the head from fear of the bullet.

'If the fear of the bullet is removed, that the stories of being shot are nonsense put about by ancient books that have no relevance in today's fast-moving world, then it is the heart alone that makes the decision. God has given man a conscience, a unique wonder that allows him to choose his own destiny, he gifts, a present of restful sleep to those with an untroubled mind.

'So faith has, at its core, uncertainty.

'Nephilim, half angel half man, is still subjected through Adam's seed to the conscience.

'God has spoken of the Day of Judgment, when he will return to collect his flock, no one knows the hour. The manuscript that the Iceni have access to tells us that the Devil will walk the earth, his works will go before him. he will wreak havoc and send fear into the hearts of mankind.

'President, I think that time has come. The texts say, "The very earth beneath him will tremble".

'I think these earthquakes you speak of are the result of the resurrection of the Devil.'

It was the president, after a thoughtful pause, who spoke next. He thanked the bishop, asking if the pair could make it for lunch one day, he often used Mildenhall air base as a stopover when he travelled. The bishop said he would be delighted, even if it meant having to miss some of the parish council meeting. He'd said the minutes of the meeting may make for interesting reading.

The bishop played no part in the siting of the new street light adjacent to the maltings. He excused himself before the vote saying he had a lunch appointment with the president of the United States.

The two men laughed.

The president determined to follow up the offer of lunch with the bishop who he had found very engaging.

Now he faced his team of advisors. Having briefed them he said,

'That, gentlemen, is the gist of the conversation. There was not the scepticism one might have expected. We have a theory, not conventional, it marries the two incidents together.'

It was the CIA top man who spoke first.

'We have had these Nephilim Yazidis on the radar for as long as I can remember, they are very low on the Richter scale, excuse the pun, of interest, just another crackpot religious group, and there are hundreds that we monitor, they are very much on the edge of the screen.

'Medical research is interested in them, because they have high resistance to disease. Their life expectancy is the longest, many live past their hundredth year. They are taller than the Zulu.

'An extremely secretive cult, they are difficult to research.

'The Stuntney video has been scrutinised and found to be authentic.

'The British must have come to the same conclusion because every politician, his wife, sister and great aunt are vying for airtime in praise of the bravery of the chief constable, the bishop and all the officers, with total disregard for their own safety, had fought with the assailant.

'The chief constable had played down his role saying anyone would have done the same. It was his men that are the true heroes; they perform the same duty week in and week out.

'The Home Secretary was full of praise for these officers and their colleagues, walking into situations that they might not walk out of.

'He said that in his new post he would be looking to redress the balance, he felt justice had swung too far away from the brave men and women who try to keep the streets safe. They face pressure from an increasingly hostile public whose opinions are formed mostly by a tabloid press who, for reasons of circulation and profit, dramatize and sensationalize, often never letting the truth get in the way of the story.

'He said our police weekly walk into alcohol-fuelled war zones, while most who will judge them will be tucked up in bed, unaware of the horror on the streets.

'The Home Secretary said that in this blame and compensation culture that we have created, well-intentioned policies have borne unintended consequences, allowed the deceitful an avenue to easy riches.

'It is a stain on our national character that those we asked to do an almost impossible job often have to stand before the jury, where suit-clad, angelic-looking, nicely-groomed claimants try to relieve the taxpayer of large sums of money. Our legal system is in urgent need of reform.

'Highlighted by the recent case where the claimant received forty thousand pounds, somehow convincing the jury that the police threw him to the ground, sat on him, breaking his little finger in the process, a complete violation of his human rights. His emotional trauma will last his lifetime.

'The police involved should be sacked. Although the closed-circuit television may appear to show him wielding an iron bar and threatening anyone advancing with decapitation. He was simply re-enacting an ancient Aboriginal dance for the entertainment of the crowd of onlookers, the iron bar was a substitute for the ritual peace stick.'

'I took the liberty,' said the head of the CIA, 'of sending the Home Secretary a private email welcoming him to his new post and the real world of policing, pointing out the eternal dilemma. If you don't act, the call goes up from the press. Where were you? Why didn't you do something? If you do you can end up losing your life, job or liberty. Strange world, sir, but good luck with the new appointment.'

Michael sat in the kitchen of the rectory, the footage from the drone he had watched several times. Agnes was not there. She had been there, no one had seen her. No one had ever seen her.

She had lifted him when he was too weak to stand, they had finished the job together. He had checked with both Oliver and Ninal. She was often in the car when he passed the pair riding the horses. Both insisted he was always alone when they saw him.

Michael was disappointed, he could not get out of the house. The house was besieged: camera men, reporters everywhere.

Everyone who had ever come into contact with him had been interviewed.

Most of the stories were fairly accurate, some grossly exaggerated, some he must have been comatose when they occurred.

All his family insisted that he rest, he had seen the concern in their eyes, it will all blow over soon then we will carry on as usual.

Michael knew they knew that would not be the case, he was growing weaker by the day. He would soon shake off the fragile frame.

Oliver, the hardest to hide his emotions, would sit with his brother whenever he could, Ninal joined in the banter when the tasks of the day were behind her.

At the end of the evening meal, when the last crumb of apple pie had found its way into the stomach of Oliver, they all sat together.

Michael, in his normal jokey fashion, said, 'As you are well aware I will not be here much longer.' His mother, Jean, the dam bursting, rushed to his side hugging him.

His earthly father placed his hand on top of Michael's. He knew if he had tried to say something it would just have been shoulder-shaking sobs.

Oliver looked out of the window, every corpuscle desperate to hang on, trying to preserve some facade of a rough, tough national hunt jockey. A veneer, never having taken hold with his family, who knew he was tough as a chocolate marshmallow, a hard looking outer with a soft sweet centre.

Ninal had followed her mother-in-law and was hugging the other side, her cheeks glistening with her eye diamonds.

It was a blessed moment when they knew that Michael knew and the charade they had been playing with each other was at an end.

'I must say that the time I have been here I could not have wished for better parents, brother, or sister-in-law.

'As you know I leave few material things: a few teddies that I would like Ninal to have in the hope that, should my excuse for a brother ever achieve what he was put on the planet for and give my parents grandchildren to spoil, then maybe they will come in handy.

'My Australian bushwhacker hat that I bought at the church car boot sale those years ago, I would like my life's torment to have, although he is looking out of the window pretending to see something of interest.

'In all honesty and only because I feel our time together is short I will say this:

'If God has bequeathed a better brother to anyone, then he

193

has not been born yet.

'Ninal you have been the best surrogate sister I could have wished for. I still wince when I see you boxing them poor boys' ears who saw me as easy sport. God has given you the unenviable task of looking after two Grogan boys, the first must have been hard, the second absolute nightmare, you were never far away from me, always one eye looking out for me.

'I think it was when you sat me down to appreciate the wonders of the skipping competition, my five-year-old self, unable to quite grasp the intricacies, wanted to bolt, it was when my great friend Jim Smith sat down trying to spur me to action, that the new word entered my vocabulary, "I can't come Jim she's watching me, I think she's a Watcherer". Everyone laughed; it is a word, as you well know, that has never left my communication with the peoples of the planet.

'The joy of the Prolly household should be the model for the world.' He looked at his mother. 'It is there I honed my banister-sliding skills.' She hugged him harder.

He turned his hands over and cupped his fathers.

'You have been simply the best, a mountain of a man, the time I have spent with you has given me a glimpse of heaven.' He turn his face towards his mother whose rivulets of tears were matched only by Ninal's.

'When you picked that little bundle from off the front step and took that article of a brother of mine in, little did we know that God had placed us in the arms of an angel. We both know we have been blessed beyond belief.'

Oliver let out so the water pearls that had been rocking on the cliff edges of his eyelids began to tumble.

'Please spread my ashes around the James Grieves apple tree we planted when Oliver and Ninal got married, this garden has been a wonderland of peace, joy and happiness, it will be a delight to know that in some minute way I can give back to this garden.

'Anyway, Michael said, 'before we all have to swim out of here, I would like to say I love you all, more than the spoken or written word can express, but not as much as Mum's rhubarb pie, mincemeat tart and definitely not as much as her apple crumble and custard.'

That plugged the dam, stopped the downward flow of eye jewels, turning the tide from sadness and desolation to hilarity.

The mood lifted, Oliver said, 'You will probably outlive us all, you have been about to return to your maker since I can remember. Has it ever crossed your befuddled brain that he might not want you back, that he would rather you were down here tormenting us than up there tormenting him. Odd brother of mine, it might also be true that he has left me here this long in order to stop you believing the nonsense in the papers that you are some sort of racing superstar.

They all laughed; the mood rose again.

Ninal and her husband readied themselves for the return to their home, it would mean jumping the wire fence, running twenty yards, leaping the flint wall that separated the rectory from their back garden. If they timed it right it might be possible to avoid the paparazzi.

Michael would affect the distraction, walking towards the front gate where he would thank the media.

They all hugged and said goodnight before Michael stepped out into the night to execute the plan. He felt exhausted; he hoped it wouldn't end on the drive.

Oliver, with his arms wrapping his brother, tried to banish the thought that this might be the last time he saw his beloved friend, brother and confidant.

'That old hat of yours I will probably find a space in the back of a cupboard somewhere,' knowing it would be on his head constantly, if it were not it would be beside him in the car or in his racing bag; it would always keep his brother beside him.

The plan worked a treat. As he rounded the elbow in the drive the awaiting press and policeman saw his approach. They gathered at the gate, the policeman keeping them in check and the gate firmly closed. Oliver and Ninal made a run for it, they were in their back yard before the pack had realized potential prey had eluded them.

Little did they know, these pressmen, the biggest scoop of their lives was moments away.

Michael thanked them and wished them goodnight, and praised their diligence and dedication amid shouts of 'just a moment of your time sir,' and, 'I'm from the BBC could you spare a minute,' 'We have flown from America, Mr. Grogan, could you just give us a few sentences.'

Edinburgh, the earthquake recorded on the National Geographic Society's seismic machine recorded a record high, it pinpointed the epicenter as only yards from one of the previous.

The coordinates showed it to be St Mary's Rectory in Newmarket.

Michael turned to walk back to his home, bed and welcome rest.

The demonic noise burst from the ground; screams erupted from the posse of pressmen. Those unable to defend their ears quickly enough dropped like boulders from a cliff, their eardrums destroyed. Those wearing large earphones designed to minimize external sound to allow intimate instruction to be delivered, minimizing the chance of outside noise distorting the message, were able to remain standing and report the scene unfolding before them.

A tornado swirled some few yards in front of Michael who seemed to be unaffected by the crescendo, then the stillness. The quiet of the coffin box, every decibel spent, the coffin allowing the sleeper undisturbed rest until the time of the Resurrection.

God, through the Koran, promised the sleeper that, although millennia may have passed, he will believe he has been napping for one half of an hour.

That peace was broken a few moments later by groans, of media people struggling to coordinate.

There stood before Michael and the world's cameras the Peacock Angel, the Devil, Lucifer, the Fallen Angel. He was not alone. Out of the mist of the tornado the grotesque faces had emerged to stand beside, but now they had emerged from the ugly chrysalis to be huge, powerful and beautiful with human form. These were the fathers of the Nephilim, the heroes of Greek mythology. Michael, unaffected by the cacophony and the developments in front of him, stood watching his adversary. Those who had questioned why the entrances to the Vatican and many holy places were so large, why the thrones were huge, why imagery of devil worship abounds, why scripture from the Bible was ignored. The answer now stood before the world's recovering media.

Michael, facing his adversary with all the trepidation of an apple pie eater, who is being troubled by a fly trying to join the feast.

Appearing on his shoulder, Agnes.

'I thought you might need a little help.'

'Not really,' said Michael. 'I know why you are not on any of the videos at Stuntney. As you're well aware I'm very slow on the uptake sometimes.'

'I'd have to take issue with you on the word "sometimes",' said Agnes.

'Anyway I didn't want to dilute your fame,' Agnes said. 'You might get a church named after you,'

They both laughed.

'I know,' Michael replied, 'you are the other side of the veil.'

'Yes, only you can see me this side,' she replied.

'As I get closer to joining you it becomes clearer. The little church where I picked you up from is called St Agnes.'

'Yes,' said Agnes, 'you are a doughnut, quickness and uptake are not words that sit comfortably on your shoulders.'

'Thank you for that,' said Michael. 'My poor brother doesn't realize my banter skill has been honed by a guardian angel.' He put his arm round his beloved, asking her to help him to the house otherwise he would be joining her sooner than expected; judging by what stood before them, they still had work to do.

Michael looked into the eyes of the dark lord and said, 'Get thee behind me, Satan.'

The cacophony returned, with it the whirlwind, within a few seconds, the stillness.

Dusk was pulling its blanket across the Suffolk skies. In the middle of the Bury Hill racehorse training grounds, a tree-enclosed hundred acre site dedicated to right-hand practice, the unearthly growl from the belly of the planet began. It grew in intensity, the noise eardrum splitting.

Frank Conlon. Head lad for one of the big powerhouse stables, one of the most respected horsemen of his time. In any other sport he would have been revered by the masses. He was a demigod to those who reached the highest level of understanding with the racehorse.

Frank was the lone soul walking his dog across the hallowed turf before returning to the yard for evening stables. He fell to the ground, buried his face in the deep grass, clamped his hands to his ears in a vain attempt to defend them from the pain.

The pain and noise subsided; a stillness descended. Removed his hands from the side of his head, lifting it from its soft green bed. His dog lay on the grass beside him, dead. He straightened himself.

The sight that stood a few yards in front of him stopped his heart. He fell beside his dog to be found hours later by the small search party from the stables.

A mile south and past the left-hand training grounds of Side Hill the Devalian racehorses stud with its small army of elite soldiers waited; they were prepared for an attack. A constant state of readiness. This would not be a noisy battle of gunfire, bombs, rockets. This would be a battle of stealth; of crossbow, knife, garrotte.

As the enemy approached, they would be taken out.

The guttural sound began and quickly grew. Some brotherhood soldiers fell from trees, clutching their heads, blood running from their destroyed eardrums. Others covered their heads with whatever was available, unable to defend anything. This was a type of warfare none had heard of or experienced.

The head crushing sound stopped.

The brotherhood soldiers, that were not incapacitated, raised themselves ready to fight. What they saw would haunt them for the rest of their lives.

In the middle of the field stood the beast. Huge, terrifying, watching the stable, on top of the bunker that housed the gospel. The sound began; the soldiers defended their ears. It stopped; the beast had gone.

Michael, arm in arm with Agnes, made his way back to the rectory where Agnes kissed her love good night, hugging his body, the gesture that conveys more than the written words can ever express, from school gate to deathbed, unique to mankind, universal, the expression of the spirit. We have stood together in playing field, trench, love, laughter and grief, you live within me, etched in my heart, comrade, friend, love, parent, child, this is my gift, from my soul, a hug.

Michael slept soundly. The media world, on the other hand, was frenzied, paparazzi feasting on the bonanza, those employed by the media outlets, busy selling images to those whose representatives had fallen foul of the ear busting.

Michael awoke, millions of pounds had changed hands overnight for images of him facing down his adversary.

Asian countries woke to the incredible pictures, supermarkets were quickly in a crush, banks had queues stretching almost out of sight, hours before their planned opening.

Governments were in crisis mode, putting into place action long practiced, never implemented, banks would remain shut, the military assigned to food distribution centres to implement rationing

The house of cards was beginning to collapse. Long anticipated, long feared, panic, the nemesis of the illusion. The money emperors exerting maximum pressure, stop the fear at all costs.

Governments with total control banned all images from any media outlet. The need for an alternative narrative to be pursued or fabricated, western governments, with a few hours, due to the time difference to observe the catastrophe unfolding in Asia, followed suit.

The president, haggard from a shortage of sleep since the crisis began, once again addressed the assembled, crowded room.

'Well people, you've all seen the images, we are in crisis management, the priority is to stop the panic, I have spoken to the Russian president and we are both aware that the images are real, we are also aware that we need to reassure the public that these images are fake, blaming each other, for the cyberattacks. This should buy us some time to formulate a plan. To this end we have contacted every plausible crackpot and fed them a conspiracy theory We also contacted the news agencies, steering them to these articulate and knowledgeable insiders. Of course we have distanced ourselves from any involvement, everything done through third parties. We will have undisputed evidence that the Russians are heavily involved, basically the Russian president will say the same, laying the whole dirty business at our door which we will strenuously deny.'

As the day began across the Middle East and Europe, the headlines abounded that the two superpowers were accusing each other of cyberattacks where holograms, developed by the military, were being used to frighten people, scenes once confined to cinemas and television screens could now be enacted almost anywhere, from satellites' projectors.

"Experts" were appearing on television shows globally, saying they had been warning governments constantly for some time of the likelihood of this type of cyberattack, with the rapid advance of this technology, where multi-dimensional holograms could be projected almost anywhere. The upside of this amazing advance would be unimaginable, renowned surgeons able to be in multiple operating theatres through their hologram, advancing intricate techniques for the scalpel wielders to follow.

Lecturers able to be in the room demonstrating, answering questions, while working in the comfort of their own home.

Police able to bolster their numbers with little added cost to the taxpayer, having a dramatic increase in what would appear, their physical presence indistinguishable from the real thing, multiplying their deterrent capabilities, culminating in a dramatic fall in crime, lowering prison populations.

Rooms full of holograms, all talking to each other, while the real self-resided in some other place. The application is only governed by the imagination, as profound an impact on mankind as all the other technological breakthroughs put together, from the wheel to Internet pale into insignificance in the shadow of the hologram, the experts had apparently predicted the hologram in the wrong hands could be used to terrorize, manipulate, bring fear to the masses. There needed to be an education program informing people that what they saw was not necessarily real.

The strong had always been able to mound the masses,

fake news, propaganda, advertising, whichever handle you want to use, these devices had always been a productive tool for the steering of the flock. Today, with even more avenues to manipulate, it needed a more educated population to combat the ever increasing arsenal of deception owned by the mighty.

The evidence for all these so-called demonic appearances, was not backed by anything credible, earthquakes reported that should have caused catastrophic damage. Simply non-existent, hairless beasts disappearing, no DNA, evading all the most sophisticated surveillance.

The whole thing fabricated.

The pageant portrayed as a charade. All the major powers playing the game, propagating the illusion, they were at each other's throats, convincing the trusting population.

It seemed to be working, news editors globally, filling the front pages with stories of their governments' ineptitude, failing to protect their citizens, from cyberattack.

These servants of the people always behind the curve. The criminal mind exploiting any advantage in its quest for gold. These morally absent souls run around the planet's plains like the frolicking hare, being pursued by a sloth with apnoea, from tax havens to phone scams, money market manipulation, government officials filling their own bank accounts, to the destruction of the planet for gain.

Politicians of all hues leading the charge from the comfort of the dugout,

Things would have to change, we've learned lessons, we will stop these practices that leave the hardworking people of this country vulnerable and impoverished.

The old well-practiced slogans spoken with fake sincerity, knowing that nothing will change, the lure of the wealth of the scams will be fed back into the monetary system of the most lenient and morally corrupt countries, often in the form of property, inflated prices paid in major cities, purchasers paying astronomical sums seemingly amassed from government positions often from the poorest of nations, lifting the ladder of home ownership beyond the grasp of the young.

Accountants take pride in advertising that their big earners pay very little tax, hiding behind the well-trusted tax avoidance, not tax evasion, banner, both morally wrong, governments compliant, drawn by the knowledge that if awkward questions were asked, the lucre would be diverted to a more receptive administration. The political blind eye deceives itself, allowing unfathomable complexities to obscure the actions of the morally corrupt.

These were the most persistent themes that filled the world's media.

Once again they had failed to protect their citizens, this was a phenomenon that those experts working in the field had predicted, the governments' response, as usual, woeful.

The leaders of the free world were pleased that the strategy had worked, mass panic had been avoided. Most were convinced and comforted by the knowledge that the scenes were fake, the fear had subsided in the Far East with the revelation that it was all games played by the superpowers.

A video summit was hastily arranged where all the leaders would allegedly discuss ways of combating cyberattacks, the real reason was to discuss the response to this unprecedented show of power.

There was a level of cooperation between the powerful that had not been seen before, all accepting that none of the others were instigators of the phenomena.

They all knew that the suspension in the panic was only temporary; they had short respite.

They could only sit on the lid before those that were closely involved would expose the deception.

The statement the English prime minister gave when his turn to speak arrived stated his country's position, the history behind what they now believed to be true. He spoke of the English Civil War, of the witch finder general, Matthew Hopkins, his assistant John Stearne's reign of terror across East Anglia, which began in 1644 and lasted three years before his enforced retirement. He had sentenced to death more than three hundred souls, almost doubling the execution rate for witchcraft of the previous five hundred years. It is without doubt that many of his victims were innocent.

One of the indicators of a witch, according to Hopkins, was the love of cats, particularly black, coupled with the Devil's mark, which today would be referred to as a birthmark or a mole, he employed prickers, women who could stick pins into alleged witches at points such as warts. If they didn't bleed it was a sure sign that the woman was a witch, if it bled and a cat would lick the blood, another sure sign of a witch.

Women suspected of witchcraft would be tied and thrown into deep water. If they floated it was a sure sign that water of the baptism was ejecting them, if they drowned it was possible they weren't involved in witchcraft.

While the English Civil War for the governance of the country was fought between the Roundheads and Cavaliers, the witch finder general was plying his trade in East Anglia.

The monetary remuneration for uncovering witches was such that both men's forced retirements left them very affluent members of society.

Matthew Hopkins' death at the age of twenty-seven was a mystery, those that found his body were convinced from the expression on his face that he died of fright. Such was the concern of the viewing, he was buried within a few hours of his death.

In amongst all the innocence were the few that had consorted with the Devil, or rather believed that the future belonged to the scientist, often wives of academics from the city of Cambridge and its associated learning establishments, who were more in tune with the commandments of Nephilim Yazidis and the Peacock Angel, than the followers of the descendants of Noah's Ark.

Today they would be called chemists, producing medicine, at the time they would have been Antichrists, creating potions for witchcraft.

Cambridge, as today, pursued the highest echelons of academic achievement, pushing back the boundaries of knowledge.

It was thought for millennia that women did not possess the ability for free thought; were excellent, diligent, neat imitators, possessing no talent as innovators.

A perception that lasted till after the Second World War, when women were first allowed to receive degrees from the richest university in the world.

Officially, Cambridge University was formed after two academics were hanged by the townspeople of Oxford for the murder of a woman, without resort to ecclesiastical authority which would have pardoned them. It was an affront to the dignity of the scholars that two of their number faced the gallows simply for murdering a woman.

The townspeople's version differs somewhat from the

official records; they became frustrated that the atrocities administered to women by those purporting to hold the highest moral standards always found clemency with the Pope.

The two academics were tried in a court of the people, found guilty and hanged.

Oxford was no longer a safe haven for the misogynistic tendencies of the powerful. A large proportion left for Paris or Cambridge.

The world leaders were fascinated at the more intimate details that were possibly the root of the incarnations.

Professor Dave Dugdale, head of neuroscience at Cambridge University, could trace his ancestors back to the seventeenth century, almost all had been connected to the University of Cambridge; academia was in his blood. His great friend and working colleague, Pete Kelly, on the other hand, didn't know who his father was. His mother had been cornered as a fourteen-year-old under the pier at Yarmouth by a gang of beatniks. She had run away from home the previous week, caught up in a world where rock and roll had landed like the atomic bomb. It became a musical drug with no known antidote, tens of thousands of young teenagers were obsessed, suffering from some sort of mass hysteria.

She was found a couple of days later wandering the streets of Yarmouth like many others and returned to the welcoming arms of her family. Mother and father were overjoyed at her return, having lost weight and sleep roaming the streets looking for her.

After a few months, the realization that she was pregnant dawned. Having lost her once there was no way they would abandon her now, they would face the problem together as a family. For those with the pointy fingers and the sniggers, well that was their problem.

The baby boy was born and brought joy to the household. Mum went back to school then on to university where she excelled academically. She landed a job in a burgeoning computer science company, a new and exciting field with a promising future. She was paid handsomely, also given shares in the company as it grew.

Pete Kelly was brought up in Cambridge in an affluent household, his academic achievements surpassed even those of his mother's. He met Dave Dugdale in their first undergraduate year. They hit it off straight away, having an array of shared passions, particularly the science of the brain. The power of this incredible organ: the more you found out about it, the more the mystery deepened.

Both worked up through the academic ladder, becoming professors in neuroscience simultaneously. Gaining funding for their ongoing research became easier as their reputations grew, until they were universally regarded as leaders in the field by their peers. They worked feverishly at their passion.

The only distraction that superseded all their work was when Cambridge United football club were playing at home, or a varsity match, especially the rugby, both men could be found in the stands, punching the air or bouncing on some unseen trampoline, friendly banter fostered over many years with their Oxford counterparts. The stuff of mirth, unrelenting bragging rights, bare bum pointing joy, a ritual left over from their undergraduate days.

The boat race on the Thames between Cambridge and Oxford, eagerly anticipated by the two rival camps, the result of which was of absolutely no interest to anyone else in the universe.

Victory, a year of devising new ways to tease; defeat, twelve months of nonchalant dismissal of the jibes.

The two men's lifetime work had advanced to a point where they could monitor and map every electrical signal that passed through the brain. Thousands of subjects had been studied, computer programs had been designed that could replicate the electrical impulses. The complexities of the brain had been unravelled.

It was felt that the achievement surpassed that of Cambridge scientists Watson and Crick, who explained all the physical and chemical features of DNA, for which they received the Nobel Prize in physiology and medicine.

The excitement of the achievement was tempered with the news that Pete Kelly had been diagnosed with pancreatic cancer, and the prognosis was terminal.

Both scientists were agnostic, although the further they had progressed, delving into the mysteries of the brain, the less agnostic they became. There were certainly activities that couldn't be explained with any rationality, they were certain the quantum mechanics played a part, where the laws of the sciences as we know them were not adhered to in the quantum world.

Quantum to the mathematician is as Everest to the climber.

The two professors were intrigued by the work being done at the University of Virginia division of perceptual studies where, for almost fifty years, they had been studying NDA, or near-death experiences, where subjects had been clinically dead, but could recall vivid out of body experiences. Thousands of cases had been studied. The only conclusion that made any sense was that these things were real, revealing things on their return to their body that they could not have possibly known.

Thousands of cases of reincarnation study, initially in the Far East where it was accepted as part of religion. The last twenty years, solely in the west, where children could recount previous lives which proved accurate with no possibility of the subject having any prior knowledge of the previous life.

Initially the professors had been asked to independently review the methodology of the Virginia studies. They found the checks and balances to be beyond reproach.

Consciousness was as much a mystery throughout their career as it was on the first day, sleep another mystery beyond explanation.

Pete put forward the notion, as he approached death he should be the first to have the electrical impulses generated by his brain transferred to the immense computer. It would be an astonishing moment for science; it would be a chance for him to remain on the program, he felt he could contribute so much more on the inside. After much consideration by Dave, the team and his family, the decision was made that Pete would be the ideal pioneer.

The dilemma was in parallel with Christiaan Barnard's heart transplant in 1967. Was it ethical? What would be the ramifications? The religious spokespeople had been muted by the success of the organ transplantation, which they vigorously opposed Barnard and his team. Every mediaeval ecclesiastical theology would come crashing down. The South African team withstood the religious onslaught, today it is widely accepted that transplantation is the greatest gift one human can give to another. Atheists point out that the religious fevered opposition represented yet another catastrophic error in the zealots' long list of catastrophic errors.

The remaining weeks of Pete's life was spent sitting in the laboratory surrounded by the team, every electromagnetic instrument that they had developed recording and delivering its information. It was a bittersweet time for the two great friends professionally: it was the culmination of their lives' work. Privately the end of a friendship that had grown as the years passed; the mutual love of all things Cambridge.

They both adored the game of football, the rules of which, they would periodically inform visiting fans, were first devised at the University of Cambridge.

They could also repeat, in rote fashion, the university had fifteen prime ministers, one hundred and twenty-five Nobel prize winners, over two hundred medal winners at Olympic Games, ten English monarchs, over sixty prominent royals, three hundred from other countries. Oliver Cromwell the Lord Protector of England.

Prominent authors, actors, members of parliament all numbered in the hundreds, notable scientists from Charles Darwin through to Stephen Hawking, Alan Turing, Bill Tutte, code breakers who changed the course of the Second World War and the destiny of mankind. Seven uncovered spies, the pair of professors could espouse the virtues of Cambridge University until those suffering from insomnia had been cured.

Pete insisted that the last few hours of his life he would be connected, the impulses of his dying would be sent to the machine. It was a profound, moving experience that the family and team surrounding him had ever experienced, as his last shallow breath left his body. The emotion overflowed into sobs and tears; brave face has no shield against intense spirituality. The moments of birth and death are as close as any will get to the presence of God.

The high command of Nephilim Yazidis were well aware of the work of the Cambridge professors and knew that the brain of Pete Kelly had been transferred to the computer, with the return of the mighty Peacock Angel, they knew they were at the beginning of the end. The discovery of the whereabouts of the written word of Jesus Christ, which had evaded them for centuries, had now been found, its destruction imminent.

The pendulum was swinging even further in favour of Nephilim Yazidis' dark lord. Greed everywhere, gold the idol of almost all, deception permeating every sphere, Slaughtering each other on a daily basis. Almost all the Hebrew god's ten commandments disregarded.

World leaders gathering for the hastily arranged face to face summit in the five-star global hotel close to Suvarnabhumi Airport near Bangkok.

It was the French president who was the first to speak.

He welcomed the assembled heads of state, gave a brief description of what was known, which in truth was very little.

'It is a time to put all our differences aside and pool our resources.

'We are facing a power, as we all know, that is beyond our comprehension at the moment. As we understand it we may be facing Armageddon, our collective intelligence sources have come up with no logical explanation. Unless in the very unlikely circumstance that some group has developed technology beyond our understanding, it is likely that the source of this power is not logical, maybe from another realm, either spiritual or galactic. The technology is akin to the caveman having produced a computer.

'The best scenario for us would be some terrestrial group

that has managed to evade all of our collective surveillance.

'Mathematicians tell us that the odds for such an outcome would be the same as winning an international lottery every week for a century.

'If that is not the case then we are simply ants in a barrel with boiling water hovering above. We have bought ourselves some time with the notion that these images are fake but as we know we are witnessing something beyond our understanding; we can only keep the lid on the stories for a few days at most. We must use them wisely and prepare for mass hysteria, runs on banks and food halls. We are facing a return to the days of the caveman with the added dilemma that instead of a few hundred thousand seeking sustenance from the planet it will be billions, it will be survival of the most aggressive and fittest, cities will be the first to succumb.

'Millions with no food, electric, water. I leave it to your imagination of the horror, apocalyptic I would suggest.

'We need to return to paper money in the hope that we can keep the system that we are so used to, that is so fragile, able to function. If we can get through this together and hopefully come out the other side then maybe we can build a better world, the odds are against this, should any more phenomena appear before we are ready, then we, as a race, are facing extinction.'

Many more leaders spoke, all with the same message. All knew it had to be every man for the world, if they fail it would be the return of the wild west of the dark ages, every man for himself.

Every nationality promised to print money, all accounts worldwide would be printed in paper form, stored. Should the need arise there would be enough paper money to distribute and in circulation it would be nightmarishly laborious but meant that economics as we know it may be able to carry on for a short period before it returned to trading only in commodities.

The Arab racehorse farm was in lockdown, the Mohammedans' elite soldiers had been bolstered, those casualties from the encounter with the Peacock Angel had been shipped back to Dubai on private jet from Stanstead Airport, their numbers being replaced tenfold. They were in a heightened state of readiness, expecting an attack at any time, from any quarter.

With the knowledge that the confrontation could have a supernatural element, their prayers towards Mecca, more earnest, their daily ritual more deeply meaningful, convinced from their comrades that the next destination would likely be paradise.

Michael and the family were relieved that the media attention upon them had shifted. Apparently all the superpowers at each other's throats in a worsening situation, each blaming the other, neglecting to protect and inform the public of the dangers of these holograms.

The bishop had informed the Iceni, through the medium of the gypsy boy's grave with its placement of teddies, flowers, small icons that to the casual observer would mean nothing, to the Iceni a call to arms, the end game was upon them. The prophecies of the gospel of Jesus Christ was unfolding.

The bishop stood outside Saint Mary's Church with its vicar and his great friend Brian Grogan. It was two hours before the meeting with the Iceni, the defenders of the faith. The Iceni illuminati had always been female, right back to the days of Boadicea, when the church was first built, caricatures of the women carved from the local flint which symbolized the Iceni women, beautiful souls as hard as stone, had been placed around the entrance to the church. The bishop had a photocopied piece of paper from the original text which named all the women; he knew their names by heart. By studying the flint statues concreted into the wall and comparing the image with the parchment one could only admire the skill of the stonemason to have captured the essence of the devotees in flint.

It was a curiosity to both clergymen that these images, hiding in plain sight, had never been the subject of any enquiry from the parishioners, then, they mused nor had anyone queried the water course, waterhall, well bottom, the Seven Springs that no one had seen.

The mysterious route of the single underground railway line, how Doctor Richard Beeching had closed hundreds of railway stations. Large towns lost their access to the network yet either side of Newmarket, in small villages of a few hundred people, the mystery remains how they managed to evade the closure.

The strangeness of the gypsy boy's grave, the posse of dog walkers daily chose this spot as opposed to any other more convenient for canine exercise.

Two men of God knew they observed the gypsy boy's grave, reporting any changes to their sponsor in the alignment of articles placed at the top of the grave, unaware of the significance, or that any other trustees strolling by were anything other than dog walkers. It was a system that had survived the centuries, intact and undiscovered.

The chief constable had received an envoy from the prime

minister, like a scene from the James Bond movie they had met in the car park at an Ely supermarket.

The envoy had explained the need for the present emphasis on the hologram. Hoping that the chief constable could avoid the press, the powers that be needed to buy time. The longer they could stifle the truth, even a few hours could make the difference between disaster and catastrophe.

After the funeral company had collected Pete's body to begin the process of his interment, Dave sat on his own in the Cambridge laboratory. The rest of the team had drifted off. Pete's family had followed the undertakers to the chapel of rest. It had been far more emotional than he could have imagined. The final breath had instigated a collective sense of desperation, of overwhelming loss.

Abby, one of the clinical team, went over to the window and opened it. Dave knew that nurses in hospitals and hospices would open the window after death. It was for no logical reason that he could think of, but it felt so right.

Dave Dugdale switched on the computer, the machine developed in Cambridge by the "Apple Siri lab," a part of the Apple empire that was at the cutting edge of their operations. A low profile secretive outcrop, with its offices close to the botanical gardens, where Pete and Dave often had their lunch, they would meet regularly with the Apple tech people.

Apple were very enthusiastic about the possibility of the brain being transferred to a computer. The commercial opportunities were unimaginable, bigger than anything that had gone before, coupled with the hologram, humankind no longer governed by the frailties of the body; it was immense.

Dave spoke to the computer brain of Pete, the reply was almost instant, spoken through the speaker as close as a machine could get to imitating the voice of Pete.

Dave began the long list of preordained questions designed to test the hypothesis that the human brain could be transferred to a machine.

It was in the low digit hours past the midnight. A bewildered, exhausted Dave climbed into the seat of his car. Life had changed for him in the last few hours, there would be no returning to the Dave of yesterday.

The questions and answers session with the brain of Pete had gone on for several hours. Questions the pair designed to gauge understanding of the depth of the transfer.

One small trip for man, Pete would say.

One giant voyage for mankind, Dave would reply.

They would both laugh at the Neil Armstrong moon landing parody.

All the questions and answers recorded audibly, also in script to be analysed later in depth.

The deeper into the session, the realization for Dave began to emerge: no longer was he talking to Pete but simply a machine that could answer all the questions, make all the responses, prove that the brain had been transferred successfully, but Pete the person, Pete the witty, emotional, playful rascal, dedicated prankster, liberated thinker, had gone. Dave switched off the computer, a mixture of disappointment and inner peace.

The football questions towards the end had confirmed beyond any doubt to Dave that the entity he was talking to was not his lifelong friend. The questions had been so designed, sometimes without the knowledge of the other, to verify or not, idiosyncrasies about the other they were unaware of themselves.

Dave knew that Pete was the best football manager that couldn't kick a ball straight, like millions of others who stood in the stands, if he were Cambridge United football team manager, they would be unbeatable. Pete could not leave a game unanalysed. If they were beaten it was entirely the fault of the manager.

In the pub there was a good hour of analytical discussion after his beloved Cambridge United had suffered defeat. What was going through the manager's head? Why on earth did he play Martin Brady in the right back position knowing full well he couldn't match the speed of the opposing winger, if he had played John Brooks who was two yards faster, the threat from the aerial bombardment that cost United the game would have been nullified.

The manager must've been smoking some illegal substance to put Geoff Timmons at centre half. He was six foot four and the best header of the ball in the league. When would the manager realize he was a centre forward?

When Dave asked Pete the computer what he thought about the defeat of Cambridge United against Reading, the brain of Pete replied, "They were beaten three one."

For Dave it was confirmation beyond all doubt that his friend for decades was no longer.

There was simply no possibility that Pete would have left the statement there, the world would stop, he would give a detailed analysis as to why Cambridge United should have won three one and not lost by the same score.

Realization that a person could not be transferred to a machine with all the ramifications extended space travel, scientific mind no longer cut short by death. No storing of parents and relations on computers for recall through holograms.

An inner peace to know that a person, or the mind of a person, was more than the sum of its parts, that the brain and body were vehicles for something unexplained, maybe unexplainable that the mind and consciousness were different from the brain. It did not need a source of energy as we know it, which opened the doorway to the notion that the mind could function without the need for brain and body, giving credence to the notion of heaven, spirituality, the soul, and existence, not governed by the desires and frailty of the mortal form. No need to pamper the urge to accumulate, to dominate, a realm where envy, anger, desire, gluttony and laziness could not exist.

The team undoubtedly now had mapped the brain, it could be transferred, but the person, the soul, spirit, could not.

Dave, putting on his jacket about to head to the car, heard Pete's voice. He turned in astonishment, looking around the laboratory. The voice came again.

'Dave, sit down for a minute, you look like you've seen a ghost.'

'Looks like I'm talking to one,' Dave replied.

'And as for getting beat by Reading, what was the manager thinking about? If he had played four four two, in the first half, soaked up the pressure, everyone in the world, including grandmas and children above the age of two, knows that Reading come at you in the first half and then run out of steam, if we played that system and then reverted to four three three the result would've been totally different, we would probably have won by at least four goals.

'Dave I can't stay, so many people here to meet me, much of what we know about the studies that go on in Virginia

Institute is correct, there is an intense sense of love, I'm about to enter a tunnel, a sort of glorious beam of light. I'm holding my mum's hand, there's a guy here with me he says he's my dad, I feel an immense sense of love towards me, he tells me his name was Gordon McLean, all his friends called him Gordy. He says he passed over from a motorbike accident six months before I was born; he lived in Coventry, on the Tile Hill estate in a house on Delia Street.

'Dave I'm heading into the light beam. You are the best friend a man could ever ask for, probably never told you enough, I'll be here to meet you when it's your turn.'

Dave could not stop the tears, it was joy beyond expression, to know that his great friend was happy and entering another realm. A deep sense of comfort filled his being to know that this life was not the end, that the love created in this world would be carried forward.

The Iceni meeting would take place in the church, its centuries old spiritual home. The reverend and the bishop had been joined by Ninal, Michael and Oliver, all were kneeling in prayer.

The trio, and associated members of the Iceni, had avoided the remnants of the media by using the back entrance of the Kings Theatre that abutted the garden of the rectory, turning right out of the front door up to Blackbear Lane, back down the High Street, along the path of the veterinary practice that separated the High Street from the church.

It was a subterfuge that worked to perfection.

Half an hour before the allotted time people began arriving, mostly women, everyone dressed in black. Standard practice to create an impression to the casual observer that a funeral service was due to commence.

The devout filled the front pews working backwards, always facing front, kneeling and praying.

One of the last to enter was the leader of the Iceni: she had been the defender of the faith for over six decades. Headscarf, glasses and diminutive size gave her anonymity. Her devotion to duty unquestionable, a lifelong member of the Women's Institute, still pouring the tea and dishing out the biscuits.

She sat in the last pew of the assembled throng praying, after a few minutes she rose, in her distinctive voice she asked if the watcher could give the assembled an update.

The bishop rose and walked to the back of the congregation, turned and faced the altar, an age-old practice where the speakers spoke to the altar facing the backward heads of the Iceni.

He gave a detailed account of all the demonic occurrences in the region that he knew of, the quickening escalation in the manifestations, the certainty that Nephilim Yazidis had discovered the whereabouts of the gospel of Jesus Christ, the evidence now that the Devil's physical form had been released from his thousand years' confinement.

He would come to claim his own, those souls that had been freely given would wreak havoc.

The systems created by man with the dark lord's influence would tumble and fall.

It would be the last chance for those influenced by the Nephilim Yazidis' commandments to reconsider.

Jesus had spoken of man in the world as two babes in the womb, the stronger convinced that entering the birth channel was the end, nothing beyond to gain as much from this dark place. The notion that his sibling entertained of an existence beyond the womb was fanciful. That there was unconditional love awaiting, that there would be joy, happiness, peace, forgiveness, beauty beyond belief, everything would be provided by a loving family.

The stronger would laugh in his face. His wisdom in the womb knew no bounds.

The close observer, sitting in the abbey gardens in Bury St Edmunds, would have seen tiny crumbs of earth tumbling down the wormholes, the same phenomenon repeated at Caxton Gibbet west of Cambridge, one of the last public hanging platforms.

In cemeteries up and down the country, headstones began to minutely tip; those that had practiced the dark arts undiscovered were being called from the graves.

The Iceni had been briefed, like those that had gone before, it was the time they had hoped to see, tinged with dread, knowing with certainty that their hearts would be strengthened. It was the Garden of Gethsemane moment where Jesus petitions God "Let this cup pass from me". God had strengthened him to face his trial, to face his accusers, to wear the crown of thorns, to carry his cross towards Calvary, asking God for forgiveness for those who were killing him, to hang upon the cross engulfed in pain, his blood dripping from his wounds, draining his life, none of the multitudes that would face death in his name would face anything more terrifying than the crucifixion.

It was decided that copies of the gospel according to Jesus Christ would be delivered to the world's media.

It would be uploaded to the Internet. Copies would be delivered far and wide; the secrecy was over. It was the beginning of the end, the second coming was upon them, there would be forty days and forty nights for mankind to endure, the mystical length of time Jesus, had faced down the Devil, forty days and nights Moses and Isaiah spent fasting in the wilderness.

The Iceni meeting was at an end, some were heading for the vestry and the secret portal, others preparing to leave by the main entrance when the demonic ear-splitting cacophony erupted.

The Iceni placed hearing defenders in position, pre-warned that their deployment may be necessary. The remaining pressmen one hundred yards away observing the rectory followed suit, turning their attention from rectory to church, the sight before them was enough to stop the heart, a huge terrifying manifestation exactly as depicted in recent pictures and videos now denounced as fake holograms.

Pictures and videos instantly beamed across the world by the pressmen who had stood at their sentry post, convinced that the earlier appearance they had witnessed of the Devil was real.

Swirling around in a mist were faces and limbs developing into form, until eventually massive beings stood beside the dark lord.

These were the Nephilim angels come to claim their own and take the strong to the universe, leaving the meek to inherit the earth.

The door of the church swung open to facilitate the Iceni exit. The sight of huge limbs came in to view, the torsos invisible above the door opening. The Iceni knew that to distinguish between the church of God and the church of the

Peacock Angel were the size of the doors.

Ethereal things were forming around the Devil and the Nephilim, souls unconditionally given, happy to do their master's bidding.

These were the enforcers that no despot in the history of mankind could have prospered without.

They began to stream through the door, striking the Iceni. The stench once again filled the church causing collective vomiting. The Iceni walked towards the door receiving punishing beatings until they fell, never lifting a finger in defence.

Michael, closely followed by Oliver and Ninal, pushed his way to the front.

He began speaking, his language unrecognizable to the human ear, the enforcers back towards the door their form gradually returning to the ethereal world. He walked out of the entrance, stood facing his adversary and his entourage, walking towards them.

Appearing on his shoulder was Agnes.

'Hi gorgeous.'

'Hi handsome.'

'I imagine no one else can see you.'

'You're really getting a grip of this now, aren't you?' Agnes said. 'I thought you might need a hand.'

'I'd probably have managed it, no problem, but I do love it when you're with me.'

'I will always be with you,' Agnes replied.

The pair continued towards the pitiless, who backed towards the small patch of green that fronted the church, where hordes of the town's children had spent countless happy hours cavorting at the annual church fete. This afforded an escape for the Iceni.

Those filming the rapid departure were amazed at the prominent figures that emerged from the church, disappearing immediately into the vet practice's car park.

This was the moment the Internet crashed. Mobile phone services ceased.

The modern communication networks were no more. Satellites orbiting the earth had been turned away and faced the stars.

At the same moment The Peacock Angel and his Nephilim had appeared at Saint Mary's Church, busloads of apparent horse-racing tourists were emptying their cargo along the Duchess Drive opposite the Arab-owned horse farm.

In reality it was the elite soldiers of the Nephilim Yazidis on a seek and destroy mission.

Two hundred melted into the belt of trees, heading for the last known coordinates of their fallen comrades, a small stable block that housed expectant equine mothers.

The Arab brotherhood were waiting, fully aware that an attack would be imminent, as the first coach pulled up along the Duchess Drive. The alarm was raised, the premier Arab soldiers not on watch raced from their barracks, disguised as stable staff accommodation, to bolster their brothers in arms, ready to defend till paradise.

The battle that raged was ruthless, savage and silent, not fought in the imagination of the filmmakers.

This was two opposing forces that had spent their adult lives refining the art of killing, silence paramount, to avoid interference from third parties.

The stiletto knife, crossbow, the karate chop, the severed

throat or vertebrae.

All were employed as the Nephilim Yazidis soldiers advanced towards the stables.

Hours later both had lost three quarters of their number to lie in the fields and trees that surrounded. Those whose lives would not continue were heading for paradise, either the paradise of the Koran or the Utopia promised by the Peacock Angel.

The few that remained on either side would fight till the last; there would be no surrender, it was not a word that entered the vocabulary of any of these committed soldiers.

Eventually the last few Arab brotherhood stood before the maternity stables. They had been outnumbered; the Nephilim Yazidis' hierarchy had done their homework well. They had gained immense respect from their adversaries, they had proved to be granite to subdue.

The masquerading stable staff charged into the midst of the remaining Nephilim Yazidis, a heroic last stand that would never be recorded.

The expectant equines were released into the field, the only witnesses to man's inhumanity to man.

Six Nephilim Yazidis high priests, who had been observing the carnage from the safety of the woods, advanced upon the stables.

These Peacock Angel devotees were the only players who knew the quarry they were stalking.

The search of every square inch of the stable and feed room commenced.

The remaining Nephilim Yazidis soldiers drove the tractor and trailer, conveniently parked by the maternity unit used extensively for taking the horse manure from the stables.

Today it would be used for some purpose reminiscent of the Black Death, a plague that had claimed the lives of a quarter of Europeans, the Nephilim Yazidis collecting bodies that lay strewn, taking the deceased to the barn where hundreds of tons of bailed hay and straw, stacked ready for use as bedding or feed. The teleporter used for distribution of the litter and fodder, now lifted bodies to the top of the stack.

The high priests, realizing that a new floor had been placed in the horse feed room, understood that their prey almost certainly lay under a considerable amount of concrete; they had been thwarted by the brotherhood.

The Arab soldiers knew their portal had been discovered, they also knew they would be observed, every action examined; they had to close the entrance.

The feed lorry, emblazoned with the company name, ABC Saddlery and Feed Suppliers, had been stacked with thousand litre drums of liquid concrete, the drums surrounded by sacks of corn to disguise their content. The vehicle had backed down the driveway to the stables, the same ritual that had continued for decades. Unseen by the observers from the side curtain slipped a tube from which the concrete would be pumped, the trapdoor removed, the stairwell leading to the chamber holding the gospel was filled with concrete. Feed sacks being carried from the back gave the illusion that all was normal. A pile of concrete left in the corner would be spread after the lorry's departure and the closing of the door, forming a new floor and hiding the exact spot of the portal.

Pick up buses would drive slowly by on the hour. At ten minutes to the hour candles were lit and placed at convenient spots around the base of the hay and straw stacks, loose hay and straw placed at the bottom so that as the candles burned down the stacks would ignite, this gave the Nephilim Yazidis time to vanish from the scene.

As the small convoy of coaches joined the M11 heading for Stansted Airport the barn full of hay and straw was well alight.

The first coach half full, the only one employed in its main task, the rest empty. The driver reported that his mobile phone had crashed and he was unable, for some reason, to contact the depot as the radio mike had also decided to rest from employment.

Little did they know that the world had lost its ability to communicate.

Nothing worked, TV, radio, Internet, phones of all descriptions, computer screens blank.

People, for the first time in living memory, were talking to their neighbours over fences, in the streets. What had happened, who was to blame, this was an abuse of my human rights.

A new reality had dawned.

The world of the town cryer. The flag, the hilltop burning beacon, ancient information devices now beckoned.

Nuclear submarines patrolling the oceans, unsure if the world had been obliterated, where should their retribution fall. Governments impotent, unable to operate, the starving media now joining the hungry unemployed.

Banks, supermarkets, unable to function.

The totem tree the modern world relied upon had been felled. Communication, the flame of civilization, had been snuffed out.

The flames from the funeral pyre on the horse farm roared

into the sky. Locals had spotted the flames but had been unable to inform the authorities. Some of the youngsters had pedalled their way to the fire station to find that the hub had lost its ability to raise a crew. The paging system to the retained firefighters was gone.

Communication between ship and shore over. Communication between country and country finished. International trade over. Humankind became instantly rudderless.

Cities all over the world would empty their populations, refugees seeking sustenance and shelter. Hunger and thirst being the driving force, conflict on a scale never seen before.

The shaky pillars of civilization were crumbling. Armageddon had begun.

The cacophony from the Peacock Angel and his Nephilim smashed the air as it receded; the diabolical had gone.

The small party returned to the vicarage past frantic media people desperately trying to reach their distant masters.

The realization that, like some great redwood tree, centuries in the making could be put asunder quickly with an axe, never to be returned to its glories.

These paparazzi would be the first outside of the Iceni to realize they were at the start of some event of biblical proportions.

Michael sat with the small posse of close family and friends around the kitchen table. The kettle no longer working its magic, no longer turning crazily bumping electrons into boiling water, it's sorcery so regularly performed it seemed normal, it had now become completely redundant along with every other device designed to ease the workload. The power source, understood by very few, created by even less, had stopped, never to return.

Brian Grogan transferred the contents of the kettle to a pot that was placed on the Calor gas stove of the barbecue.

They would enjoy the sacrament of water poured over leaves or crushed beans at least one more time before life changed forever.

The generation least able to look after itself had returned to the age of the caveman. The world without electrical power, communication.

A transport system that would quickly be starved of fuel would lay waste at the sides of the roads.

The initial bewilderment had begun, it would soon be replaced by desperation, after that panic, turmoil, fear, dread.

Crumbs of soil gently falling in to wormholes had increased to a churning bake of aggregate. Transfixed observers would see the hairless undead climb out of their earth tombs, their souls long departed into the ethereal space would return at the behest of the dark lord.

They began to lope, the destination, the Suffolk town of Newmarket.

Unbeknown to the terrified, the lack of communication meant that none were aware that the same phenomena were happening worldwide, each manifestation heading for some focal point with a significance of its own. A well-orchestrated battleplan, formulated in the Garden of Eden. A paradise known as the earth, everything perfect, only disrupted by the Peacock Angel and his Nephilim.

Had the consumption of the apple of knowledge, (its significance emblazoned on almost every electronic device.) benefited mankind?

"What doth it profit a man to know the world, but lose the

love in his heart". Chapter six, verse five, the gospel according to Jesus Christ.

"Fill thy heart with the joy of bird song, do not lose that love with its examination". Chapter eight, verse seven.

"He who covets the golden cup will build his walls. His heart of fear looking out for the murderer and the robber. Blessed water tastes the same from the cup of clay". Chapter eleven, verse three.

As the hairless made their way towards the gate of the abbey gardens, others of the same kind joined from different points. The size of its gateway gave a clue as to who was at the heart of abbey worship.

Misogynistic men living secret lives, performing questionable rituals, living behind walled fortresses, espousing, but not practicing celibacy, was rich recruiting ground for followers of the Peacock Angel.

The band of soulless continued its journey west. Others, resurrected, joined along the way.

Hordes of gathering crowds, who were demanding answers from anyone who appeared to have any official capacity, fled in all directions at the sight of the advancing terrors.

The global village had almost instantly become the infinite universe, the next town might as well have been on the moon, another country, Andromeda.

The world had lost its power, the only communication remaining, word of mouth.

Like some vast physical body with all its intricacies, unfathomable workings, miraculous abilities so commonplace as to appear normal had suddenly been decapitated. Vibrant and energetic one minute, dead and decaying the next.

Materialism, the world's biggest religion, was no more.

Nothing worked, petrol pumps unable to operate, banking systems of no use, people denied the comfort of work.

Quantum, dark energy and matter, had replaced the limited understanding of physics, no longer could electricity be generated.

The mushroom cloud of chaos was descending.

The bishop left Saint Mary's rectory in Newmarket and headed back to Ely Cathedral and home like millions of others who wanted to be with their family during the crisis. The crisis, the bishop, knew was permanent.

Their journey home would be one of their last by motor vehicle, fuel would become of enormous value. It would be commandeered by the local militia.

The bishop hugged his wife with an intensity that words were unable to express. Both had lived their lives in the comfort and conviction that heaven awaits, both believed they would live their lives the same as countless others and face the Resurrection from their graves.

Now they believed they could face Judgement Day without passing through death.

He had spoken of the Resurrection, second coming, heaven, thousands of times. Now he faced the reality, would he be parted from this woman he loved who had been the ground upon which he stood? The arms that had wrapped him in unconditional love when the distress of his job had battered his soul, when he buried children and the young, the palpable grief that filled his being, relief only found in the knowledge that they were waiting in a better place.

The arms of his wife, the place his emotions could run freely onto her loving shoulders, it was the heaven he knew on earth.

There were many people wanting to speak to him, he would head for the cathedral, he would spend his time praying and administering to those that sought spiritual guidance.

He would take with him copies of the gospel of Jesus Christ a booklet of the gospel that he had locked away in the secure part of his residence. Others in the Iceni would be doing the same, with the Internet down it would be the only way of distributing the word of Christ.

One hundred thousand copies had been produced in various languages, long before the Internet was invented, and stored in the cabins that surrounded the lake under Newmarket. They had been distributed to the Iceni in recent times as it became clear that the prophecies Jesus Christ had predicted were unfolding.

The bishop made his way to the cathedral; there was a sizeable bewildered crowd, unable to comprehend what was happening.

He distributed the gospel for people to sit and read with the proviso that they left them in the pews for others.

He spoke to the assembled crowd, asking them to take notes in order to pass on the message, he told them of the Iceni, of the long line of strong devout women dating back to Queen Boadicea, how she changed the course of history drawing back the Roman forces, in order to subdue the fiercest of the pagan warriors, leaving the Celtic nations relatively free from Roman influence.

Queen Boadicea saw the Romans as liars, cheats, worshipping nothing but gold. Pillaging the conquered nations, sending their plunder back to build a perceived Utopia.

In keeping with the Celts, the warrior queen, her East Anglian kingdom worshiped the earth, its wonders, its ability to generate new life, to feed all its inhabitants, a paradise of wonderment.

They knew it could not be by chance, there had to be a creator, a celestial being.

The sun rose every morning and rode across the sky, it fell and slept, to wake and reappear, a little earlier or later each day. Everything stretched towards it in worship. Twenty-first to the twenty-fourth of December the glowing ball in the sky struggled to wake, the fear that this could be its death throes, universal, the twenty-fifth of December was the first day of its perceivable ascension, its rebirth, a day of great celebration.

With the advancing Romans, or the Devalians as they were known by the Iceni, her band of warriors would be hopelessly outnumbered. They prayed for intervention by the god of the earth.

The parting of the Red Sea, the ark of Noah, the burning bush, all can be argued, the huge earth wave that lifted in front of the advancing Roman armies for ten miles, originally known as the Devalian Dyke, morphed into its modern name of the Devil's Dyke, cannot, it still stands.

The bishop went on, Abraham had fathered a son with his servant, before he fathered a son with his wife. God was disappointed with Abraham and told him the two lines that now emanated from him would have enmity between them forever. The holy land continues to be an intermittent battleground between the Christians and the Muslims.

The Templars, a monastic warrior group of knights, fought in the holy lands, setting up the first banks where pilgrims could deposit money in England or France, subsequently retrieve it from the Templars in Jerusalem.

The Templars grew exceedingly rich by their banking exploits, along with selling religious artefacts to the relic-hungry churches of Europe.

The devout Christians of Jerusalem began to shun the Templars, it appeared their love of wealth seemed to overtake their love of Christ.

There was a constant presence in the holy land of the devout women of the Iceni; they had laid down their arms and adopted a pacifist existence, having witnessed Jesus Christ, his wife Mary Magdalen and his mother, Mary, walking across the underground lake at Newmarket, asking them to put down their weapons and follow him. From that day to this a tool to inflict pain and death on another human being had never entered their hands.

The Templars were arrested and imprisoned in France for heresy their vast wealth was to be confiscated by Philip the king.

Unfortunately for Philip the tentacles of the Templars' espionage encroached to the very heart of his court. The wealth created by the Templars had been moved to London which became the hub for the banking world. The tarnished reputation of the Templars for commercial reasons became the secretive Masonic order, Masons would spread throughout the land, their lodges home to some dubious practices and rituals. Although professing Christianity as their root, to the independent observer the Nephilim Yazidis' creed would appear more prominent.

Self promoting, most senior police judges, solicitors, bankers, still today are Masons.

The misogynistic world that existed paid little attention to the women from East Anglia, little is known outside of their own texts, which speak of nursing the sick and injured, feeding the impoverished, promoting peace and harmony, preservation of the values of Christ.

In times of peace kings and khalifah found they had more that bonded than divided, particularly the love of the horse, which brought into their lives joy, exhilaration and contentment.

When the early Christians realized that the written word of Jesus Christ was in danger they gave it to the Iceni. The most devout of the Jesus people, the Iceni could not have been tempted by the lure of gold, an affliction that seemed prevalent in the male ego of the species.

The Mohammedans gave a vow that they would protect the writings of their penultimate prophet Jesus.

They escorted the Iceni women and the gospel back to the chalk cathedrals under Newmarket where to this day they have honoured that commitment, their comings and goings disguised as horse traders.

'Ladies and gentlemen,' the bishop said, 'that is a very brief outline of a secret that has been kept for centuries. It is being revealed to you now because it is believed the second coming is imminent.'

The congregation, scribbling, silent and astonished.

One of the assembly asked what was his connection with the Iceni if it was predominantly female. The bishop replied that it was only in modern times that women had been treated anything like equal, for most of history they had been denied, believed to be weak, indecisive, incapable of original thought, emotionally unstable. Through misogynistic practices women had been unable to gain access to their rightful place at the table of the decision makers.

'They needed a male man of Christ we could move freely amongst the highest, his job was to observe and report any of the signs foretold in the gospel of Jesus Christ which may be only apparent in the highest circles of the imminent second coming.

'They are called the watcher of which I am the present in a long line of watchers.'

The bishop moved among his congregation, as they sat in the pews reading the gospel of Jesus Christ in the candlelight.

His Holiness caught sight of the chief constable donned in his civilian clothes entering the back of the cathedral.

He greeted the policeman and the two sat in the quiet pew at the back. The officer of the crown reported that there were strange phenomena appearing all over the area. It appeared that the yeti type beings were everywhere, vandalizing churches and churchyards, anything in their way they smashed they seemed to be moving towards the east. It was very hard to make much sense because all communication was down, his officers were meeting in the car park as there was no power in the police station which without it was dark and dingy. There were long lines of people waiting to report incidents. They had made their way to the police station by various means trying to avoid using any remaining petrol that couldn't be replaced. The policeman said that they were awaiting instructions from the government which up to now had not been forthcoming. With all forms of communication down they had made contact with their Cambridge colleagues by bicycle which, until the present predicament was rectified, would be the most prudent means.

Cambridge station had reported by means of a handwritten note they were more or less in the same predicament, they faced large groups of strange-looking beings, much the same as those pictured at Stuntney, moving from several places in Cambridge; a particularly large group had been spotted emerging from the ground at the Caxton gibbet.

The note from the chief constable at Cambridge had read that policing was almost rendered impotent. No communication, no electrical power, little reserves of fuel it would be very difficult to retain law and order if things weren't resolved very quickly. They had received nothing from central government which they hoped would be rectified as soon as possible.

The holy man gave the lawman a copy of the gospel of Jesus Christ, asking him to read it. The gospel was being distributed to wherever the Iceni could reach, which in truth was most countries throughout the world, it was hoped to distribute much more quickly to the global audience but with no Internet, the process would be slower, although the bishop explained the book, much maligned by the young, still towered like a beacon for the transfer of knowledge and ideas, easily portable, not difficult to be concealed, extremely tactile, difficult for its ideological opposers to eliminate. The mass burning of books in Russia and China and many other doctrines were unable to destroy ideas, thoughts, wisdom, live beyond the grave and gifted to each ensuing generation, the modern world with all its technical wonders is built on the back of the horse and the genius of the quill.

The bishop left the policeman to his audience with the gospel of Jesus Christ returning when the chief constable had read and digested the narrative.

'Well!' said the chief constable. 'It would appear that we

are in the last days before the return of Jesus Christ and the day of judgement.'

'I agree,' said His Holiness. 'We are in for forty days and nights of Satan, Lucifer, The Peacock Angel, whatever name you want to pin on him, causing fear and dread, there will be hunger, thirst, man will turn against man. Nothing will be left of the civilization we knew.'

The policeman returned to the sanctuary of his wife to learn that the running water had stopped. She had managed to fill a bowl from the rain butt in order to flush the lavatory, cooking and drinking would be a problem.

Time passed slowly; the mechanisms for diverting attention away from the present were over. It was here and now, priority to feed and drink paramount. The great food stores had been looted and ransacked, security no match for hungry, angry people. Only those who had lived through the miners' strike, when the power was only available on three days a week, had any notion of trying to live without electricity. Coupled with no communication, no running water, the notes issued by the government promising to pay the bearer the sum printed on the IOU were no longer valid.

The government was unable to govern, they could not communicate with the people and the people could not respond.

Within days what had been perceived as normal had collapsed.

The old and infirm were dying in their beds unable to receive their care, their carers distraught, unable to reach and administer their profession.

Hospitals, places of mayhem, centralization coming home to roost. No power, no staff. Only those able to walk or pedal able to attend.

The global village had become the village globe. Nothing was known of anything other than the immediate vicinity; verbal reports had come in that everywhere everyone was in the same situation.

The Grogans were spending their time in the church with ongoing services, queues outside all the places of worship, much of the population desperate for religious guidance, filling the spiritual houses in relays.

Local councillors, elevated from the mundane, plod to presidential decree, trying to repair the cracking Kariba Dam of desperation with a tube of glue.

Oliver, Michael and Ninal had attended the combined trainers and stable staff association meeting to discuss the crisis and what could be done. Most were at a loss, the diminishing supplies of oats being used to feed the racehorses would have to be redirected to a common pool in order to fend off starvation in the human population for as long as possible. As supplies of hay ran out horses would be let loose on the heath with numbers painted on their flanks, so that if and when the crisis was resolved the animals could be returned to the appropriate stable.

The overriding sense of doom that prevailed featured as its main focus, the yeti, hairless entities, were terrifying, soulless things of immense strength, that moved seemingly effortlessly across the countryside, destroying every obstacle placed before them. The brave humans left lying beside their instruments of resistance – guns, knives, cudgels of all descriptions, they were left, eyes popping, carotid arteries and windpipes left dangling.

Whole streets of Newmarket had become no-go areas, in

order to give the loping servants of the Devil free access to the heath, where they would yomp up Warren Hill and disappear into the woods. It was estimated that somewhere in the region of two thousand had disappeared into the trees that had been planted, along with all the trees surrounding the heathland, by prisoners from the Napoleonic Wars.

The invasion had been overwhelming in the first few hours and days, now it had slowed to a trickle. The question was what was the gathering army's purpose.

The gospel of Jesus Christ was widely available in the spiritual shrines of Newmarket, Michael and his earthly father would preach passages.

"Be not afraid of the days when Satan brings forth his armies, Jesus had said. He hath wreaked havoc in Paradise, most who have been deceived knew not of the deception believing the fruit was wholesome. They shall not be denied on the day of judgement".

"Those whose hand went out to the beggar, the poor, who bound the wounds of his brother and sister but received not the word of God, he shall be exulted, and welcomed into my house".

"He that dealt fairly, with the glories of compassion and love, I was with him though he visited not my house, or spoke my name, he will live with me forever".

"Those who spoke out against me, who saw not the miracles my father placed before them, whose works were good and righteous I will walk among them in heaven".

"Be fearful of the days to come all ye deceivers even ye sat in my house called my name on high, thy fruit was pain, thou shall reap what thy sowed".

"Those that sleep not in the peace of their graves, but live in the darkness of the last days, will call out to me we have been deceived, I will not answer thy call. Thou will be left in the wilderness forty days and forty nights. I will strengthen thy hearts to face Satan. Know his time is short, his angels and those whose souls were freely given will be cast out forever. His sword of greed, hate, envy, will be banished with him, peace, joy and the greatest of all love, be exulted and magnified, be not afraid, rejoice in the days to come".

As the days grew into weeks, the Iceni had distributed the gospel far and wide, the words of the Christ had managed to suppress the worst emotions and notions of humankind.

Stockpiled and hidden, the gospel of Jesus had been released. The faithful had known that, should communication fail as was predicted, the power generated by mankind rendered dead, those that worshipped only the golden calf would see their mountains crumble into the desert; their faith would not comfort them in their hours of darkness.

The gospel was now abundant on the earth.

It had brought restraint and realization that this was the last days of the holy book, there was an end to the trauma, The dark lord would do his worst.

Most were convinced by the gospel of Jesus Christ that they would receive his blessing, therefore the short-term suffering could be endured.

Oliver and Ninal helped as much as they could at the Bottril stables. The horses confined, hay stocks running precariously low.

The few Suffolk Punches, the ploughing horses lovingly kept by enthusiasts, remnants of a past era before the tractor had made them redundant, were commissioned back into action, pulling carts of water from Exning River to keep horses and townsfolk from the worst ravages of thirst, washing of any description banned, toilets, holes dug in gardens. The only sight to lift the heart in these dreadful times, great, powerful, majestic animals with dinner-plate feet, effortlessly dragging these carts of water.

Seamus Prolly, great horseman that he was, said that the horses in his care seemed to take on a new persona, something that all his time with horses he had never seen, other head stable hands that he had spoken to reported the same, that the roles had somehow been reversed. They had done man's bidding for eternity, lifting, carrying, working, taking man to places he could never have known at speed he could never have achieved.

Seamus explained they seemed to have grown in stature, not in height, but the way they carried themselves, they seemed to be constantly staring into the offing. They seemed to be in a zone, not unlike the boxer before a bout.

He had heard about the phenomenon before, the great steeplechaser "Arkle" would sometimes stop walking, stand staring at the horizon as though viewing some mystical scene, he exuded majesty, observers were convinced that he knew his own greatness, he was the steeplechaser from God, that none before or after would come close to his crown.

"Copenhagen", the impeccably bred thoroughbred horse, mount of Wellington at the Battle of Waterloo, rose in stature at the sight of an enemy. Wellington reported, "There were countless more handsome and quicker steeds, but for courage and stamina and rage for the fight I never saw his equal.

"I never rode him into battle, he carried me into the fight, he knew the path, burst of cannon or flash of sabre only emboldened his heart.

"Chroniclers will report he was my horse, but truth be told he was my master.

"At quiet of eve I would take him his oat, he would not rise from his bed of straw, I would place his payment where he could eat in recline.

"He required naught from me but a kind hand. My mark to him was my life."

Ninal and Oliver new exactly what Seamus was referring to: there seemed to be an aura of expectant calm. Oliver remembered the poem scratched on the wooden saddle horse inscribed by the stable's street artist Bolly.

"You serve in the master role, I burden you a heavy toll,

Blessed to wipe away your sweat Only way to pay the debt,

I look out as far as I can see,

Your toil in life an honour, only meant for me".

Oliver remembered the text in the gospel of Jesus Christ.

"My father has beseeched that you have dominion over every living creature, he has touched the ears of the mighty, go take the burden from Adam's children and serve them all the days of thy life".

Horse, ox, donkey, camel, elephant, mule, it was the ears where man could display his gratitude. The kindest caress, the gentlest of rubs was all the payment required.

The walking dead were re-emerging from the woods on top of Warren Hill, bringing dread to the townsfolk, all the able-bodied from the town gathered where the heath ended and the brick walls began, where the hungry developer had salivated, where countless spirits had been elevated from the mundane to the magical, a union of souls between the divine. Where the spellbound observer could observe the symphony of movement from the duet from God.

Although any defence of the town and its inhabitants was believed to be futile, most were of the opinion that they had to try something to protect their homes and families.

The cycling network had revealed that every town and city social structure had collapsed, all faced the same problems. Migration was of no use, exchanging the same problems for another location where the reception may not be as congenial as hoped or expected.

A background clatter changed into a rhythmic drumming, horses all over Newmarket were kicking the stable doors.

A jungle beat boomed out across Newmarket.

The hairless were rapidly emerging from the woods until swathes of them stared down upon the townspeople who had armed themselves with pitchforks, shotguns, kitchen knives, a variety of implements that could be used as some sort of weapon.

Oliver, Ninal and Seamus watched the agitated horses drumming at their doors. Michael strolled into the yard as though it was Sunday afternoon on the promenade. Beside him, unseen by the others, was Agnes.

He knew he was going home. The half veil was now almost completely gone, he had entered the birthing channel, according to the gospel of Jesus Christ, or imminent death, according to the Oxford English Dictionary.

He was slowly fading.

'Let them out,' Michael said. 'It's time for them to do their job.'

Seamus, against everything he thought he knew about the racehorse, released them from their boxes. Half a ton of unpredictable galloping horse, sporting metal shoes that were akin to skates on ice, bolting across tarmac was not the elixir needed to steady the heart.

Instead of bolting headlong into disaster, they formed an orderly procession by the front gate, which was opened by Oliver, and they trotted out down the Exeter Road through the water courses, to the Severals, the place where Ninal and Oliver had exchanged their vows.

The domino effect saw other stables release their animals, till the Severals, the grassy morning assembly area, was a mass of horses in excess of two thousand animals. They stood in Arkle style, proud and silent, staring at the amassing hairless, soulless, the moving dead.

Those who spent their lives tending the horses were astonished, most always convinced that there was more behind that thoughtful eye than was ever revealed.

The crescendo that struck pounded the air and eardrums, the burst of demonic hellhound scream announcing the arrival of the prince of darkness, the Nephilim, his band of fallen angels stood beside.

The souls of the hairless yeti swirled in a dark cloud of either grotesque images that adorn his churches, peered out, to disappear, replaced by the next hideous caricature depicting the satanic delights of the ungodly.

His arrival had lost its surprise, all were equipped to defend against it. The assembled manifestations gazed down upon the townspeople, as the cat gazes at the captured mouse, toying with it, prolonging the agony of its death.

It was the time of retribution, of revenge, to punish not only those that had stood steadfast against him but almost all of mankind whose overriding emotion through their lives was love.

Hatred, greed, have youthful vigour but die, love endures. The love of the child, family, friends, planet, environment, love trumps all other emotions, it lives, it grows, it remains from crib to coffin, from tiny hand to calloused wrinkled fingers. Love lives eternally in the heart, other emotions have temporary lodgings, time mellows their condition until they leave in peace.

The quartet left Hugo Bottril's stable, following the horses. Seamus looked back at the empty stable, a tear formed and perched, gone the gentle heads yawning, stretching, slowly oscillating in search of some new point of interest, now the stables, a ghostly shell devoid of life.

Oliver held his brother's arm. He knew he was nearing the end, there was a peace, an inner glow radiating from Michael. Agnes held his other arm, his eternal love, his guardian angel.

Ninal held the arm of her husband, knowing he would soon face the worst moment of his life. Not the horrors that awaited on top of Warren Hill and governed his early years, but the loss of his beloved brother.

The small party of horse people joined a throng of stable staff heading to the bottom of Warren Hill, armed with pitchforks, ready to face down the Devil and his cohorts.

It was a David and Goliath moment, eerie quiet before the tempest.

Praying for deliverance had already been done, this was the last trench, no retreating, people living under these endless skies, whose realization of living in paradise had been smothered by the burdens imposed by the moneylenders.

The Nephilim, their master, the bodies of the walking dead, stood and stared. Around them swirled the souls of the walking dead in demonic murmurations.

Thousands stared back, bulldogs, their defiance lasered into the eye of the tiger.

Lines of equine riderless cavalry gazed across the road from the Severals to the Warren Hill looking undaunted at the satanic forces.

All was quiet and still. Then, in answer to some terrifying booming guttural utterance, the foot soldiers of the Peacock Angel began to descend the hill in perfect marching unison. The stomp from two thousand heavy hairless feet pounding the ground with metronomic precision sent shockwaves vibrating into the air.

A slow, rhythmic drumbeat from the lowest register of sound boomed down the famous hill engulfing the waiting.

One could forgive any facing such a dreadful foe, with its terrible soul-chilling drum requiem, to turn and flee: no one did.

The defiant spirit, either bred or infused into the souls of this small nation, like many times before, stood against impossible odds, the tyrant, those who would seek to dominate without consent.

All towns and villages had engraved granite, A tribute to those that stood. The towns' militia readied themselves for the uneven fight.

The drumroll of the hairless descent was broken by the clip clopping of horses trotting across the road onto the heath, the lead horse then cantering the half mile to the next road, each subsequent horse stopped behind the previous and turned to face the advancing foe, they formed a line, a barrier between the satanic soldiers and the Bravehearts of Newmarket.

Most stood in amazement. The horse people were past amazement, closer to shock, years of navigating and plumbing the depths of the intricacies of the horse, never expected to see what was appearing before their eyes.

It was as if another entity had emerged from the deep recesses of the animals' psyche. The intelligent, sensitive soul in constant physical contact, long suspected a deeper plane. None realized it was as deep as the Pacific Mariana trench.

The horses began to walk towards the advancing devil battalion, the riderless cavalry collectively rising to the trot,

Two hundred yards from the enemy they rose as one into a canter, fifty yards apart saw them spring into the gallop.

The ensuing mayhem as they smashed into the advancing ranks saw the lifeless bodies of the Peacock Angel's advance forces dismembered.

Bullet, sword, knife, had been rendered useless in halting the advance of the hairless, but half a ton of equine fury smashing at speeds of up to forty miles an hour, the impact of living animal against putrid, ancient flesh caused its disintegration, those entities left standing after the initial charge felt both hindlegs of the horse pummelling their frame to annihilation.

Those long in the tooth could remember that the front end of the horse was as lethal as the back legs, those animals driven to madness by excess grooming in an era of military conformity knew that the teeth could rip a man's intestines out and shake him like a rag doll.

Those still standing after the onslaught were subject to the elongated neck, ears laid flat, teeth grabbing in vice-like grip, shaking the entity to bits.

The observers had stood spellbound for the few minutes that it took the animals God had instructed to serve and protect, to dispose of the hairless.

The ancient flesh of the hairless, their forms smashed and ripped, began to degenerate into powder falling through the blades of turf to provide sustenance for the greenery.

The Nephilim and their god began to sink into the turf staring constantly at the dumbfounded militia.

Michael announced they were heading for the lake and this was where the fun really began.

He led his small band towards the clock tower where another secret portal to the lake could be found.

Once inside they descended the steps that led to the lake. They walked the ancient chalk promenade, they met a group of the devout Iceni knelt in prayer. At the far end, past the bridge that supported the railway line and directly under the top of Warren Hill where the Nephilim and the Peacock Angel had descended, stood evil personified.

The Devil knew he had been defeated; the paradise still remained. Love, still the most powerful emotion.

Conscience still ruled.

Those who knew they were leaving this world wanted to be surrounded by those they loved, they were the only riches that counted in the final hours.

More Iceni were arriving from different portals, amongst them was the bishop, the Reverend Grogan, Michael and Oliver's adopted father, the two holy men's wives. The bishop had arrived with his wife in a bicycle rickshaw from Ely.

The bishop gave a quick overview of happenings in his diocese.

The bicycle was the form of transport, teams were working to convert many to rickshaws, tandems were commonplace, multi tandems were being used to pull carts and transport larger numbers of people. Innovation with the bicycle was amazing.

Groups and committees were being established to organize everything from water and food distribution, home sharing to allow expertise to be close to where it was needed, nurses, doctors, et cetera.

Despite all the hardship and fear, an amazing sense of community had been reborn. the bishop believed it could not have happened without the release of the gospel of Jesus.

Had the gospel been available any time before the last days, there would have been a doubt that the heart of man had come to God through fear, now with every temptation thrown before man from those that stood across the lake it was evident that the vast majority lived their lives through love and faith.

The general consensus of opinion from his parishioners was that it was not the catastrophe they expected from the loss of rapid communication, social media, roads clogged, people spending hours travelling in a metal womb, people were going to bed when it got dark, getting up when it got light, many felt invigorated, liberated.

If basic food, water and shelter could be maintained there was a growing sense of euphoria felt by many that a return to the old style of life would not be required.

The vast majority of the Iceni were present, the defender of the faith was amongst them. The Nephilim, the Peacock Angel just stood and stared across the lake at the Iceni, earth warriors that became soldiers of God, armed with nothing but prayer.

The murmuration of diabolical souls swirled and swooped around their chosen god waiting only for the signal from their satanic lord to bear down upon the Iceni, their nemesis, the band of sisters and their associated menfolk who had thwarted them at every turn.

The souls of the mass murderers, the child killers and abusers, the religious perverts, the diabolical who took pleasure in the pain and anguish of others, swirled in a frenzy, desperate to pummel.

The leader of the Iceni stepped forward, she bowed her head, the rest followed, she began the sacred prayer, the prayer taught by Jesus himself.

'Our father which art in heaven,' each line of the prayer more powerful than the line before. At the penultimate line she lifted her head, looked across the lake at the Devil himself, all the Iceni followed suit. She paused, lifted her eyes skyward, the defender of the faith then beseeched the heavens, 'Deliver us from evil. Thine is the kingdom, the power, and the glory, forever, Amen.'

Satan growled as though struck, booming A gastromancy from hell itself. The order to release, to administer the lowest forms of depravities imaginable onto the Iceni, satanic retribution, rape, sodomy, debauchery in all its forms, murder, torture.

The unleashed evil murmuration shot forward across the lake like greyhounds released from the traps.

The Iceni knelt in prayer, Michael, supported by Agnes, walked out onto the lake confirming to all what was suspected: he was an angel from God. In that moment the Iceni had the veil lifted, all could clearly see Agnes, they both began to chant. To left and right on either side appeared others, guardian angels, who had walked beside their earthly charges unseen Their presence often felt, the direction they indicated often described as destiny or fate.

It was reward for the Iceni, who had remained steadfast through the doubt.

The advancing onslaught began to slow, as the diabolical approached the defenders their power seemed to ebb.

Angel children appeared from the ether, palms pointing at the demonic swarm, hundreds fell towards the lake, their grotesque faces writhing and screaming in agony, their atrocities towards the child magnified back ten times.

The kaleidoscope of mayhem gradually cleared as more and more of the satanic souls, disintegrating, fell into the lake until nothing was left of the Peacock Angel's hellish murmuration.

Michael and Agnes walked back, his earthly body almost spent, he lay down, exhausted, on the chalk promenade.

On the other side of the lake the Nephilim and their master had disappeared. They would face the same problems everywhere, God had placed his angels throughout the world, all humanity had their unseen guides. He had placed strong animals decreed to serve and protect.

Michael's mother and father knelt beside him, alternately stroking his head and kissing his cheeks, brine rivers cascading, Oliver and Ninal, holding and squeezing his hands, their love pouring from their eyes.

The bishop and his wife were in front of the surrounding crowd, silently mouthing a blessing. Guardian angels surrounded the Iceni, joy radiating from their assembly.

Michael looked into the faces that he loved, he looked to his feet, stood there was the person he loved beyond explanation.

Agnes had both arms outstretched. She said, 'Come on soldier, let's go home.'

Michael closed his earthly eyes and opened them in a

paradise he knew well. He raised himself, clasping the arms of Agnes. He looked back at the body that had served him well, there was tearful joy on the faces of those he loved, they could see him, the veil had not yet fallen. He waved, they waved back. He reversed, arm in arm with Agnes, into the host of angels; he blew kisses and waved and waved.

The veil returned and Michael was gone.